"So? It's mine, isn't it?"

"Yes." Madison sighed. She braced herself for the lecture.

"That's what I thought," Collin said, looking eager...and even...excited? That took her by surprise. She hadn't expected him to *want* the baby. He'd been all hands and mouth that one night they spent together, but then the next day, it was as if she didn't exist. Now he liked the idea of her carrying his baby? Maybe she'd been wrong about him. Maybe he wasn't the hard-nosed prosecutor without a heart.

He dug around in his pocket and pulled out a black velvet box. He put down his backpack on the terra-cotta stone tiles of the foyer, and then turned to her.

"If it's mine, then we need to do this." He flipped open the black box lid, revealing a brilliant solitaire diamond that caught the sunlight and sparkled like fire. Suddenly, all coherent thought fled her mind.

Collin Baptista was asking her to *marry him*.

Dear Reader,

I'm excited to share with you my new book, *Practicing Parenthood*, a story about how sometimes the best way to learn how to love is to dive in, headfirst.

After Collin Baptista has a night of fiery passion with opposing counsel Madison Reddy, neither believe it's a relationship with legs. But then Madison discovers she's pregnant, and Collin surprises her by proposing. Madison, however, has no intention of getting married just to get married. Instead, she heads to her uncle's beach house on beautiful North Captiva, Florida.

Collin follows and he and Madison find a stray puppy on the island and adopt him, and in the process discover they have a long way to go to learn to be parents.

I recently adopted a goldendoodle (half poodle, half golden retriever) myself that my daughters named Teddy as well (since he, too, looks like a teddy bear), and so I knew firsthand the difficulties of having a puppy, and it reminded me of how similar puppies and babies can be. You can't turn your back on either one for a minute!

I loved the idea of a couple at odds coming together and learning to be parents while fostering a puppy and realizing that they are stronger together as a team. Sometimes, the biggest obstacles to love are the ones we put in our own path.

Because this is my last Harlequin Superromance title, I also wanted to thank you, the reader. It's been an honor and a privilege to write for you. I hope you enjoy *Practicing Parenthood* as much as I enjoyed writing it.

All my best,

Cara

CARA LOCKWOOD

Practicing Parenthood

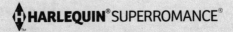

HARLEQUIN® SUPERROMANCE®

Recycling programs
for this product may
not exist in your area.

ISBN-13: 978-1-335-44920-7

Practicing Parenthood

Copyright © 2018 by Cara Lockwood

Printed in U.S.A.

www.Harlequin.com

Cara Lockwood is the *USA TODAY* bestselling author of more than seventeen books, including *I Do (But I Don't)*, which was made into a Lifetime Original movie. She's written the Bard Academy series for young adults and has had her work translated into several languages around the world. Born and raised in Dallas, Cara now lives near Chicago with her two wonderful daughters. Find out more about her at caralockwood.com, friend her on Facebook, Facebook.com/authorcaralockwood, or follow her on Twitter, @caralockwood.

Visit the Author Profile page at Harlequin.com for more titles.

For Hana, Miya, Sophia, Pete and Sarina,
the true joys in my life who let me practice
parenthood every day.

PROLOGUE

COLLIN BAPTISTA SLID through the metal detectors at the Lee County courthouse, grateful for the cool air-conditioning that fought off the humid air of southwest Florida. He grabbed his keys and wallet from the conveyor belt and nodded at Joyce, the armed guard who wore her hair in tight braids. She was a regular, like all the staff he saw almost daily at the courthouse.

"Looking good today," she told him, her eyes sliding down the length of the new dark suit that fit him like a glove, a splurge he'd allowed himself after winning that high-profile murder trial last month. He patted the top of his thick black hair, courtesy of his Filipino mother, a contrast to his green eyes and the lopsided, roguish smile from his Irish dad. Collin was anything but boy-next-door, but he could command a courtroom with persuasive arguments alone, one of the many reasons he hadn't lost a case in two years working as a prosecutor for the state attorney's office.

Still, he felt nerves dance in the pit of his stomach, but they had nothing to do with the hearing this morning, which was a routine case—a drunk driver who'd smashed his car into a tree but thankfully hadn't hurt anyone. Yet. Collin planned to take the driver's license to teach him a lesson. That was an open-and-shut case, something he could do with his eyes closed. The man's blood alcohol had been three times the legal limit. No, what made him anxious was the thought of seeing Madison Reddy again.

Madison. Her dark thick hair, her light brown nearly hazel eyes... The curves that simply didn't quit. Her father's family had immigrated from India, her mother's side was from Scotland. She was biracial like he was, and the only woman he knew of who could make an off-the-rack gray suit and sturdy heels look almost pornographic. He'd been haunted by her eyes for a year, and even more so now since they'd fallen into her bed two months ago after happy hour gone wrong.

Or, he thought, *very, very right*.

Collin walked through the courtroom and found he was early; no one sat at the defense table. He felt a tug of disappointment. He'd wanted every extra minute before or after the hearing to see her. That she wasn't waiting for him left him feeling a little empty.

You were the one who didn't call her, a voice nagged inside his brain. *You were the one who deliberately avoided her these past couple of months.*

He'd told himself he hadn't called because he was worried about violating the state attorney's policy of not sleeping with the opposing counsel. He could've gotten around that, he supposed. But he knew the real reason ran deeper than that. He liked Madison. He liked her too much. He had career plans that didn't include staying in Fort Myers, and if he started a serious relationship with her, he'd be tempted to toss those ideas out the window.

He only had three rules in life: 1) Don't lose; 2) Bad guys deserve more than the book thrown at them; and 3) Never sleep with the enemy (in other words, defense attorneys). He'd broken one of his *three cardinal rules* for Madison. That was how amazing the woman was.

In his opinion, most defense attorneys were liars or exaggerators, relying on smoke and mirrors rather than facts. Every prosecutor felt that way. He'd vowed never to go to bed with one of them. Yet, Madison had somehow managed to sneak past all his defenses. She stood by her own set of principles and wasn't afraid to give him a piece of her mind.

Instantly, afterward, he realized how reckless he'd been. If word got out that he'd slept with opposing counsel, it would tarnish his career and hers.

They'd faced off on a number of different cases, including one that involved a fairly high-profile white supremacist who'd tried to murder a black man but had ended up shooting a twelve-year-old girl by mistake. After their one night together, he'd avoided her steadfastly for a couple of months. Yet, as much as he tried to forget her, he kept thinking about her smooth legs, soft stomach, her light brown eyes alight with mirth. It was only his career that kept him from picking up the phone and calling her.

But none of that mattered now. He wasn't going to be her opposing counsel for much longer.

He sat at the prosecutor's table and opened his briefcase, checking out the letter one last time. He'd accepted a job at the US attorney's office in Miami, a huge promotion, beginning in four months. Not bad for a kid whose father went to prison for drugs when Collin was just two and died there when Collin was ten. He was proud of being a success despite the odds—son of a single mom and raised in the poorest of poor neighborhoods. Sure, he was a hard-nosed, hard-charging prosecutor, but life had never given him any real breaks. He'd had plenty of temptation to run drugs, to steal, to cut corners—but he'd never done any of it. He'd worked the worst jobs on janitorial staffs at two in the morning to put himself through college and law school, and eventually he wanted to be the highest prosecutor in the land, the attorney general. But for now, he'd accept a position as a federal prosecutor in Miami.

Collin planned to take some time off before then. This was his last case before he took an extended sabbatical. And the months he wasn't working as a prosecutor, he wanted to spend with Madison, getting to know those curves he fought to remember through the fuzz of alcohol he'd consumed that night. He glanced at the defense table. Where was she?

Then attorneys from her firm, Reddy, Chester and Todd, arrived. Collin recognized one of them, Matt Todd, a guy he'd gone to law school with. Collin momentarily felt disoriented. Where was Madison? Surely, she hadn't left the firm. Her uncle was a partner and there were rumors he'd make her a partner one day, too.

"Matt? I thought Madison was on this case," Collin said, getting up to shake Matt's hand.

"Not anymore," Matt answered, trying to balance a briefcase and a large Starbucks cup while clasping Collin's hand. "You haven't heard?"

"Heard what?"

"She's on sabbatical." Matt placed his briefcase and coffee on the defense table. "Rumor has it she's *in the family way*." Matt lowered his voice as if this were the antebellum South when polite company refused to talk about pregnancy.

"Pregnant?" Collin felt like he'd been slapped. "How far along?"

Matt shrugged. "How should I know? All I can tell you is she was granted a few months off to figure it all out. At least, that's the rumor. Everybody's calling it a *health issue*, so it may be cancer for all we know…"

Matt continued to talk, but Collin was barely listening. Madison was *pregnant*? Collin remembered that they'd used a condom, although little good it had done them since it had broken sometime during the act. Or acts… He'd made the assumption she'd been on the pill because she'd told him, "Don't worry about it." Looked like he should've been worrying about it.

"...she gets to hang out on North Captiva for the summer, so it's nice to be related to a partner."

"What do you mean? She's on North Captiva?"

"House-sitting for her uncle Rashad," he said. "For the summer. That's why I'm here, picking up her caseload while she has a health sabbatical or whatever." Matt rolled his eyes, clearly annoyed by the new developments, but Collin hardly noticed.

"The rumor is she's pregnant, though?" Collin pressed. Suddenly the neckline of his crisp new shirt seemed too tight. Why hadn't she told him if she was?

"That's what Rashad's paralegal said. She's a notorious gossip, but she also sits outside the man's office and has bionic hearing..." Matt shrugged again.

Collin felt hot and cold all at once. Madison was pregnant? With his child. *Had* to be his. She'd said that she hadn't slept with anyone in more than a year...and something in his gut said Madison didn't sleep around. She just wasn't the type.

He needed to find out if it was true.

Because if she was carrying his baby, there was only one thing he could do.

He wasn't going to be like his own father

who had never been a true parent. The man who'd never bothered to marry his mother, even after she'd given birth to two children. No, he'd vowed to be the opposite of that man in every way possible. Then he remembered the timing. He had the next few months off. He'd get on a boat, head out to North Captiva and find out if Madison was pregnant or not.

Because if she was, there was no way he'd abandon his son or daughter. He'd have to marry her.

That was all there was to it.

CHAPTER ONE

MADISON REDDY CLUNG to the edge of the small ferry that was shuttling her from the Pine Island Transportation Center to North Captiva, a small island on the west coast of Florida, just north of Sanibel Island. Known for the big shells swept into the Gulf from the currents in the Atlantic and for its lack of cars, North Captiva housed three hundred residents. They navigated the four-mile long island via golf cart and bike. Madison's uncle Rashad had been more than generous in giving her time off from her job and a place to stay for a few months while she figured out what she was going to do. Her uncle had married but never had children, and in some ways, he had adopted her as his own.

"Go there. Take a little time off," her uncle had told her in his office when she'd revealed in tears that she was pregnant. "If you don't want to have the baby, there's an excellent clinic in Fort Myers. If you do, then that's fine. You can spend your pregnancy there, have the baby and come back to the firm. Your job will be waiting for you."

It sounded like a plan from a hundred years ago—hide an out-of-wedlock pregnancy, have the baby in secret and then pop back up in society. But frankly, Madison was just grateful that Uncle Rashad had saved the lectures and was simply letting her, as a thirty-year-old woman, make her own decisions.

Rashad had been like a father to her, ever since her father died when she was fourteen. Rashad was even more generous, she thought, than her father would've been, but that was how seriously he took his responsibility to look after her—and her mother.

Still, she did need some time off to work this out. Her brain felt like muddled mush, and she needed some distance and a few weeks to decide what she'd do next. Her gut already told her there was nothing to decide. She was going to keep the baby, but she had to figure out *how*.

"You can live with me, and we'll raise her together," her mother had offered over tea the previous afternoon. "Or him." Her mom had retired from the firm last year, so she had ample time on her hands.

"Mom, I can't...ask you to do that. You've earned your retirement." More than earned it, being a single mom. Her mother, whose cool blue stare never left her face, tucked a strand of dark auburn hair behind her ear as she studied Madison.

"There's no *asking*," her mother had said as she leaned over the small table at the coffee shop and gave her only daughter a big hug. "You don't have to *ask* me to do anything. It's my pleasure. Whatever you decide, I'm with you."

It had felt good to have her mom in her corner, but her mother had always been on her side, the two of them an inseparable team since her father died. Even with the support, though, Madison wasn't sure how she'd make it work. Could she really ask her nearly seventy-year-old mother to watch a baby for fifty or sixty hours a week? It didn't seem right. She could get a less demanding job at another firm, but then what? Less money? Now she had a baby to think about.

You could tell Collin, a small voice in her head whispered. *Doesn't he have a right to know?*

She instantly swatted the annoying thought away like it was a mosquito. *Tell him, so he has an opportunity to weigh in and insist she get an abortion? Forget it!*

She assumed he'd be anti-baby. There wasn't anything soft and fuzzy about the man, and he'd made it more than clear these last few months that he considered their one-night stand exactly that—one and done.

But right now, all she cared about was holding down her meager lunch of saltines and water. She clung to the ferry's railing at the back of the boat, willing herself not to hurl as the crystal blue ocean sped by. Madison always prided herself on having a stomach made of steel; she never got food poisoning, and only once in her life ever had the stomach flu. She never even got a hangover. But…this…this was different.

Her stomach roiled and she leaned over the side of the railing but managed not to throw up. Not yet.

"Seasick?" asked a sympathetic elderly tourist sitting near her in the oversized pontoon boat, wearing a bright pink flamingo visor, raising her voice over the wind.

Madison's face flamed as she hurried to wipe her mouth. This was so embarrassing. Seasickness? Never once in her life. "Uh, yeah," she lied.

"Try to look at the horizon, that will help," the lady offered. Madison nodded and then stared off into the distance, but she knew it would do no good.

Collin Baptista. She'd fallen victim to his

green eyes, and the fit, muscular body that looked so good in those suits. Never mind that he was the most arrogant know-it-all prosecutor she'd ever met. Collin was all the things she hated about prosecutors—his full-of-himself, holier-than-thou attitude that somehow failed to rub juries the wrong way. He'd never met a defendant he thought might be innocent or, at the very least, deserve his sympathy. He'd once asked a jury to put James Miller, a nineteen-year-old kid with a partial scholarship to the University of Indiana, away for three years for shoplifting a pair of earbuds. Forget that the kid was stealing them as a Christmas present for his single mom who worked two jobs. True, he'd hit the security guard, who'd tried to stop him, although the guard had gotten away with just a black eye.

Collin had told the jury the kid was violent, but Madison thought the punch he'd thrown was a mistake he regretted. In some ways, they might have both been right; the kid could've gone on to be more violent the next time. Or he could've learned his lesson. Now, locked away in jail, he'd almost certainly *become* more violent in order to survive.

Madison saw the world in a hundred shades of gray, but Collin Baptista saw it in stark black and white. Guilty or innocent, right or wrong, no in-between. She couldn't believe she'd fallen into bed with the man. But then again, she knew why: Jimmy Reese, the horrible white supremacist. They'd faced off as opposing counsel on that case, but in that one instance, they'd both agreed. The violent, hateful man needed to be in jail. The fact that they had common ground at all was a turn-on, one she hadn't expected.

Besides, she knew herself. She was attracted to overconfident men, and Collin was their poster boy. He possessed unwavering confidence, an ability to command the room and a certain fearlessness. Once, when a convicted murderer got loose in the courtroom, he'd simply clotheslined the man as he made a run for the exit, laying him flat on the floor before the bailiff could even react. Nobody would ever accuse Collin Baptista of being a pencil-neck lawyer. He oozed alpha-male sex appeal, and she was the first to admit she liked it.

And she wasn't the only one. He had a reputation for loving and leaving the ladies, had slept with half the female clerks in the courthouse. He was known for never being serious, never having a steady girlfriend, always playing the field. After their night together, when Collin pretended it had never happened, she ought to have seen that coming. She'd only been yet another challenge, the charismatic young prosecutor who had women falling at his feet. Still, the rejection had hurt her pride.

Just add it to the list of jerks I've slept with. Not that it was a big list, but still. If there was a jerk in the room, she'd find him every time.

She was *not* going let him know their one-night stand had resulted in a pregnancy. Sure, she could go after him for child support, but she wasn't a charity case. She could take care of herself...and this baby. She just needed to work out a plan. He'd left her messages lately, but she'd doggedly refused to respond to them. He'd only said, *We need to talk*, which could mean anything, and besides, the last thing she wanted to do was be on the phone with the county's most dangerous cross-examiner, known for his ability to eviscerate an unwilling witness. She knew if she talked to Collin, her resolve to keep the pregnancy secret would dissolve. Another wave of nausea hit her as she leaned over the side of the railing and lost the saltines she'd tried so hard to keep in her stomach. *Baby, you're making this really hard on us both*, she mentally scolded. *How am I supposed to feed you if you eject everything I eat?*

She wiped her mouth with a tissue and sighed. Nobody ever mentioned that morning sickness could actually be morning, noon and night sickness. One more thing about pregnancy she never knew. Just like the bone-tired fatigue that would creep up on her at all hours of the day and the pregnancy hormones rushing around her body, inducing her to cry at the drop of a dime. She'd even gotten teary at a car rental commercial last night. Madison shook her head. The pregnancy was already making her soft.

If only her friends from high school knew. They'd voted her least likely to have a family and most likely to own a business by twenty-five. Madison had always focused on her career and made her personal life secondary. But Madison wasn't about to apologize for her ambition. She wasn't going to be like her mother: a stay-at-home mom who'd been completely unprepared for the workforce when her husband had suddenly died. They'd had several hard years, with her mother cleaning homes and working odd jobs, before her uncle helped her mom get paralegal training and then hired her in his own firm. Madison had watched her mother struggle and vowed never to be so unprepared. Family and kids weren't her priority—financial security was.

The shore of North Captiva came closer as the small ferry approached the dock. Madison recognized the North Captiva Island Club, home to swimming pools, boat rentals and the island's best restaurant. She saw the golf carts lined up in the small dirt parking lot near the office, the bright Florida sunshine bathing everything in a warm glow. She remembered the island from when she was a kid and her parents had taken her there on vacation, using her uncle's house. Now, as an adult, she welcomed the getaway. Here, she could think. Figure out what she planned to do. Alone.

"Hope you feel better, dear," the woman in the flamingo pink hat said as she moved past her to climb off the boat. Madison followed, and once her sneakered feet hit the wooden dock, she instantly felt better. Either it had been the boat making her morning sickness worse, or she was just relieved to be back in the place that held so many prized childhood memories. Uncle Rashad had been very generous to her mother and her, hosting them every summer, even after her father died. The clubhouse had received a new coat of paint since she'd last been to the island, a few years back, but otherwise, everything seemed the same.

Madison glanced at the line of golf carts parked near the tennis courts and didn't see her uncle's telltale silver four-seater, the one that looked less like a golf cart and more like a dune buggy. Usually the North Captiva club staff had everything waiting for guests, including transportation from the dock. Burly workers flexed their muscles as they took cargo from the ferry to the shore—crates of food, luggage, coolers. The island might be remote, but it was hardly rustic. As the crew unloaded her luggage and her plastic bin of groceries, Madison headed into the main office.

She saw Yvana Davis, the resort's manager she adored and had known most of her life, standing behind the counter. The woman wore a uniform of a golf shirt and khakis, accessorized with sparkling dangle earrings and a colorful scarf around her head. There was no way Yvana was going to let the club dress code cramp her style. Now, however, a frown replaced her usual smile. She was trying to deal with what seemed to be an unruly tourist.

"But there are spiders," cried the forty-something brunette, who wore a floor-length wrap dress and sparkly slip-on flats and held a quivering lapdog in her arms.

"Inside your house?" Yvana asked, raising a dark eyebrow and putting one hand on a generous hip. Yvana made eye contact with Madison and gave her a nod of recognition.

"No, *outside*," whined the woman with the Boston accent. Madison, meanwhile, felt the nausea return. She didn't know if it was because of the woman's nasal voice or the fact that it was a little hot inside the office, but she was definitely feeling sick again.

Yvana pursed her lips. "Honey, this is *Florida*. We got bugs bigger than your dog. Hell, our bugs will *eat* that adorable little thing."

Madison hid a smile. That much was true.

"Well, I'm just asking someone to spray," the indignant woman said. "And...the garbage just... It just stinks. It's thoroughly disgusting. The dumpster's full of rotten fish and goodness knows what else, and it was full *before* we arrived..."

At the idea of fish rotting in the hot Florida sun, Madison's stomach lurched. *Please stop talking about trash. Or I'm going to hurl. Again.*

She glanced around for a bathroom...a trashcan...but found nothing. *I can hold it*, she thought. *I can will myself* not *to throw up... And the woman will stop talking about trash. Any minute now.*

"Trash pickup isn't till tomorrow," Yvana said, tapping her pink nails on the counter and clearly starting to lose her patience.

"Well, *something* needs to be done. There's rotten eggs in there, something that smells like spoiled meatloaf and probably some awful shrimp salad and..."

Madison lost it. Her reaction came hard and fast with no time to react. Even as she tried to cover her mouth, she threw up what little was left in her stomach—she was surprised there was anything—all over the tourist's sparkly shoes.

"Oh…my Gawd!" shrieked the woman. "What on earth…" Her face twisted in revulsion.

"I am so very sorry. I…" Madison wanted to say she was pregnant, but she couldn't get the words out, not with the angry woman glaring at her. "Let me see if I can help…" Madison moved forward but the woman batted her away with one hand.

"Get away from me!" she cried, backing off while clutching her dog.

Yvana obviously couldn't resist, as she instantly emitted a cackle. "Well, goodness me. That *is* something. Want a tissue?" Yvana held out a tissue box to the tourist, who frowned at the offering as if it had spider legs. Yvana gave one to Madison instead.

"Maddie, here, child." Her expression softened instantly. "You okay? You look like death warmed over!"

"I'm not contagious… I'm just…" She clutched at her mouth once more.

Yvana jumped into action, tugging a trash can from behind the counter up to her. "Here, honey."

Madison grabbed the metal wastebasket. Luckily, nothing more came up.

"These were *designer* shoes. They're ruined and…they cost $200 retail, and now…" The tourist stomped her feet.

"I'm happy to pay for them," Madison said, wondering where she was going to find an extra $200. Her budget was tight, and even with the money she'd tucked away, she was about to take unpaid leave from work and she needed every dime she had.

The woman wasn't placated. "I ought to sue," she threatened. The tiny white dog in the crook of her arm barked as if he agreed.

"Careful," Yvana warned. "*This* lady is one of the best lawyers in town. If you sue, you're going to lose, sister."

The tourist's face grew more pinched. She opened and closed her mouth, seemingly at a loss for what to say. Her cheeks grew redder than a ripe tomato.

"Well, I've never had such poor service in all my life. Do I have to call your supervisor?" The annoyed woman hugged her little dog to her chest and delicately lifted one foot to shake off some of Madison's vomit.

Madison just shook her head. Yvana didn't *have* a supervisor. She damn near ran this place and nobody was foolish enough to go toe-to-toe with the woman who owned a fourth of the island and knew *everyone.* An older resident on the island had left his entire share to her when he passed away five years ago—she was the one who'd cared for him and he'd had no living children.

Yvana had a heart bigger than the Gulf of Mexico but also a temper that was legendary. You got on her good side, and Yvana would do anything for you, but get on her bad side, and you might not have your power turned on for days.

Yvana narrowed her eyes at the indignant tourist.

"Mm, hm." Yvana gave her a once-over. "*My supervisor* is out," she lied, since she was her own supervisor. "But I'll write a note and make sure she gets it."

"Well," the tourist muttered. "I…"

Yvana glared at her and then turned back to Madison.

"Maddie, honey. Sit down before you fall down." Yvana put her back to the other woman who, with nothing more to do, stepped out of her shoes and bent down to pick them up, careful to keep her fingers clean. She headed out of the office in a huff. Yvana ignored her and moved Madison over to a chair, then scurried over with the tissues she'd held out to her earlier.

Madison reached out as if to start trying to mop up the spill.

"No, no. Sit. I'll call someone from the janitorial staff to handle that," Yvana said.

"I am *so* sorry. God, how embarrassing. I normally don't do this. I never get sick." Madison sat down in the chair still feeling a little woozy as Yvana fetched an unopened water bottle from her desk and handed it to her.

"Not every day that you're pregnant, either," Yvana said, tilting her head to one side.

Madison stopped mid-drink, stunned. "How did you know that?"

"Oh, I just *know.*" Yvana looked so serious that for a second Madison worried that she'd somehow begun to show, although her stomach was still flat. Yvana threw back her head and laughed. "Oh, I'm kidding, honey. Rashad told me."

"Uncle Rashad! He wasn't supposed to tell anyone!" Madison grumbled, wishing she'd been more explicit with her uncle about this being a private matter.

"Oh, he swore me to secrecy, don't you

worry," Yvana said. "He just wanted me to know because he asked me to keep an eye on you. And by the look of things—" she nodded at the mess on the floor "—you might need a little bit of TLC."

"I'm fine." Madison wiped her mouth with a tissue. "I just need some rest and—if this baby will ever let me keep anything down—some food."

"Soda water, then, and I might have something that could help settle your stomach. Something I ate when I was pregnant with my twin boys." Yvana rolled her eyes. "Thought I'd about die from that pregnancy. I threw up right till the end of the second trimester. I never let those boys forget it, either."

Yvana grinned, and Madison had to laugh. She shook her head and glanced out the window to see the tourist throwing away her shoes in a nearby trash can. Then the woman hobbled in the hot sand over to a waiting golf cart that a man—her husband, Madison presumed— was sitting in and got into the passenger seat, fuming.

"I should apologize to her again," Madison said.

"You'll do no such thing. One apology was enough for *her*. She's been in my office every day since they got here, complaining about everything under the sun. She once came in here and complained about there being too much *sand*. On a beach. Can you imagine?" Yvana slapped her side. "She's worse than my ex-husband. He'd complain about the heat if the sun was shining and the damp if it was raining. Never could be satisfied, just like that woman. That, Maddie, was pure payback."

Madison smiled. She hadn't heard anyone call her Maddie for a long time. It was a name reserved for people who'd known her since she was little, the nickname her father gave her when she was a baby. She'd visited North Captiva all her life, but it had been her special refuge after her father died. She and her mother had lived in her uncle's house for nearly a year. She'd known Yvana most of her life and was grateful to the big-hearted woman who'd always looked after her.

"I didn't see Rashad's golf cart..." Madison said, nodding her head toward the window.

"No?" Yvana peered out. "Huh. I told Gus to get it, but he must be backed up today. Don't you worry. I can drive you. The front office can watch itself for five minutes. But first, let me call someone to deal with this mess."

YVANA EXPERTLY MANEUVERED the small tan-and-green golf cart emblazoned with the North

Captiva Club logo through the sand trails of the island. A simple white post marked most turnoffs and to a visitor's eye, easy to miss. Ahead of them, tourists who were new to the island studied a map, then scratched their heads. Yvana pulled over to help them find their way. Phone GPS didn't work well here, and one sand-lined trail looked pretty much like another. As she waited, Madison craned her neck back to catch the sun's rays, feeling comfortably warm and much less sick to her stomach. *It must be the island weather*, she thought. She was already starting to feel better. More hopeful.

Yvana asked the tourists if they needed help, but they waved her off, determined to find their own way.

"Tourists," Yvana said as she waved at them and hit the gas. "They *might* get to their place before the end of the week." Pity laced her voice. She took a sharp left then by a big white house with a wraparound porch, and a moment later, they were speeding along a little lagoon spotted with ducks and a couple of white cranes. Above them, a canopy of palm trees provided shade as they sped by in the little cart.

"Not any of my business," Yvana said, "but

you know what you're going to do? About the baby?"

"I'm going to keep it. I'm not sure how. Mom offered to babysit, but I think that's a lot to ask of her."

"You got time to sort it out," Yvana said, keeping her eyes on the road. "What about the father? What's he doing in all this?"

Madison sucked in a breath. "Haven't told him." She thought of Collin's smug face, his always-right smile. *Won't ever, either.*

Yvana's head swiveled, and she glanced at Madison's profile.

"Is it because he's the running type or the marrying type?"

Madison let out a long, tired breath. "I don't know. Which one is the me-first type? Hell, me-first and me-*only*?"

Yvana chuckled. "Oh, then, well, that ain't going to work at all. He'd get a rude awakening when he found out the baby always comes first." The breeze ruffled her colorful head scarf. "But don't you worry, honey. You'll figure it out."

Madison hoped so.

Yvana took a hard right onto a road nearly covered by brush, and a yellow daffodil hit her knee as they turned into her uncle's long driveway. It almost felt as if they were ducking into some deserted rain forest, but then the path widened and she saw the sandy yard, the big blue two-story house on stilts, making it as tall as your average three-story building. Yvana swung the cart into the little circular sand drive, letting Madison off at the steps.

"Looks like the guys already brought your luggage," Yvana said. Madison saw her suitcase and grocery tote sitting on the front porch near the front door.

"Thanks for the lift, Yvana."

"No worries. And if you need anything, you call me, you hear? Anything at all. Pickles and ice cream, even."

Madison turned and leaned into the golf cart and gave Yvana a big hug, tears pushing out from behind her closed eyelids. *Damn these pregnancy hormones.*

"Thank you," she whispered.

Yvana returned the hug. "You bet," she said. "Take care of yourself. And I'll be by later with that remedy I told you about. It'll settle your stomach in no time."

"Thank you," Madison said once more, brimming with gratitude. Looking at Yvana's smiling face, she couldn't help thinking that everything would somehow be okay.

"See you later!" Yvana called. Madison nodded as Yvana took off around the circle. She walked up the front porch steps, a whole story's worth, to accommodate the stilts. Most homes on the island included two livable stories, but stood three stories high. Flooding was common on the island, especially during hurricane season. She marched up to the front door, framed by full-length glass windows, her first objective being to put away the groceries she'd brought in a cooler from Fort Myers. Meantime, her stomach rumbled. If it wasn't nauseated, it was hungry. *Decide already*, she thought. She didn't know how much more of this yo-yo effect she could take. This was going to be a *long* nine months.

CHAPTER TWO

COLLIN SAT ON the ferry beneath the blistering afternoon sun and just wanted to *be* there already. He'd driven to the ferry station, parked and then taken an old passenger van down to the shore, where he'd boarded a small pontoon-style boat with about ten other tourists headed to North Captiva. He was currently sitting between a little boy kneeling on the seat and facing the water, hands on the edge of the boat as if he might fly off any second, and a teenager whose eyes had never left her phone. It was the only seat left, and he was lucky to have it, but now he simply wished the ferry ride to be over. He needed to see Madison.

Collin *knew* the baby was his. He wasn't sure how, but he knew it. The second Matt had said Madison was pregnant, he'd felt that it was true. Sure, he could be wrong. Hell, Madison might not even be pregnant, but he trusted his instincts. Collin's mother had been extremely superstitious; she'd claimed ESP— or what she called *really good hunches*—ran in their family. Collin had never put much stock in it. He didn't believe in hocus-pocus, but he *did* believe in good instincts. That was exactly how he could tell a witness on the stand was lying—or about to lie. He'd become notorious for trapping shaky witnesses, dominating the cross-examination. Maybe that was the family hunch at work.

All he knew was that Madison was doggedly refusing to answer his calls. He'd left her a dozen messages, had texted, emailed— basically, he'd done everything but try to send her a telegraph. She was avoiding him, and he was going to find out why.

Collin glanced at a couple on the other end of the boat beneath the shade of the awning. The woman had a baby strapped to her in a sling, and her husband was making faces at the little one. He wondered how old the infant was—he or she was so tiny. He realized, with a start, that he'd only ever held his niece, but that was long after she was six months old and big enough to hold her head up—not like this fragile newborn across the way. He had no idea how to hold a baby that small. His niece, Sari, was six, loved knock-knock jokes and was easy to entertain. He'd missed the first half year of her life because his sister and her husband had been in the Philippines for work when she was born. Now, they were stateside again, and he'd spent the last four Thanksgivings at their house.

He reached into his pocket and felt for the small black velvet box there. He had a brand new one-carat princess-cut solitaire set in platinum inside. It probably wouldn't fit Madison's finger, but the salesclerk had assured him it could be sized. Collin knew the power of a big gesture, and he had one planned—although, the roses he'd bought at the grocery store stop-off before he'd reached the ferry were looking a little wilted in the heat. *Not unlike me*, he thought. He wore shorts and a polo, but he wished he had his swim trunks on so he could just jump into the bay and swim for it. The Florida sun was brutal today. It had beaten down on him mercilessly since he'd gotten one of the only seats in the sun. He swiped at his brow.

He'd been running through everything he planned to tell Madison when she swung open that door: *Do me the honor of being my wife* or *Let's be a family* or *This means we're meant to be together.* Suddenly, more sweat rolled down his temples. Was it the sun or were nerves getting to him? He felt jittery.

He texted his elder sister, Sophia. They'd been thick as thieves growing up, relying on each other as their single mom worked long hours to care for them after their father went to jail. It had been a poor childhood, and in some ways hard, but not an unhappy one. Sophia had made sure of that, even though she babysat him when she was barely more than a child herself. She could easily have slipped into poor choices, but instead she'd taken her responsibilities seriously, and she'd managed to make straight As. She'd pushed him to do better as well, which was the reason he'd opted for law school.

On the ferry... I'm nervous.

Collin had already talked to her about Madison and the baby and his plan the night before.

You have no reason to be nervous. Any woman would be lucky to have you.

Collin wasn't sure that was true.

Yes, but she wasn't exactly happy with me, remember?

Whose fault was that?

That is NOT helping.

Collin was beating himself up about the way he'd handled the aftermath of their night together. He'd not exactly been sensitive. Or, even nice about it.

Listen, guy-who-got-asked-to-the-prom-by-FIVE-different-girls, I think you'll do fine. Really, I do. And what's the worst that can happen? You offer to do the right thing and she turns you down? Then, you avoid a shotgun wedding, and it's probably for the best.

Collin felt a pit in his stomach open up. That was *not* what he wanted, actually. He wanted a family; he wanted this situation to work out. It might not be the way he'd planned it, but as far back as he could remember, he'd wanted kids, a traditional family, like he'd never had. Sophia texted again.

You sure you want to do this? Propose to a stranger?

They weren't exactly strangers. He remembered flashes of their night together—a melding of bodies, heat, desire. He recalled being wowed by her, that her body was even more perfect than he'd guessed. The fact that he might see that same body *tonight* sent a shiver of anticipation through him.

Besides, he knew couples who'd dated for years before tying the knot, only to get divorced half a dozen years down the road. You could live with a person for a decade and he or she could still surprise you, so why *not* marry a stranger?

I don't have any doubt that we can make this work. I want a family. I want my child to be raised right.

Sophia sent him a heart face.

That's why I love you, little brother. You've got a big heart. Don't worry. You'll do fine. She's lucky to have you.

The sun relentlessly bore down on his head and Collin wondered if he should've worn sunscreen. He wiped his brow again as he saw the island before him grow larger. Almost there. The baby at the other end of the boat let out a cry. The mother bounced the child in her little sling, but the cries just got louder. Collin glanced at the dad, who helped the mother untangle the baby and then took him in his arms, but he wailed even louder. He wore a blue onesie, so Collin assumed he was a boy. No matter what they did, the baby just kept fussing, growing ever more red-faced and angry. Collin wondered why they couldn't make him stop crying.

Then the mother lifted up her shirt and Collin glanced away, hoping to give her some privacy. Did Madison want to breastfeed? Didn't doctors say that was healthier? He didn't really know. He glazed over when that kind of news came on. His interest in breasts had nothing to do with babies or milk.

The boat landed at the dock with a little thump, and the passengers started to file out—all but the mother, who sat with her baby a little longer. Collin moved past, careful to keep his eyes averted as he stepped out onto the dock. The father of the baby struggled with the gear, and Collin lent a helping hand, picking up the stroller and assisting the father in maneuvering it down to the dock.

"Thanks," the man said, looking tired and sporting deep dark circles under his eyes. Collin wondered when the man had last slept through the night.

"No problem," Collin said. "Beautiful baby you have there," he added, even though the baby's head was covered in a burp cloth as he finished his afternoon snack.

"Yeah, good thing, too." The tired dad shook his head. "They're a handful."

Soon I'll have a baby, too. I'll be just like this dad.

He glanced at the man whose shirt was wrinkled, his socks mismatched. Collin noticed a white stain on his shirt. Baby drool? Baby spit-up? The momentary unease left him, and he felt like his old confident self again. Collin had never met a challenge he hadn't happily faced head-on. Not that women had ever been a problem, at least not since his freshman year of high school—after he'd had the growth spurt that launched him from five-one to five-eleven in a single year. He'd spent most of his twenties and, so far, his thirties leaping from one casual encounter to another. He hadn't ever pursued a serious relationship, in large part because his job was so demanding. He barely had time for anything more.

But now, he'd have to make time. Somehow. He'd do it.

There was no way he'd ever be like his own father.

Collin remembered daycare, when the other kids were making gifts for their dads for Father's Day and he'd been one of the few who hadn't. The teacher had told him to draw a picture for his mom instead, but Collin never forgot the slow burn of embarrassment, feeling the hole in his life where his father should have been.

No. He wouldn't do that to *his* son.

Because, oddly enough, he knew it would be a boy. That certainty had just come to him...

The other guests from the boat ambled over to the waiting golf carts, apparently regulars on the island. *Probably homeowners here*, he thought, as they seemed to know exactly what to do. He still found it weird that there were no cars on North Captiva.

The island was prettier than he'd expected. Colorful tropical flowers lined the dock and the sandy path leading to the parked golf carts. He could see tennis courts in the distance and signs that led to a large pool and bar.

Collin, at a bit of a loss, wandered into the front office. He'd looked up Madison's uncle's house in the public record, but he wanted to find out if he could rent a golf cart to get there.

Inside the office, he found a large amiable woman behind the counter, wearing sparkly, dangling earrings, a colorful scarf over her head and a big smile on her face. Her age was impossible to guess. Forty? Fifty? Her name tag read *Yvana*. He presented her with his most charming smile as he set down his backpack that held two changes of clothes and his laptop. He didn't know how long he'd stay, but his plan was to convince Madison to come home with him.

She gave him a slow once-over in response, a sweep of judgment, and he could sense he met her approval.

"I'm Collin Baptista," he said, leaning on her desk.

"You have a reservation, hon?" she asked him.

"Uh…no, not exactly." This was where it might get odd. "So, I need your help… Yvana."

The woman's eyebrows rose, and he knew she was trying to decide whether or not he was worthy of her help. He was an excellent reader of people. *Tread carefully here.*

"Well, that depends on what you need." Yvana studied him.

"I want to ask your advice. If you were going to propose to a woman, where would you do it?" Collin pulled the velvet box from his pocket and flashed the engagement ring.

Yvana fanned her face. "Oh, *my*, that is gorgeous! You sure you don't want to just propose to me? That ring would look perfect on me."

He laughed. "Don't tempt me," he said, and she laughed, too.

"Who's the lucky girl?" Yvana tapped a bright fingernail on the counter.

Collin hesitated, wondering if he should be so forthcoming. But he knew he'd have to be. He needed her help.

"Oh, sugar, you can tell me. I've got to have the details if we're going to make sure she doesn't say no."

Collin shrugged. What was the harm? He wanted Yvana's help, and pretty soon he and Madison would be engaged, anyway, so what would it matter?

"Her name is Madison," he said.

Yvana just stared at him for a second. "Madison *Reddy*?"

"You know her?" Collin couldn't hide his surprise.

"I've known her for years. Since she was this big." Yvana held up her hand about waist-high. Now she studied him even more closely, like a bug under a microscope. "You going to make her happy?"

"I plan to try," he said honestly.

"Hmm." Yvana nodded thoughtfully. "Does she know you're coming?"

"Nope."

Yvana put one hand on her hip. "So, you show up here *without* a reservation and a ring and think...you're going to propose, just like that?"

The doubt on Yvana's face made him pause.

"Uh…right. That's right." Collin nodded. He glanced out the window, as he saw a golf cart speed by. "Something wrong with that plan?"

Yvana shrugged one shoulder. "Oh, honey, that's not for *me* to decide." She chuckled, then picked up the phone. "Let me call her and see if she's willing to see you."

Willing to see me? Now Collin was definitely feeling anxious. He thought about all the times she'd refused his calls.

"How about you just tell me how to get to her house and I'll surprise her? It's number fifty-nine, Harbor Bend Road?" He pulled out the printout from his pocket, the result of his search for her uncle's property.

"Oh, I know where it is." Yvana picked up the phone and punched in the number. "Maddie, sugar?" she said.

Maddie? Collin had never heard her called that before.

"I've got a male visitor here for you. His name is…" She cupped the receiver with one hand. "What's your name again, hon?"

"Collin."

"Collin's here. He wants me to take him to you, but I thought I'd…" She paused, listening. "Oh, I see. Mmm, hmm. Is that right? Well, now." She studied him, frowning. What was Madison telling her? "Oh… I see." She eyed him. "All right, then. Don't you worry none. I can handle this."

Was Madison refusing to see him? That didn't compute with Collin. He'd driven all this way, paid for the ferry, lugged this one-carat perfectly cut diamond from Fort Myers—and it had never occurred to him that it might be a wasted trip.

"You take care of yourself, you hear?" Yvana said and then hung up. She focused her dark brown eyes on him.

"What was all that about?" Collin asked, but Yvana ignored him. Her body language made it clear that she had no intention of sharing any details.

"Well, how about you wait out there on that bench?" Yvana said sweetly, pointing to the bench near the line of parked golf carts bathed in North Captiva sunlight. "I'll get Gus to drive you. He's running a few patrons out to their houses, but he should be back in fifteen or so."

"Maybe I could just walk?" he offered. He didn't want to wait that long. The ring felt suddenly heavy in his pocket. It belonged on Madison's finger.

"Oh, honey, you'd get lost." She shook her head, then gave him a big smile. "Wait right there. Gus will come by. You sure you don't want me to hold on to that ring for you?"

Collin chuckled. "No, I'd rather keep it, thanks."

"Suit yourself." The phone rang and Yvana picked it up. "Hello, North Captiva Club," she sang. Collin let himself out, the cool breeze from the beach ruffling his hair. He looked at a line of tropical flowers. There were worse places to wait, he figured, as he headed to the bench in the shade. He slumped down and checked his watch. He'd come this far. What was another fifteen minutes?

CHAPTER THREE

COLLIN BAPTISTA WAS HERE.

Madison paced her uncle's third-story deck in a panic. She bit her thumb as she glanced out over the treetops toward the ocean, which sparkled blue in the distance. Collin had found her. *How?* Did he know she was pregnant? God, she hoped not. Then again, she remembered that her uncle had spilled the beans to Yvana. Was he trying to play matchmaker with Collin, too?

No. He couldn't do that. She hadn't told him who the father was, after all.

Would Collin have been able to find out some other way?

She'd steadfastly refused his calls. Surely, he would've gotten the message that she wasn't interested. Besides, why was *he* even interested? And why now? He'd been more than clear that he didn't want a relationship. *I don't date defense attorneys.* Wasn't that what he'd said? *No, he doesn't date them. Just sleeps with them, that's all*, she thought bitterly. *And then dumps them like garbage the very next day.* She remembered how coldly he'd treated her. She got that it had been *one* night, but she had assumed he'd enjoyed it as much as she had. Obviously, that hadn't been the case. She'd thought the sex had been…exceptional, and yet he'd treated her as if it had been the worst night of his life. Maybe it had been. That idea was painful. He hadn't felt the connection, the spark that she had.

She ought to see him, but part of her felt scared. She wasn't sure she'd be able to keep the baby a secret, and the anxiety of seeing him roiled her stomach so that her morning— now officially afternoon sickness—had returned. She told Yvana to stall him while she figured out what to do. She couldn't flee; the next ferry wasn't for an hour at least, and she'd have to walk right past him to get on it. She could hope he'd get tired and leave, but what she knew of Collin told her he was a tenacious fighter who wouldn't give up easily.

What was he doing here?

Calm down, she told herself. *Just calm down and think.* A million different thoughts flooded her mind.

He knew. He had to know about the baby. Was he here to tell her to get an abortion?

She clenched her teeth at that possibility. She wasn't going to do it.

What to do?

Her brain suddenly didn't want to work. Ever since she'd stared at those two pink lines on the pregnancy test, she'd felt that her brain had gone into slow-mo mode, and she'd lost all ability to make a decision. Now, faced with Collin here, on North Captiva, she'd need to decide. If she told Yvana to get rid of him, she would. But was that what she really wanted? She wasn't sure.

What she did know was that she still wasn't over the sting of rejection she'd felt when he failed to call her the morning after their drunken tryst. She'd texted him—twice—and he hadn't bothered to respond. The curt nod she'd gotten in the courthouse the next morning had told her all she needed to know—she was a one-night stand, a mistake he didn't intend to repeat. She should've seen it coming. *I don't date defense attorneys*, he'd warned her over drinks. *It'd be a bad career move.*

She ought to have walked away from him right then and there. Yet, she hadn't. *It was his green eyes*, she thought, *almost gray, striking with his tanned complexion, set off by his jet-black hair*. He wore it longish and wavy on top, short at the sides. He was shrewd, but that wasn't what had made her stay for a drink. It was his surprising show of empathy that day.

"Nobody said this job was easy," he'd murmured as he sidled up to her at the bar at Pete's, down the street from the courthouse in Fort Myers. "I know you had a rough week. Buy you a drink?"

Rough didn't begin to cover it. Two days ago, she'd had to tell the mother of a nineteen-year-old that he was going to prison for seven years. He stole a car because someone had left it running with the keys in it. A crime of opportunity. But he'd messed up badly—because the car had had a baby in the back seat. That automatically made it a felony.

The teenager wasn't a bad kid, just rudderless; he'd spent his life in an impoverished neighborhood. Nevertheless, his carelessness had left a mother in a panic, and worse, he'd abandoned the car with the baby still inside. Thankfully, a cop had spotted it, but if that hadn't happened…the baby could've overheated, could've died. Poor decision-making and bad luck meant he was going away for seven years, and he'd come out harder. Maybe even more violent. There was nothing reforming about the prison system.

And then, in the afternoon, she'd had to represent a white supremacist—her! Madison was about as brown as a person could get. But Jimmy Reese was a KKK member who'd tried to shoot a black man and hit a white twelve-year-old instead. She couldn't imagine getting a worse case. She'd lost the one case and then gotten another that she hoped very much to lose.

"You planning to cut a deal for Jimmy?" he'd asked her.

She slowly shook her head. Jimmy had made it abundantly clear that he didn't want to cop a plea. "No, he wants to tell the whole court how patriotic he is for trying to kill anybody who isn't white."

Collin just rolled his eyes. "You gonna defend that?"

"No," she said, shaking her head again. "It's indefensible."

"I say we both need a drink," he said. "Come on, let me buy you one. A drink can make you feel better," he promised. "Or it'll make you feel much, much worse. Either way, you won't be where you are right now."

She'd had to laugh at that.

That was why she'd accepted Collin's offer of a drink. And the second. And the third.

And that led to…a night she wouldn't forget. Boy, the man had skills. He was gorgeous and he possessed a magical touch. It almost wasn't fair.

Her phone rang. She picked it up.

"You still want me to stall this guy?" Yvana asked. How long had it been since she'd called the first time? Half an hour?

"I don't know what to do," she admitted.

"Well, this Collin guy has been in here twice, asking me when his ride is coming, but you and I both know there ain't no ride. Not unless you say so."

"Where is he now?" Madison bit her lip. She didn't want to see him, and yet how long could she really stall?

"Waiting on that bench, but he's going to start walking soon, and you know how this island is for newbies... He'll be wandering around for days trying to find your house." Yvana clucked her tongue.

"I know, I just..." Madison hesitated. Her mind whirled like an old computer with long outdated software. She couldn't decide. Talk to him and get it over with? Should she do that?

"He's cute. You didn't mention that."

Madison felt a blush creep up her cheek. She knew he was and that women noticed him, but hearing it confirmed didn't help.

"I mean, I can see why you knocked boots. He's got muscles that go on...forever."

"Yvana!" Madison cried. Yvana cackled her delight into the phone.

"Just stating the obvious," Yvana said. "Don't worry, sugar. He's far too young for me. So, it's not his looks that are keeping you away. Why not let this fine man—the father of your baby, I assume—come see you? What's wrong with him? Aside from the fact that you could bounce quarters off those abs. Which isn't a problem unless you want a softer man to snuggle with."

Madison laughed. "He doesn't know. About the baby."

"You sure about that, honey?" Yvana sounded suddenly very skeptical.

"Thought I was. I didn't tell him."

"Well, he *sure* is anxious to see you, and I don't think it's got anything to do with asking you out for drinks."

Madison considered this. She glanced out her uncle's kitchen window. Since the house stood on stilts, even the first floor was raised. She could see the tops of some shorter palm trees swaying in the breeze outside. "I just… He wasn't very nice to me." Ignoring her *wasn't* nice. Not nice at all. And now, he'd shown up out of the blue… He *had* to know about the pregnancy. There could be no other explanation. "And there's no way he's ready to be a parent." She remembered how easily he'd fought to have a nineteen-year-old put behind bars. What kind of father would he make? A heartless one, probably. "He's full of himself, so how can he even focus on a baby?"

"Hmm, well, that *could* be trouble," Yvana agreed. "But maybe he's turned over a new leaf. He's been waiting in the sun for half an hour, so that gets him points in my book. Why don't you let me bring him to you? I've got a feeling you'll want to hear what he has to say."

What could that be? Madison wondered.

COLLIN GOT TIRED of waiting, so he set off down the sandy path in what he hoped was the right direction. He glanced back at the office once, but Yvana wasn't moving fast enough for his taste. Patience had never been his strong suit. He would wait for a golf cart no more. Collin pulled up the address on his phone, but the signal was weak and the map kept spinning—and at one stage, his phone told him he was walking in the ocean when he was a good twenty feet from the bay. He adjusted the heavy backpack on his shoulders, now second-guessing the idea of bringing his laptop. What "work" was he going to do? He'd said goodbye to the office before he left, and they'd had a send-off with cake and everything, and he was now happily enjoying all those vacation days he'd stockpiled but never used. Yet, he'd never been without work for so long in his whole career that he'd packed the laptop as a matter of course.

The hot North Captiva sun beat down on him. Sweat poured from his forehead and dripped into his eyes, making them sting. He wished he'd had the foresight to bring a hat. Or some sunscreen. But when was the last time he'd been on an island? On a vacation of *any* kind? He thought a moment. It had been before law school. *Ten* years without a proper vacation. He spent what little time off he took during holidays at his sister's house with her family. His sister was expecting again, and he'd be an uncle soon—for the second time.

Collin trudged down the sandy path, singing birds flitting from tree to tree beside him. Sweat continued to sting his eyes, and he squinted at his phone. It was useless. He'd have to ask someone for directions. He came to the first fork in the road, and paused, swatting at a mosquito buzzing around his face. This was beginning to get silly. He'd have to turn around and head back to the front office, or maybe flag down someone who might know where he needed to go. He couldn't believe an island that was just four miles long and a half-mile wide could be so confounding.

That was when he heard the whirl of a small engine behind him. He turned to see Yvana driving a beige golf cart with the green logo of the North Captiva Club on the hood.

"Well, Lord, aren't you in a hurry?" she cried. "You want to get heat stroke out here? Get in."

Glad to have a lift, Collin climbed into the cart, his shirt damp with sweat. "Thought you forgot about me."

"Oh, there's no way I could, believe me." Yvana eyed Collin as she drove down a path that led them by a large lagoon. A big white crane stabbed at a fish in the middle of the water, coming up with a mouthful and gobbling it down. "So, you plan on getting down on one knee or..."

Yvana let the question hang there.

Collin hadn't thought about it.

"I don't know," he said because he hadn't thought much about that part.

Yvana slammed on the brakes, nearly sending him out the open front of the cart. He grasped his bag, which had almost went flying as well.

"You want her to say *yes*, don't you?"

"Oh, she's going to say yes." He had a steady job and he'd offer security, and this way their son wouldn't be a bastard. Not that legitimacy seemed to matter anymore, an old-fashioned concept as most people saw it these days. But still. It was the principle of the thing.

"You think so?" Yvana eyed him with doubt.

"I know so."

Yvana threw her head back and laughed. "Oh, she's right. You *are* a little full of yourself, aren't you?"

"What did she say about—" Collin didn't get to finish the sentence because Yvana took the next turn at a speed she probably shouldn't have, and he nearly fell out of his seat. Once he'd righted himself, he heard Yvana laughing.

"*This* is going to be fun. Yes, it is."

MADISON WATCHED YVANA drop Collin off at the rounded sandy drive in front of her uncle's beach house, and she sucked in a breath. She was used to seeing him in his dark tailor-made suits, and the casual polo and cargo shorts he wore caught her off-guard. The bay air ruffled his dark hair. He seemed less severe, less…imposing. She approved. *So, this is what Collin Baptista looks like when he's not putting people away. Approachable, affable….handsome.*

Madison felt unnerved. His strong shoulders and muscular chest were as impressive in a polo as they were in an expensive wool suit. She had a flash then of his bare skin, of the feel of his strong pecs beneath her fingers. He was a surprisingly fit attorney, one who somehow found time to hit the gym. *Collin was one of those people*, she thought, *who woke at five a.m. just to life weights. An overachiever.*

Still, she felt an odd mix of delight and dread as she watched him walk up the stairs to the front patio door. Yvana steered the golf cart back out to the road, throwing her hand up in a wave as she left.

There was no more time to stall. Madison heard the doorbell and headed for the entryway. What was she going to say to him?

She padded down the staircase inside the house, her bare feet slapping the smooth dark wood as she made her way to the patio, anxiously fiddling with her hair. *Why do I even give a damn?* she asked herself as she went to the glass door. Collin was already knocking, peering in.

She'd forgotten how tall and broad he was. So broad. The normal-sized backpack slung over one shoulder looked…undersized.

She swung open the door.

"Is it mine?" he blurted immediately.

So he did know. Still, the *it* rubbed her the wrong way. The baby wasn't an *it*. The baby was…a boy or a girl, but first and foremost, a baby, a human being, *not* an it.

"How did you find out?" she asked as he moved past her into the cool air-conditioning.

She hadn't exactly invited him in, but he didn't seem to care about that little detail. She closed the door behind him, shutting out the swarm of gnats on the patio.

"Heard a rumor. Is it true? You're pregnant?"

She felt the intensity of his gaze. She wanted to lie but knew it was futile. He'd sniff out a falsehood in a heartbeat.

"Who told you?"

"Matt. From your firm. He said people are talking about you taking a sudden leave, and the rumors are either that you're pregnant or you have cancer. Which one is it?"

Madison bit her lower lip. She hadn't told anyone but Uncle Rashad about the pregnancy, and she was sure he'd never tell anyone at work. Yvana was an exception, but then she'd been a close family friend for decades, and the spilling of that secret really was about her protection. Uncle Rashad wouldn't gossip about something like that at the office.

"Is it true?" Collin asked again. He wasn't going to let this go.

"No one was supposed to know," she murmured.

"So, it *is* true."

Here's where he argues about the benefits of getting rid of the baby, she thought. *Here's where he subtly, but firmly, tells me the best thing is to terminate the pregnancy.* She remembered Collin's ruthless precision in the courtroom, his cold heart when it came to pleas and to empathy. He allowed for zero errors—whether it was a teenage kid making a stupid mistake or a mother who'd left her child in the care of someone who wasn't fit to look after anyone else.

"So? It's mine, isn't it?"

"Yes," she sighed. She braced herself for the lecture.

"That's what I thought," he said, his expression eager and even…excited? That took her by surprise. She hadn't expected him to *want* the baby. He'd been all hands and mouth that one night they'd spent together, but then the next day it was as if she hadn't existed. Now, he liked the idea of her carrying his baby? Maybe she'd been wrong about him. Maybe he wasn't just the hard-nosed prosecutor, the man without a heart.

He dug around in his pocket and pulled out a black velvet box. He put down his backpack on the terra-cotta stone tiles of the foyer and then turned to her.

"If it's mine, then we need to do this." He flipped open the black box lid, revealing a brilliant solitaire diamond that caught the sunlight and sparkled like fire. Suddenly, all coherent thought fled her mind.

Collin Baptista was asking her to *marry him*?

CHAPTER FOUR

MADISON FELT STUNNED as she stared at the ring. Could this really be happening? He was asking her to be his wife? She glanced up at Collin. His green eyes were serious; this was no joke.

"So?" he asked, handing her the box. A respectable diamond, she noticed. It must've cost a pretty penny.

He ducked down quickly, opened his backpack and pulled out a bouquet of wilted roses. "Oh, and here." He thrust them at her. She took the flowers but ignored the box.

That was his proposal? There was nothing romantic in it. Hell, she wasn't even sure he *liked* her, much less *loved* her, and he was proposing marriage? Why? Because one of his little guys had slipped past her goaltender? The ring was impressive; he, however, was not.

"That's your proposal." Madison crossed her arms, feeling a flare of anger in her chest. This was the best he could do? He couldn't even muster up an actual question? She'd always imagined when the time came for a man to propose marriage, it would go very differently than this.

"Well, yes. I'm making an honest woman of you."

What? She glanced at his face, so smug, so confident, so sure she'd only have one answer for him. He hadn't even gotten down on one knee. Not that she was the kind of girl who demanded old-fashioned subservience, but… why wasn't he trying harder?

He attempted to hand her the velvet box, and her heart thudded in her chest.

"What year is it? 1812?" Madison jabbed a fist into her hip.

"Hey, *hey.*" Once more, Collin held out the box, and the diamond glinted brightly in the sunlight, but Madison wasn't about to take it.

"I'm doing the right thing," he said.

There it was again, Madison thought, *that tone of superiority. The right thing.* He was so certain about what that was, and yet, he hadn't even asked her opinion. He'd made a unilateral decision.

"What makes you think I'm keeping the baby?" she asked, and she could tell by the expression on his face that that threw him for a loop. Even though she was, she hated that he was deciding *for* her.

"Because…you're always the softhearted

lawyer. You're always telling the jury about how they should have pity on this client or that client, and I assumed..." He frowned at her and stopped talking, then ran a hand through his hair. "You *have* to keep this baby."

"I think it's *my* decision."

"Oh, no, no." Collin was pacing now, a bundle of furious energy. "That's *our* baby. It's *our* decision."

This just made Madison more furious. He wasn't the one who had to carry the baby, give birth to the baby, nurse the baby. How was it half *his* decision?

"I came all this way, *and* I bought this ring, and you're telling me you're really considering an abortion?"

The word *abortion* felt like a slap. She didn't like to think about it. She knew plenty of women who had no issue with it, but Collin was right about one thing; she had a tender heart. That also meant she'd never in a million years judge another woman who decided to get one. She understood now with perfect clarity just how your life could be sidelined in a heartbeat with too many drinks and one bad choice. She'd already made the decision to keep the baby, but now that Collin was here, that decision had just become more complicated. Collin wanted to be *part* of the relationship between her and the child. That was a possibility she'd never considered. Now, having the baby meant…having Collin in her life to some degree. She hadn't planned on that.

Suddenly, the room felt airless, stuffy. Madison wanted to get away from Collin. She moved to the kitchen to get herself a glass of water. Her throat was dry and she was starting to feel light-headed. All she wanted to do was lie down.

But Collin wasn't finished as he trailed her into the kitchen. "And you weren't even going to *tell* me about it? I have a right to know. That's *our* baby."

Madison snorted. "*Our.* There's no *our* anything," she grumbled. After all, it was Collin who'd made it abundantly clear that he wanted nothing to do with her.

Collin followed her to the refrigerator. His shoulders seemed to take up all the space in the kitchen, and she felt trapped. "I'm doing the right thing, and you should, too," he said.

Oh, here it was again. Collin's obsession with right and wrong. It made him a fantastic prosecutor but also generally insufferable. Heaven forbid anybody should actually be a *human being* around him. Madison set down her glass of water near the sink and scowled at him.

"There he is... Mr. High-and-Mighty. I wondered when he was going to show up." Madison crossed her arms. "Do you ever get tired of your high horse? Isn't the air thin up there?"

"I don't know what you're talking about." Collin crossed his arms and glared back at her.

"You're full of yourself, that's what." Madison poked Collin in the chest, her finger bouncing off his muscles. "You never returned any of my calls. Or texts. You wanted *nothing* to do with me, but now you hear I'm pregnant, and suddenly you show up thinking I'm going to what...be grateful?"

The stunned look on Collin's face told her that was exactly what he'd thought.

"But...why *wouldn't* you be...happy or grateful or whatever?" Collin asked. "I'm offering to *marry* you. I never even *date* defense attorneys. But I'm willing to put all that aside and make up for my mistake, because now there's a baby on the way and... I'm offering you my support and my name and—"

"Don't talk about me and my profession like we're somehow less than human. *Defense* attorneys are people, too," Madison snapped. "And, for your information, I don't need your support." Madison was growing fed up with this kind of thinking. It wasn't the 1800s. Or, hell, even the 1900s. "I don't need your *name*, either. You may not know this, counselor, but I probably make more money than you. Those defense attorneys you hate so much often make more than you prosecutors."

"Not always."

"Pretty much always." Madison glared at him again.

Collin looked uncertain. The prosecutor who almost never lost a closing argument seemed adrift. "You *have* to keep the baby. You *have* to marry me," Collin said, still looking dumbfounded. Apparently, he hadn't considered the possibility that she'd say no, which irked her even more.

"I don't *have* to do anything," Madison said. But as the words left her mouth, she knew that was partly a lie. She was compelled to look at Collin's full lips, his perfect squared-off chin. Even in this moment of annoyance, she found herself attracted to the man, a feeling completely and utterly out of her control.

"I don't get it. You don't want to marry me?" The disappointment in his eyes caught her by surprise. Her rejection *hurt* him, something she hadn't thought possible. Madison's head pounded; she was tired and strangely sad. Why did she feel like she was going to cry? She hated the look of hope on his face—and the feeling of hopelessness in her own chest.

"I think you should go." Madison pointed to the patio door. "I have a headache. And I need to rest." Fatigue hit her, and suddenly all the energy left her body. And then there was the feeling of sadness that threatened to crush her.

She ushered Collin to the door.

"But…"

"You need to go. I am not making any decisions until the end of the week, okay? Right now, I need to lie down before I fall down." She opened the front door and he went, almost in a daze.

"You don't want to marry me," he reiterated.

"No, Collin, I don't," she said. Then, she shut the glass door in his face.

"THAT DID NOT go well," Collin said aloud, but the only one who heard him was the little green gecko darting by his feet on the porch. He stared at the closed door. Madison had closed the blinds, so he couldn't even look in. Still, Collin stood on the porch, swatting away mosquitoes.

What the hell do I do now? A nagging mosquito bit his neck and Collin slapped it hard. Damn bloodsuckers. Sometimes he hated Florida. He'd been raised in the Bronx and there, mosquitoes never got this big. But he'd gone to law school in Florida, since they'd offered him the biggest scholarship, and after graduation he'd gotten an internship and then a job in the state attorney's office. And he'd stayed, but he sometimes wished he was back in New York.

"If only I could put the entire mosquito population in jail," he mused as he adjusted his backpack on his shoulders and headed back to the main office on foot, the ring feeling heavy and suddenly way too expensive in his pocket. He was still reeling from her rejection. He hadn't been *one hundred* percent sure she'd say yes, but he realized he'd never really entertained the notion that she'd say no.

Where had he gone wrong? He knew Madison wasn't like other women he'd dated. She was fiercely independent, and she hadn't bothered chasing after him when he hadn't returned her texts, but still… Why hadn't she accepted his help? Then again, maybe she didn't *need* his help.

He shook his head as he wondered whether or not he ought to see if he could get a refund on the ring. He also had no idea what to do if Madison terminated her pregnancy.

Part of him felt strongly that she wouldn't do that, though. She was one of the biggest-hearted defense attorneys he knew. She couldn't spin those sob stories to the jury if she didn't believe them, and Collin's gut told her she'd be even more protective of her own baby.

Then it's my job to convince her we ought to get married. He didn't see it as a sexist thing at all. Madison might be convinced she didn't need him, but he was convinced the baby did.

After two wrong turns, he ended up back at the office. The door opened with a telltale ding of the bell, and Yvana glanced at him with pity.

"She said no, huh?"

"Why aren't you surprised?" Collin asked, leaning against the counter, wondering if Yvana knew more than she let on. He swiped at his sweaty brow and tried to enjoy the air-conditioning in the office.

"Oh, I've known Maddie a long time," Yvana said. "Babysat her when she was little. She's as stubborn a girl as I ever met. You couldn't get her to do anything unless she thought it was her idea."

Collin chuckled ruefully. "I learned that the hard way."

Yvana shook her head slowly, her golden hoop earrings catching the sunlight. "What're you gonna do? Pack it in? Ferry comes about half an hour from now."

"No," Collin said, suddenly feeling a new wave of determination. He hadn't given up on law school when things had gotten difficult.

He wasn't about to throw in the towel now. That was something his no-good father would have done. Quit when the going got tough. Not him.

Madison wasn't the only one who had a stubborn streak. "Do you have a house to rent? Preferably close to Madison?"

"Well, well, *well*." Yvana raised her eyebrows in surprise. "You're determined. I'm starting to like you," Yvana said as she clacked away on her keyboard. "You're in luck. The Petersons' house next door is available for rent. You want the whole week?"

"How about just one night?"

Yvana laughed. "Oh, honey, you're gonna need longer than that," she said. "I'll put you down for the week. Maybe two. You can always change the reservation if you convince her earlier—but, honey, let me warn you. She ain't an easy one."

CHAPTER FIVE

COLLIN WOKE THE next morning inside the little two-bedroom cottage on stilts, wondering for a second where he was. Then he saw the black velvet box on his nightstand, and all the events from the day before came rushing back. He sat up and yawned, still remembering the steely look on Madison's face when she'd refused to marry him. Clearly, Madison had been angry with him, and he guessed, if he really thought about it, he understood. He hadn't exactly been nice after they'd...done the deed. Worrying about office protocol and breaking office rules was probably something he should've done *before* they got naked. But Madison was just irresistible. He supposed he should've told her that after they'd slept together instead of ignoring her texts.

He'd messed up. He got that, but a baby changed things, didn't it?

And why wasn't he getting any points for standing up and taking responsibility? That was what he didn't get. Then again, since when did anyone ever give him points for that? His childhood on the poor side of the Bronx should've taught him that much. Guys who cut corners—like his father, like the hoods on the street—they got the instant payoff. Good guys had to work harder for theirs. He knew that, had always known it.

The sunlight beamed in through Collin's open bedroom window; the blinds were permanently stuck in the "up" position. He was normally an early riser, but dawn was earlier than even he normally got up. He glanced around the small room. Everything about this house was smaller and less impressive than Madison's. Or, rather, her uncle's. His, too, was on stilts, and stood three stories high, though only two were enclosed, the first being open to the elements, with an outside shower and a small shed for garden tools. The two properties faced one another, and all that separated their properties was a small green space of a shared yard, and a few trees. Their porches and balconies faced one another, though as he glanced at her home now, he couldn't see her. She must be inside. The yard was surprisingly manicured, most of the island was brush and trees where it wasn't beach—like a series of crisscrossing sandy trails through bits of tropical jungle. This house badly needed a new coat of paint—and a kitchen and bathroom remodel. However, it was close to Madison's, which was all that mattered.

He wondered what he ought to do. Call Madison? Go over and offer to get her breakfast? Neither of those things seemed likely to impress a woman who was totally pissed at him. He looked again at Madison's deck and checked for signs of life. He didn't see any. Collin sighed. He had no idea what his next move should be. If he was prosecuting a defendant, he would have been able to call his next witness or file a motion before the judge, but now, he felt at a total loss. Madison had told him flat-out no, and it wasn't as if he could appeal her decision to a higher authority. He rubbed his face and dragged himself to the bathroom where a brown gecko darted across the tile floor. Collin swished mouthwash around to rid himself of stale morning breath and glanced at his bare chest in the mirror. He worked out. He took care of himself. He was a good-looking guy—if he did say so himself—with a promising career. None of that seemed to matter to Madison, though.

He sighed again. Maybe he was a little egocentric, but he was proud of his accomplishments and of his career. He'd put in a lot of effort and defied all the odds to get where he was. He thought about the two jobs his mother had done, her late nights and early mornings, all by herself, working to support him and his sister. She'd passed away of a heart attack the year after he graduated from law school, but at least she'd gotten to see him land a job at the state attorney's office. She was so proud of him, and he had every right to be proud of himself. Was that ego or just fact?

Collin headed to the kitchen, where he found a refrigerator empty of everything except a bottle of ketchup and a cabinet that had coffee filters but zero coffee. He hadn't expected to be staying alone or in this house. He'd imagined being wrapped up in Madison's arms...or at the very least, sharing a meal with her. He hadn't brought groceries, and now he realized he'd probably have to go to the small convenience store near the pool for supplies, or simply eat out every meal. He groaned.

Peering up at the line of windows, he looked out on the treetops below and Madison's backyard. When he opened the sliding glass door, he could see all of Madison's yard from the porch on, since the first floor of the house was raised a story and a half above the ground. He went out onto the wooden deck barefoot and shirtless, wearing only his sleep shorts. Just then, he saw Madison emerge from a path near the shrubs carrying a watering can. She walked leisurely to a couple of potted plants nearby, where she watered some blooming bright pink flowers.

Collin watched for a second, risking the chance that she might look up and see him. Madison's dark hair hung loose past her shoulders, her eyes focused on the task. Usually, she wore her hair up in a tight bun in the courtroom. He remembered that on the night they'd shared he'd run his hands through it, and it had been thicker than he'd imagined. He could tell that she wore no makeup and just a pair of gym shorts and a tank top, but the sun hit her glowing skin in a manner that made her seem younger than thirty. He wanted to touch that smooth skin again, almost forgetting what it had felt like. *Damn those drinks that fogged my memory*, he thought. She moved gently, easily. Was she a little thicker around the middle? He wasn't sure, although, she did seem softer somehow, her curves curvier. He tried to see where a baby bump might be forming, but saw nothing except a perfect figure. The woman was breathtaking. *That was why she was so impossible to reject that night*, he thought. He remembered the way she'd reached up on her tiptoes to kiss him, the energy flowing between them, the attraction neither one could resist.

This woman is carrying my baby. The very idea still shook him.

Then a yellow blur dashed across his peripheral vision. He turned, glanced around the low-lying green leafy trees. What was that? He saw another blur of light colored fur. Yellow? Gray? He couldn't be sure. Too big to be a cat. A dog? It was close to Madison's backyard—and she didn't have a fence. What if it was a rabid dog? A dangerous one? Did they have coyotes on this island? Suddenly, he felt fearful. For Madison. For his baby.

"Madison!" Collin shouted, but she kept her back to him. That was when he saw the white earbuds, their wires trailing from her ears. Dammit! He watched, frozen, as the blur he'd seen in the trees broke free and headed at top speed toward Madison's turned back. Collin was already on the move, skidding down the wooden steps that led to their shared drive, nearly falling over himself as his bare feet hit the rocky path. He didn't feel the pricks of the tiny shells and pebbles on the soles of his feet as he sprinted over shrubs and through thorny bushes to Madison's yard. He heard a loud screech and went faster, breaking through the cover of thick branches in time to see a shaggy yellow dog licking Madison's face. She was flat on her back, and he had a single paw on her chest. He looked tame, but the adrenaline rushing through Collin's veins told him she'd been knocked to the ground by this... animal, no matter how adorable he seemed.

"Get off her!" Collin roared and rushed forward to push the dog away.

"Collin!" Madison chastised. "It's fine... He's just a puppy."

"That thing? That's no puppy!"

"He is," Madison insisted. "Look at the size of his paws. He's all clumsy... He's just a *big* puppy."

Collin glanced down at the dog's enormous paws, oversized for its body. Though, now that he was closer, he saw that the dog was smaller than he'd first thought. He was mostly fur. The dog probably weighed only thirty pounds.

"What if he's rabid?"

"I'm sure he's not," Madison said. He saw that she took notice of his shirtless chest, her eyes momentarily on his torso. Was it his imagination or did her eyes linger there a bit longer than they ought to? *Well, let her look.* He hadn't had time to throw on a shirt. He'd thought she was being mauled by a rabid dog.

"He knocked you down." Collin still felt his heart thudding as he reached out and helped her to her feet. "Are you okay? Is..." He couldn't even get out the word *baby*. "Is *everything* okay?"

"I'm fine," Madison said as she shook a leaf out of her hair, then batted his hands away. "He didn't knock me down. He surprised me, and I slipped."

"Same difference." He shifted, the sandy soil filled with shells poking at his bare feet. "You all right?" he asked once more.

"Fine," she snapped. "I told you. And what are you even doing here? I thought you went home."

"You thought wrong. I rented the house next door."

"Why?"

He heard a note of annoyance in her voice. He was worried about her—was that a crime? For a second, she reminded him of his mother: stoic, stubborn, refusing to admit she ever needed help. The woman would work until she collapsed, never complaining.

"Because we need to talk."

Before Madison could answer, the shaggy yellow dog barked. He looked like some dog experiment gone wrong. His poofy, curly yellow fur hung in his eyes, and his shaggy coat made him look, at a guess, part poodle and part sheepdog. Or maybe part golden retriever. The little guy had big floppy ears and a long fluffy tail that curled up like the feather on a musketeer's hat. He wore no collar, and bits of leaves and brush were poking out of his thick fur. Collin had never been much of an animal person—living with a single mom in the Bronx meant he'd never had a dog growing up. His mother barely had enough money to buy *them* food, much less food for a pet. Collin had spent most of his childhood convincing himself he'd never wanted one, anyway. He studied the dog with suspicion.

Madison, however, leaned down and ran her hands through the dog's furry head, scratching him behind the ears.

"Who's a good boy?" she said. "You look just like a teddy bear."

"If a wolf can look like a teddy bear," Collin grumbled.

She continued to rub the dog and his back foot instantly began bobbing, as if he was trying to scratch an invisible itch.

"Aw, you're adorable, yes, you are." Madison's voice went high and baby-like, and Collin felt a stab of jealousy. Why did she like this strange little stray mutt more than him?

"He probably has fleas," he said, noticing how much the dog seemed to appreciate being pet nearly anywhere, as Madison continued massaging his back and he kept moving glee-fully to divert her attention to a new spot.

Madison ignored Collin's remark. "You don't have a collar," she said. "Who's your owner, boy?" She waited patiently as if the dog might answer her.

"You know he can't speak, right?" Collin pointed out, but Madison just frowned.

"You're thirsty, aren't you? And hungry. When was the last time you had a drink?" She shook her head. *Why was that her prob-lem?* Collin wondered. "Wait with him. Don't let him leave," Madison ordered, as she ran up the wooden staircase to her front door.

"But…" Collin didn't like dogs. Or cats. Or anything with fur and teeth. He stared down at the dog, who had a big pink tongue hanging out its mouth as it panted, and he had no idea what he was supposed to do. The dog pushed his nose up against his crotch to sniff.

"Hey, back off," he said, squirming in the opposite direction. Then, as he was trying to maneuver farther back, the dog gave his hand a big sticky lick. *Ew. Probably all kinds of germs in that drool*, he thought with dis-gust, as he wiped his hand on his shorts. The dog leaned forward again and licked his toes. Collin nearly leaped a mile straight in the air. "That's it… You…" He jumped away from the dog and nearly fell. He had half a mind to scare the dog off. A stray wasn't their problem, no matter how much Madison wanted to make it hers.

She emerged with a bowl of water, a small belt and a white nylon rope. She put the bowl down in front of the mangy mutt, and he began lapping up the water as if he hadn't had any in days.

"Thought you looked thirsty, boy," she said as she bent down and wrapped her belt around the dog's neck, using it as a makeshift collar. She attached the nylon rope and tied it to one of the posts of her front steps. "Now you won't run off before we can find your owner."

"We?" Collin asked, anxious. "Let's call animal control. Then he won't be anybody's problem anymore. They can take him to the pound."

"The pound!" Madison cried, shocked. "No way. Besides, this island is too small for that. We've got one fire station and not even a police station."

Collin frowned. "What if there's trouble? Does everybody just hope it goes away?"

"Usually there isn't, but in an emergency, we call the shore, and the police can helicopter someone over."

"But they can't get here that fast," Collin

noted, not liking the idea of his future wife and future baby being on an island where the police were a helicopter flight away.

"It's a peaceful place," she said. "Or *was*. Till you got here."

"What's that supposed to mean?" Collin asked, defensive. Near his feet, the yellow dog lifted his now-wet snout from the bowl of water and whined.

"Never mind. Anyway, there's no pound, so we're going to find his owner."

"What if he doesn't have one?"

The dog cocked his head to one side. "We're on an island, so I don't think he swam here." She glared at him, and he felt the sudden urge to march back to his rental house, grab his things and head straight for the first ferry off this little rock.

"What if they don't want this ugly dog back?"

"He's not ugly! He's adorable."

Collin sighed. Here went the softhearted defense attorney, wanting to give everyone a second chance.

"I think he's a poodle mix. Maybe a labradoodle or a golden doodle."

"He's a no-doodle, if you ask me." Collin frowned at the dog.

"You're so mean!" Madison exclaimed. "Can't you have a heart, for once?"

"I have a heart," he argued, a little taken aback.

"Really?" She looked skeptical and that stung.

"I'm not that bad. Only to the *bad guys*."

"Look, why don't you go back to…" Madison lost her train of thought. "…wherever you came from and I'll take care of the dog. I can go knock on doors."

"You? Take this disaster around and knock on strangers' doors?" Collin was horrified. "In your condition?" He suddenly imagined a host of problems—heat stroke or an accident—or even worse, serial killers lurking behind every palm tree.

"I'm pregnant, not paralyzed," Madison said, narrowing her eyes. "And you don't care about this dog, so I'll do it."

Collin let out a sigh. He'd have to go with her. He didn't want her wandering around the island with a dog nearly as big as she was. Puppy or not. "I'm coming with you."

"I didn't ask for your help," she said, lifting her chin.

"You're getting it anyway. Can you let me put on some clothes first?"

Madison glanced uneasily at his bare chest. "I guess so."

The yellow dog barked his approval.

CHAPTER SIX

BY THE TIME they'd walked nearly a mile and asked about the dog at a dozen houses, Madison was starting to tire…and her empty stomach grumbled, reflecting her increasingly darker mood. She looked at the yellow fluffy ball of fur trotting ahead of them. So far, nobody they'd talked to owned a dog or knew of anybody who owned a dog, aside from the Ruben family and they had a German shepherd. The hot North Captiva sun hung high above them, nearly overhead, signaling that it was drawing close to lunchtime. Madison had long since burned off her breakfast of an English muffin and a cup of decaffeinated tea. Collin insisted on holding the dog's "leash" as he fretted over her as if she were made of delicate china. She wasn't sure whether she liked his nonstop worry or hated it. She might be pregnant, but she wasn't some little weakling.

Although, her hungry stomach told her that if she didn't find some food—and something to drink—soon, she might start to feel like one.

"Are we really going to knock on *every* door?" Collin asked her. "Why don't we just let the dog go? He seemed fine on his own, and maybe he knows where home is."

"No! How can you say that? He's dying of thirst."

"Not dying. Just thirsty," Collin muttered. The dog bounced happily ahead of them, tail wagging as Collin held on to the rope attached to Madison's skinny belt, which she'd looped twice around the dog's neck.

"He's been on his own for a while… Maybe his owners even left the island."

"And left him behind?" Collin asked.

"Sometimes people do bad things." Madison shrugged.

"Says the defense attorney," Collin quipped. "Can I get that *on record* for the next time you're defending one of your guilty clients?"

Madison whirled, feeling anger squeeze her throat. Plus, her empty stomach made her short-tempered. "Not all of them are guilty."

"Uh-huh." Collin rolled his eyes. "Are you going to tell me *another* sob story about a thug who just fell in with the wrong crowd?"

Madison crossed her arms as they walked side by side down the narrow sandy path.

"You don't know everything, Mr. Prosecutor. Some clients are innocent. Like James Miller," she said.

"James Miller? The gangbanger? Are you serious?" He stopped, and the fluffy dog stopped with him, pink tongue out as he sat on the trail, watching them argue.

"He wasn't a gangbanger," Madison insisted. "He was a nineteen-year-old who stole a gift for his mother. That's all."

"I know that's what you told the jury, but I can't believe you really bought that. He was best friends with one of the most notorious gangbangers in his neighborhood, and he'd been seen riding around near where a shooting took place."

"He never shot anybody." Madison was absolutely sure about this. "And he knew bad people, but he wasn't in a gang. Besides, *you* know he didn't shoot anybody, or you'd have been prosecuting him for it."

"He punched the security guard, or don't you remember that footage? It was a violent act, and he was likely going to get more violent," Collin said.

"He made a mistake," Madison countered. They were now standing toe to toe, but Collin was so much taller that Madison had to arch her neck to meet his eyes.

"Okay, fine…and we're supposed to set him

free so his next 'mistake' is killing someone? And what about Jimmy Reese?"

Madison couldn't defend Jimmy. Well, technically, she *had* defended him, but he'd been a white supremacist who'd sprayed a supermarket with bullets, aiming for a black man, but killing a white girl and wounding half a dozen others.

"I tried to get him to take a plea," Madison said. *I didn't want to defend him.* "Besides, he's in jail for…what? Twenty years?" *Not that even twenty years would help the girl's parents sleep at night.* "And anyway, James isn't Reese."

"No? Reese also had burglary on his record. Just because James hadn't shot up a grocery store yet and killed someone's little girl doesn't mean he wouldn't have."

"James doesn't want to kill people just because of what they look like." How could he equate a neo Nazi with a kid who made a mistake?

"No, but gangbangers kill innocent people all the time," Collin countered. "Do I need to remind you how many kids were victims of gangbanger bullets last year alone?"

Madison felt her blood begin to boil. She hated this "if one's guilty, they're all guilty" attitude. It was why people assumed that everyone who lived in a certain zip code or looked a certain way must be a criminal.

"Maybe *you're* so concerned about being right that you can't see an obviously innocent defendant when you see one." Madison hated the way he always put labels on people. *Bad. Good.* Life wasn't that simple.

"And maybe *you're* such a bleeding heart you can't see that the guilty clients are guilty... and that this dog is just fine without us." Collin nodded at the dog, who still sat panting in the shade.

Was this how Collin would be as a father? An authoritarian know-it-all? How would he be understanding with a child, who would inevitably make mistakes? "This is why we shouldn't be parents," she said, waving a hand in the air. "We're too different."

"What does *that* have to do with being parents?" Collin took a step closer, his green eyes flashing in the sunlight. He was tall, imposing, intimidating, ever the prosecutor.

"You. Me. We see the world so differently. We'd make a terrible couple, and we'd make terrible parents," she said, taking the leash from his hands and walking ahead of him, the dog prancing out in front of her, happy to be moving again.

"Whoa, I'm going to make a great dad." Collin jogged to keep up, his sneakers sinking in the white sand.

Madison blew hair from her face, irritated. "Oh, yes, Mr. Authoritarian?"

"Kids need discipline." He didn't waver in his conviction.

"No." She turned and stared at him. "Kids need love."

"Well, of course, but they also need boundaries. They need rules."

She looked up at him again. "They need both."

Seeing the stubborn lines near his mouth, she recognized the expression. The one that crossed his face at the end of a trial, anytime things weren't going his way. That was when he dug in, readied for the hard fight. Was this how it would be forever? Would they be fighting, like opposing counsel, for the baby's entire life? The thought made her feel exhausted.

"This is why we can't be married," she said, gesturing to the tense space between them.

"Really?" He took a step forward, so their feet nearly touched. Now the tension disappeared, transformed from anger to something even hotter. His full lips… Madison remembered what those lips felt like on her skin, the searing trail they'd left down her collar bone. Memories of their night together filled her mind as she inhaled the smell of his after-shave, salty and sweet.

"Maybe we'd make the best kind of parents," he said. "Maybe we were meant to be together."

How did he do that? One second, she wanted to strangle him, and the next, she wanted to kiss him. She inhaled and took in a hint of his aftershave, something sweet and spicy. He smelled so damn good. He reached out and took her hand, and she momentarily froze. In that instant, she realized it was much easier to be angry and cold toward Collin when he wasn't standing right in front of her, when she didn't have his broad shoulders and his bright smile to contend with. He was too handsome, too charming...

"We're too different," she said for what had to be the third time, recalling how everybody, even opposing counsel, loved him. She was the book-smart girl, the quiet one, the contemplative one, the one who didn't have a favorite color because they all seemed to have pluses and minuses.

Collin was the kind of guy who wore charisma like a jacket and when he entered a room, everyone took note.

"Different is good," Collin said. "I couldn't stand having two of me around."

Madison laughed, unable to help herself. "I hate it when you're self-deprecating."

"Why?" He seemed puzzled by that.

"Because…" *It makes you so damn charming, nearly irresistible.* "Because you're harder not to like when you're funny."

He reached out and stroked her bare arm. At her feet, the dog got restless and whined, tugging at his leash. "Well, then I'll be funny some more." He stared at her a second or two longer, and Madison worried that he might kiss her, and then all that was left of her self-restraint might just sail out to the sea.

"Why are you trying so hard?"

"Because we belong together," Collin said, and in that moment she almost believed him.

"Why?" she asked again. She could never let anything go, never take things at face value.

A slight frown creased his forehead. "Because we're having a baby," he said. "No other reason?" *Like you love me, like you can't live without me.*

"What other reason?" He looked as if the zinger he'd planned for closing arguments had fallen flat. Madison let out a frustrated breath, too annoyed to respond, so she kept moving. The dog, happy to be going again, trotted ahead. Goodness, what she'd do for a cheeseburger and fries right about now. Her stomach rumbled so loudly, she was sure Collin must've heard it. The heels of her flip-flops sank into the sandy path and she struggled to keep the dog on the substitute leash, the belt collar and the length of rope together not being ideal. Not to mention the fact that the nylon rope dug into her palms whenever the dog pulled, which was every two seconds.

"Heel," she told him, although the dog seemed unfamiliar with the command. She wondered if he'd been trained at all, and how long he'd been running free on the island. Surviving on what? Trash? She looked at the golden fluff ball, his fur matted in places, twigs and leaves still in his tail. Poor thing.

"You're not going to say anything?" Collin prodded.

"What do you want me to say?" Madison glanced back at the man walking just behind her, craning her neck to see his face. Even now, her body reacted to having him so close. More than anything else, it was his eyes, his green, almost gray eyes that moved her. She speculated, fleetingly, if their baby would have them, too. She realized she hoped so.

She'd been thinking about the baby inside her growing daily, no bigger than a bean, and every time her mind wandered, it was usually to thoughts about what the child might look like. Rarely did she think about herself alone, childless, throwing herself back into her career.

"I'm that baby's father, and I do get a say," Collin said, interrupting her thoughts and bringing them right back to him. "I know, technically, you get to decide, but before you do anything rash, just…just…promise you'll talk to me first, okay?"

Madison stopped in the middle of the path. The dog wanted to continue, but she tugged at the rope and he stopped, looking at both of them with his pink tongue lolling out.

"Why do you care?" she asked him. That was the question she'd been dying to ask, ever since he'd shown up on the island. "You never cared about me before."

After our night together, you never called. Worse, you avoided me in court. She still remembered the way he'd glanced at her and given her only a tight smile, a please-don't-talk-to-me smile. The way he'd turned his back on her.

Then, when she'd asked for a plea deal for her new client, he'd flat-out refused. As if trying to prove she had even less sway than before.

"You know I don't date defense attorneys. I told you that." Collin sounded matter-of-fact.

He'd told her the same thing that night, in the bar. Although, warning her up front that she *wasn't his type* didn't mean it was okay to treat her like a stranger the next morning.

"But now you'll marry one."

"Because it's the right thing to do."

Madison let out a bitter bark of laughter. "Right thing to do! That again. For someone who's so concerned about the *right* thing to do, you sure are *wrong* a lot."

"What do you mean?"

"Well, for one…" The length of rope in Madison's hand suddenly went slack. She looked down, and that was when she saw the makeshift leash had come loose and the dog was darting ahead into the bushes.

"Doggie!" she called. "Doggie! Come! Wait!"

The dog glanced back once, then took off, the loose belt collar whipping around his neck in circles as he ran full speed. Madison, not thinking at all, ran after him.

CHAPTER SEVEN

"MADISON! NO!" SHOUTED COLLIN, but it was too late. She was already halfway into the heavy brush after some lost mutt. "You're…"

He was about to shout "pregnant" and then realized she was so far ahead she wouldn't hear him anyway. Shouldn't she be taking it easy? He wasn't up on prenatal care, but he thought running after a half-wild mutt in near 90-degree heat wasn't the best of ideas. She'd raced after the dog, her flip-flops kicking up sand, focused on catching the dog. He saw a million horrible scenarios—her tripping and breaking her ankle, falling and hitting her head, tumbling forward and landing on her stomach and…

Collin ran, too, not wanting to let her out of his sight, and hoping that somehow he could convince her to stop.

"Madison! Don't run! Don't…" *bother going after that stray! It's not worth the risk to you or the baby.*

Madison sprinted behind a palm tree, down

an old path to a house that looked like it badly needed repair—not to mention a good lawn guy, since the flowers were overgrown and the small patch of grass at the side was at least a foot high. He saw a flash of yellow. The dog. It rushed past the house and down a small sandy path flanked by seagrass swaying in the breeze that was coming off the ocean. In the distance, he could hear—but not see—the water.

Madison stumbled a bit, and then Collin caught up to her, grabbing her by the elbow.

"Stop!" he commanded, wheezing as he sucked in a breath. "Just…stop!"

"The dog!" she cried, trying to pull away from him, toward the seagrass, following a set of fresh dog prints in the shallow sand.

"Let him go!" Collin suggested.

"How can you say that? He's *our* responsibility."

"No, he's not." Collin shook his head.

"How can you say that?" she repeated. Tears shone in her eyes. Now he'd upset her and he had no idea why. They'd known the dog for about fifteen minutes. He was a stray. What was the big deal? He wasn't starving to death or hurt. He was fine on his own.

"I…"

"Forget it. Just go. I'll find him." Madison stalked off, carrying the slack rope in her hand.

Collin watched her leave, wondering why this dog had become so important all of a sudden. Weren't there other people on the island who could find him and take care of him? Why was it *their* responsibility?

"Madison," he called, jogging to catch up. "Come on. I'll help."

"I don't need your help," she ground out between clenched teeth.

Collin felt the pain of those words. She'd made it more than clear yesterday just how little she needed him.

"I know. You mentioned that," he said. "But you're getting it anyway." Collin sent her a sidelong glance. She angrily swiped at her hair, revealing cheeks flushed red from the exercise. She was gorgeous and always had been. Collin had noticed her the very first day she'd stepped inside the county courthouse. She had a runner's muscled legs and a beautiful heart-shaped face. Full kissable lips that, as he recalled, did a fine job kissing his. He'd been drawn to her from that first moment, and he'd been fighting the attraction for months. Yet... despite that, she obviously didn't want him.

So, what was keeping him here? Yes, he wanted her to have the baby. Still, something more was compelling him to stay in this fight. It was Madison herself. He wanted to be with her, to be a family. How could she not want it, too?

He grinned to himself. They *belonged* together. The baby was simply fate at work. He just needed to convince her of that, and then they could hurry up and start their happily-ever-after. Why couldn't she see it the same way he did? Black/white. No gray.

Madison headed down the narrow path near the seagrass and behind the sloping dunes, and they came closer to the sound of water. They rounded the corner of a small, hastily thrown-up stake fence and then the blue ocean rose before them. So did a long expanse of sandy beach. But the dog was nowhere in sight.

"Doggie!" Madison shouted.

"That probably won't do much good," Collin pointed out. But Madison sent him a warning glance that made him shut up. He wasn't doing himself any favors.

"Here, puppy, puppy!" Madison called, this time moving away from Collin and closer to the seagrass, which was so thick the yellow dog and about a hundred others could hide in it for days. Collin scanned the green but saw no sign of the dog. Where had it gone?

"Here, boy!" Collin yelled. He half-hoped the mangy mutt was gone for good. The dog smelled awful, *and* he'd tackled Madison once, which could mean the thing was dangerous. It might not have rabies, but it could have something else. Fleas, maybe. Ticks.

Then, out of nowhere, a burst of yellow fur sprinted out from between two sand dunes about fifty feet from them.

"Doggie!" Madison shouted. "Come, boy! Come here!" The dog stopped suddenly, front paw raised, as he glanced at the two of them on the beach, and for a second Collin thought he'd run right toward them. Instead, he bolted away.

"No! Come, boy!" Madison ran and instantly Collin saw that it was a game to the dog, who looped back into another wider circle up the dune. Whenever Madison got close, the dog would switch directions, looping back the other way. At this rate, Madison would chase the damn pooch around in circles for hours.

"Madison! Stop running! He…" But then Collin glanced down and saw an old piece of driftwood. An idea hit him, and he picked it up.

"Here, boy!" he called and then whistled. He threw the stick high in the air so the dog could see it. The dog, excited, stopped in his tracks. It was clear the animal knew what to do. "Come on, boy! Fetch!" Collin cried and wheeled back to toss the driftwood in the opposite direction. It landed between the crashing waves and the sand dunes behind him. The dog took off at full speed, eyes aimed at the stick bouncing away. He grabbed it and raced back to Collin, dropping the ball at his feet.

"That's a good boy," Collin said. He reached down and grabbed the dog by the collar. Madison, red-faced and out of breath, exhaled a sigh of relief.

"You were just lucky," she said, blowing hair from her face as she marched, barefoot, up the beach toward him.

"I think what you mean to say is clever. I'm very, *very* clever." He flipped the stick in the air. Madison just shook her head, but even he knew he'd won points. The dog, at their feet, barked once and wagged his tail, oblivious to all the trouble he'd caused. Collin took the rope from Madison's hands and bent down, securing it with a double knot around the belt-collar. "Now, why don't we take this little guy to the front office?" Collin suggested. "Maybe Yvana will know if anybody's lost a dog recently."

Madison crossed her arms, as if she was preparing to argue with him. She opened her mouth and then reconsidered. "Fine," she sighed. "*You* walk him this time."

"With pleasure," Collin said, grabbing the rope. He stuck the driftwood halfway in his pocket and the dog happily pranced behind him, furry tail waving.

THEY'D GONE BACK to Madison's and taken her uncle's golf cart to the main office. By the time they arrived, with a very thirsty shaggy dog trailing behind them, neither was speaking to the other. Outside sat a huge golf cart with a front end that looked like a miniature Rolls-Royce. Workers were hustling big bouquets of flowers from the office and carrying them to the pool house nearby, where other staff had set up two dozen tables and chairs and were busy covering them with white tablecloths and wrapping the folding chairs in swaths of fabric.

Collin led the dog past the workers, and he sniffed at their shoes as they went into the front office. The place was full of floral centerpieces—white roses and oversized lavender hydrangeas. Yvana was on the phone. "Yes, I told you, the couple wants the chocolate fondue fountain. It should be in the kitchen closet behind the mixer. Go look for it and let me know if you can't find it. Thanks, hon!" she said and hung up the phone.

She saw the couple and sighed. "Wedding this evening," she said. "Reception in less than an hour! Pretty much gonna be a wedding a week—or many a week—until August.

It's been *in-sane*." She frowned at them. "You two look like you've been through hell." Then, Yvana saw the mutt between them. "*Oh*, my. Who's that?"

"Teddy," Madison said confidently.

"Since when does he have a name?" Collin asked, wondering when she'd decided to name him *Teddy*?

"Since right now," Madison said, sending him a glance that could cut glass. "He *looks* like a teddy bear, so... Teddy." She raised her chin in defiance.

"He is kind of adorable," Yvana agreed, nodding. "I'd say he looks like a Shaggy, too."

More like a pain in the ass, Collin thought but didn't say. Sure, he'd tricked the dog into coming back for the stick, but it didn't mean the two of them were friends. He was just as anxious to get rid of the dog as he'd been the second "Teddy" knocked Madison down. The women fawned over the dog for a while, calling him a handsome boy, although Collin just saw a mangy mutt, one that smelled, honestly, like a horse. A horse that had rolled around in manure.

"Is he a poodle?"

"I think he's a golden doodle," Madison explained. "You know, part golden retriever, part poodle. He showed up in my yard, and we've been trying to find his owner, but no luck so far. He's so sweet, and I don't think he's been looked after in a while…"

"He's doing perfectly okay on his own." Collin nodded at the mutt. Madison ignored him.

"Is there anybody you know of who might have lost a dog?" Madison asked.

Yvana, who obviously hadn't missed the tension between them, shrugged her shoulders. "Can't say as I have," she said. "I didn't even know there were dogs on this island. Except for Onyx. The German shepherd, who belongs to Dr. Ruben, the vet, but he isn't on the island right now."

Collin felt his hopes sink. *What now?* The last thing he wanted was to hold on to this dog one more minute. He was a distraction. They needed to focus on what to do about the baby. The dog was…just a dog.

"Can you keep him here?" Collin asked hopefully, holding up the leash.

"Collin!" Madison squatted by the dog and scratched him behind his floppy ears. The dog cocked his head, enjoying the affection.

"Sorry, sugar," Yvana said. "No can do. The wedding and all. Plus, I'll be honest with you, dogs make me sneeze. Not bad, but bad enough." She gave a single shrug of her shoulder. "If you want, we could put him on the last ferry back. Gus could take him to the pound in Fort Myers."

"No!" Madison threw her arms around the dog's neck. "They'll put him to sleep."

"He might get adopted," Collin suggested.

"And he might not," Madison said. They glared at each other, and Collin didn't break the stare until he heard Yvana clear her throat.

"Dr. Ruben is coming tomorrow, I think, so y'all could ask his opinion on the dog." Yvana nodded toward the mutt. "But until then, think you two could watch him for a night?"

"Yes!" Madison cried without hesitation, which annoyed Collin. Why was she so determined to keep this dog? His overgrown fur almost entirely covered his eyes. His paws, he noticed now, had somehow become covered in both sand *and* dried mud. *How had he managed that?* Collin just shook his head.

"Why don't you two go get a drink or some food by the pool? Wedding reception isn't for an hour, and they're still serving everybody at the bar." Yvana looked at them as if they were squabbling toddlers, and Collin had to admit they were acting like it. "You could take the dog with you. Tie him to a table on the patio?"

"Food would be great," Madison admitted.

"Food does sound good," Collin said, although it would sound better *without* the dog in tow. He glanced down and saw the over-sized puppy gnawing on the edge of Yvana's desk leg.

"Hey! Stop that," he said, yanking the leash so that the dog moved away.

"He's probably hungry," Madison said, grabbing the leash from him and frowning. What did *he* do? He was just making sure the dog didn't destroy Yvana's desk, but Madison was looking at him as if he'd kicked "Teddy" in the ribs.

"Do you think the convenience store has any dog food, though?" Madison asked Yvana, nodding toward the small store across from the pool.

Yvana shook her head. "I really don't think so," she said.

"Was worth a try," Madison said. She smiled down at the furry mutt at her feet. "Come on, little one. You get some people food!"

Collin followed Madison and the dog out of the office. He was closing the door behind him when he heard Yvana shout, "Told you it would take more than a day." And then she giggled to herself.

Great, Collin thought. *Is every woman on this island against me?*

MADISON DUG INTO the hamburger in front of her as if she were a starving woman, and maybe she was. Between morning sickness and running after the dog all day, she'd burned up what little calories she'd managed to keep in her stomach. The food, thankfully, was settling well, and she took another big bite of the juicy burger. Across from her, Collin picked at a club sandwich and sipped a cold beer while he studied her and the dog.

Teddy sat at attention, head cocked to one side, watching every bite she took. His attention was focused like a laser on her plate. She hesitated a little, glancing at her burger.

"Don't feed him," Collin warned. "Wait until we're done…"

But that just tipped Madison over the edge, and she broke off a piece of hamburger and fed it to him. He swallowed it in one gulp and then happily licked his snout.

Collin let out a sigh. "Now, he's just going to want to eat hamburgers," he moaned. "He'll just beg at the table forever."

"You trick him in *one* game of fetch, and all of a sudden you're acting like a dog expert," Madison pointed out. "Did you even have a dog growing up?"

"No," Collin admitted. "But I don't need to

have had one to know how a dog who gets hand-fed hamburger is going to act."

"Well, we had two dogs when I was growing up," Madison said. "And I can tell you that this one is hungry and needs the food. He's starving!" Madison tossed the dog a couple of french fries, too, which he gladly ate.

"He's not starving." Collin took a bite of his own sandwich and chewed. "He's fat, actually."

"That's just fur."

"So says you." Collin shrugged. Why did the man seem to get on her last nerve? Madison didn't know how a person could be so handsome, and yet, every time he opened his mouth she wanted to tell him to shut it. The man was beyond irritating. "So...you had dogs growing up," he said. "Where was that?"

"Fort Myers."

"Family still there?"

"Just my mom. And Uncle Rashad and my aunt. Dad died of a heart attack when I was fourteen."

"I'm sorry to hear that."

"My parents fought constantly before he died. I think if he'd stayed alive, they would've divorced."

Collin nodded once and dabbed his mouth with his napkin. "So is that why you don't want to marry me? Your parents?"

Madison whipped her head up, surprised. "Yes. No. I mean, I wouldn't marry you, anyway. I don't even know you. But my parents… Well, they were miserable all the years they were actually married." She absently dunked a fry in ketchup. "That much I remember." She popped the fry in her mouth and chewed thoughtfully. "They argued all the time. That's what I remember about them in my childhood— the constant fighting."

"It's not how all marriages are," Collin said as he ate a french fry. "And how long did your parents know each other before they got married?"

"They met in high school and didn't get married until after college," she said. "So, a long time."

"See? Just goes to show that even if you know someone really, really well, marriages might not work out." Collin took a sip of his beer. He studied Madison, and she felt the weight of his stare. "I don't think you can ever truly know a person."

"How come?"

"Because you can't. Not unless they *let* you. And even then, most people keep secrets."

Madison felt that Collin might be speaking from personal experience. He had a forlorn look on his face. "What about your parents?"

"Mine?" Collin took a deep swig of beer. "My mom's family was from the Philippines. Her parents came over in the nineties. She dated my dad for years. She had me *and* my sister, but they never got married. He wasn't interested in being a dad." Collin frowned. "My dad had an opioid problem. He started using it and selling it and went to jail when I was just two. Was killed in there by another inmate who stabbed him when I was ten."

"Oh." Madison felt the sting of that truth. She had no idea Collin had come from such a rough background. She'd just assumed he'd had everything handed to him. He acted entitled in the courtroom, and she knew he'd gone to a high-end school. She'd assumed he'd been born with the proverbial silver spoon in his mouth. "I didn't know. I'm sorry."

Collin shrugged, a steely look of determination in his eye. "Well, it doesn't matter who he was. He wasn't part of my life. My mom worked multiple jobs to feed us, and I got a scholarship to a prep school because of my grades and the fact that Mom worked in their cafeteria. Then I got a full-ride to Penn and a scholarship to law school in Florida, and here I am."

Madison had a renewed appreciation for Collin, now that she knew he was a completely self-made man. He'd grown up as poor as some of the clients she herself represented.

"So why don't you show more mercy? You understand what happens to these kids. Like Miller. He was the child of a single mom, who was just trying to make ends meet. *His* dad was in jail. Couldn't you relate?"

"Growing up poor? With a dad in jail? Yeah, I know what it's like." Collin finished his beer, tipping the bottle to get the last swig. "But I also know that you can always take the easy way out...sell drugs, steal, whatever, but the fact is each of these kids *knows* what he's doing is wrong. Even James Miller. He wanted that gift for his mom? He didn't have to steal it. He could've worked for the money to pay for it. But that would've been harder than stealing it. And he could've even stolen it without hitting that guard. And Jimmy Reese came from a single mom, too. Does that mean it was okay for him to shoot a twelve-year-old girl?"

"No, of course not!" Madison shook her head. "You really are a tough one, aren't you?"

"There's only one way to be—tough."

Madison tried to imagine the overconfident prosecutor as a young boy, fatherless, with a mother who was never home, working odd jobs. How easily he could've fallen in with the wrong crowd. Made mistakes. She guessed she understood why he took a hard line.

"Well, it's dangerous to think the world is so simple," she said.

"Why?" Collin signaled the waitress as she walked by and ordered another beer.

"My uncle had a case that involved this client who was charged with arson. His own house, insurance fraud. Except that his son from college comes home late at night, but neither he nor the wife know he's in the house. He dies of smoke inhalation."

"That's terrible," Collin said. "But let me guess, your uncle was a bleeding heart. Tried to frame it as a poor father who was… what? Framed by the insurance company? Racked by guilt? What victim card did he play?"

Madison slowly shook her head again as she took a sip of ice water. "No, actually, my uncle thought he was guilty. And he was annoyed that the man refused to plead guilty. In fact, my uncle said he tried every day to get the man to plead, because your office was offering him ten years, which they thought was fair, when a jury might give him fifteen or more for murder."

Madison remembered her uncle telling this story. It was one of the first ones he'd told her when she'd gone to law school, one of the first examples of how easily a lawyer could miss things.

"The man just refused to admit guilt. My uncle thought he was being stubborn. I mean, he'd taken out a life insurance policy on his son and wife a month before. But as bad as it looked, it turned out he was telling the truth."

Collin sat back, the sun shining on his dark hair. He folded his arms across his chest. "Really? His neighbor burned the house down? Or…no, his mistress?"

"Nope. He was found guilty. The jury sentenced him to fifteen years. The man, distraught, hanged himself in prison." Collin's eyes glinted in the sun as he listened. "Then, after his death, his wife confessed. She was the one who'd set the fire. She'd never intended for her son to get hurt. Or for her husband to go to jail. The insurance policy on her son was accidental. What she wanted was to have the home insurance pay for a new house." Madison took a deep breath. "So, even when you're sure someone's guilty, sometimes they're not."

Collin seemed to consider the story, and for a second, she thought maybe he was coming around, maybe he'd see the world in a more complex way, like she had after she'd heard her uncle's story. She'd worked hard not to jump to any conclusions—not with her clients and not with any cases before her.

"Okay, so one innocent guy in the mix. There might be that. But most of them, and you know this, are guilty."

"But if even one is innocent! That's one too many."

The waitress put a fresh beer in front of Collin. He took a sip. "But that's the price you pay to lock up the bad guys,"

"How can you be fine with that?"

"Because I know that most of the guys I put away *are* bad guys. Like Jimmy Reese."

Madison let out a frustrated breath. Maybe they'd never agree. Yes, she wanted horrible, violent murderers behind bars! But that didn't mean everyone who was charged with something was guilty.

She glanced over at the pool and saw the wedding reception tables in place around it and beneath the awning nearby. A DJ had set up turntables near the front, and the music wafted over to them, some happy pop song. All the tables looked pristine, each place setting perfect, as some guests began to wander in. They wore suits and dresses.

"Um… Are we supposed to still be here?" Madison asked, nodding at the well-dressed guests as they began to arrive.

"Yvana said the bar would be open during the wedding," Collin said. "I don't see why not."

Just then, the DJ cued up the microphone. "Ladies and gentlemen, on behalf of the newlyweds, the Gattas, I want to welcome you here to their reception! Now, I'd like to introduce the bridal party…" He pointed to a nearby arch, covered in hydrangeas, where the bridal party was assembled and ready to join the reception.

"I really don't think we should be here," Madison whispered. They had a front row view of the bridesmaids entering in their lavender shift dresses and the groomsmen wearing coordinating lavender ties.

The bride and groom were announced last, arriving in a flurry of applause as they kissed beneath the flower-covered arch. Madison couldn't help feeling moved; the couple seemed to be so in love, and that emotion spread through the reception. She could practically feel its warmth from here. Waiters dressed in white jackets roamed with trays of champagne, and the bride and groom both took a long-stemmed glass and toasted each other, their happiness obvious on their faces. Suddenly, Madison felt a pang of envy. She wanted that. Wanted what they had—love, commitment and a beautiful way to celebrate it. What she *didn't* want was to be somebody's afterthought. Or obligation...

The DJ put on some music, a slow song. "And now, let's ask the bride and her father to take a spin around the dance floor," he said. Madison watched, feeling a surprisingly sharp longing in her chest. She could feel Collin studying her as she concentrated on the first dance until its end, and then the DJ put on an upbeat dance song and called for everyone else to join the couple on the dance floor.

"Hey," Collin said, his voice low. "Why don't *we* join them?"

"What?" Madison was taken off guard. Was he seriously asking her to dance? That was almost...romantic. Since when did he care about romance?

"Want to dance?" Collin offered her his hand.

CHAPTER EIGHT

MADISON FROWNED AT her ratty T-shirt and her
cutoff shorts and cheap flip-flops. She was decidedly underdressed. How could she join the
well-dressed guests on the dance floor? Her
face felt hot just thinking about it.

"No! We can't. I mean…" She gestured at
the half-dozen dancers moving to the beat on
the small dance floor.

Collin stood, pushing back his chair. Teddy,
who'd dozed off, looked up, his blond shaggy
mane falling in his eyes. Collin came to her
side, lifting her by the elbows. "Of course,
we can," he said as she stood uneasily. "They
won't mind."

Madison paused, staring at the man in his
cargo shorts and golf shirt, his sunglasses
tucked up in his hair. He had an air about him,
that confidence; jurors always recognized it,
too. Madison couldn't quite resist his charm,
either. And she didn't object as he led her out
onto the dance floor. The music suddenly

turned slow. A love ballad came on, the notes drifting into the dusky sky.

Madison felt a tiny moment of panic. Not only was she going to be way underdressed, she was also going to *slow* dance with the man? Then Collin stopped at the edge of the dance floor, between the wedding party and the pool, and pulled her into his arms, expertly, easily, without hesitation. They held her fast as he snugly drew her to him, his hand firmly at the small of her back. And suddenly...she was right back in that night with him. God, the man had expert hands. He'd guided her to each position, had deftly made her come *twice*. She had trouble resisting a man with such confidence, a man who knew what he wanted and how to get it. A man who knew what *she* wanted...

A couple drifted by a few feet away on the actual dance floor and the woman gave them a smile and a nod.

"See? Not so bad, is it?" Collin asked.

"No," Madison admitted, acutely aware of how close they were. Madison could feel the heat from Collin's body. She remembered the weight of him on her chest that one night, the delicious feeling of his body against hers. Instantly, she felt her inner thighs warm. *What was wrong with her?* she wondered. She was pregnant, so why did her body scream for sex?

Was it Collin?

Or hormones?

"I went to a team-building retreat once," Collin said as he pulled her closer. "They told us that to build trust, you need to build mutual respect. And one way to do that…is to give honest compliments."

"Honest compliments? What other kinds are there?"

"Fake ones," he said and grinned. "Like, a fake one would be, *Madison, you are…so shy. It's adorable.*"

Madison burst into laughter. She was many things, but shy wasn't one of them. "Oh, like, *Collin, you're so humble.*"

Collin laughed, a low growl in his throat that Madison felt in her stomach. "Yes, exactly." His eyes sparkled.

"So, I'm going to give you an *honest* compliment." Collin paused.

"What? Can't think of one?"

"Nope. That's not the problem. Can think of too *many.*" This made Madison's face grow hot.

"You're damn well one of the best defense attorneys I've ever seen," Collin said. "You defend every client—from the poorest to the richest—with the same effort."

"Why wouldn't I?"

"Because a lot of defense attorneys only care about money," Collin said. "But you actually care about giving them their constitutional right to a good defense."

"They're not all guilty," she said. "I keep telling you that. A lot of innocent people wind up going to jail. Like the supposed arsonist."

Collin diverted her in a spin. "Yes, and some guilty ones go free." He drew her even closer. "Do you know what we call you in the state attorney's office?"

She had a nickname? She wasn't sure she wanted to hear it. "Dragon lady?" she offered, half-joking. She hoped it wasn't worse than that.

"We call you the Earthquake," he whispered in her ear. "Nobody ever wants to see the Earthquake on the docket. You make even the most slam-dunk cases not so easy. You shake foundations. Topple the best-built cases."

"I do not," Madison protested as she enjoyed the warm feeling of Collin tightening his grip on her hand, guiding her a little closer to the pool. Their slow sway matched the music, beat for beat.

"You do. And you do it without slimy tactics

or lazy finger-pointing. You'd make an impressive prosecutor, you know that?"

"What? And be full of myself like you guys?" Madison joked, because she'd heard the refrain before. Prosecutors considered themselves the heroes and claimed that defense attorneys acted as their obstacles to true justice. But, Madison had never thought of her job that way. James Miller, for instance, deserved a good defense attorney—somebody to stand up for him.

"You don't want to put bad guys away?" he asked her.

"We've already had this discussion," she said. "I'd rather make sure good guys don't go to jail."

Collin laughed again and pulled her even closer. Now their torsos were pressed together, and she could feel the firm muscles of his chest. Their legs worked seamlessly as they moved in time with the music. The sun had dipped below the horizon, and above them, the sky turned pink and lavender. The song ended, and suddenly she heard the tiny plink of forks against wine glasses as the wedding audience demanded a kiss from the newlyweds. Madison watched the couple—young, dazzling, happy—and when she turned back to Collin, she saw he was staring at her.

"Madison," he breathed, his voice low. He'd become serious in that moment, deliberate.

And before she knew what was happening, he lowered his head and covered her lips with his. Everything else disappeared—the wedding, the music, the guests in suits and fancy dresses. All she knew then was the feel of his lips, the insistent way he claimed her and the desire that rose up in her to answer his call. Their bodies pressed even closer as he gently moved his mouth on hers. She stood up on tiptoe, sliding her arms around his neck. Suddenly, she didn't care that she was underdressed and in public. She didn't care about anything but this single moment.

He broke the kiss first and sucked in a breath, the look on his face mirroring her own shock. Had that really happened? Had that really been so...good?

"Whoa," he murmured, as her own heart hammered in her chest, beating so hard she thought it might pop out of her ribcage.

His amazement felt like her own.

She remembered now, with full clarity, the wonderful night they'd spent together, the way their bodies fit as if they'd been made for each other. She'd half-buried the memory, but now all the sensations came flooding back—a blur of hands and legs, tangled sweaty bodies, an urgency that she'd never be able to repeat. "That's how you got into my bed. With a kiss," she said.

She remembered the way he'd kissed her at the door of the Uber, and how she'd immediately invited him back to her place, her head spinning.

"It was?"

She stared at Collin. "You don't remember? By the car? The Uber? Outside the bar? You kissed me there."

Collin's brow furrowed.

Madison took a step backward. "What do you remember from that night?"

"I remember you were damn sexy," he said.

"And? And what else? Where did we go?"

He thought a minute. "Your place."

"And what did we do there?"

"Well, obviously, we…" He pointed to her belly. Madison took another step back and thrust her fist against her hip. "You have no idea what happened."

"That's not true," he said.

"What color was my underwear?"

He looked like a deer in the headlights then. "I don't know. I'd had a couple of drinks. Besides, I was too busy getting it off."

"Black." Madison was angrier by the second. How could he *not* remember a night that would forever be seared in her memory? Did he take home so many defense attorneys that they blurred together into one big orgy? "So, you really don't remember what we did that night?"

"I do, I promise. I do remember." Collin reached out and pressed his hand against the small of her back. "How could I forget the best sex of my life?" He pulled her close, his breath on her ear. "You were the best I've ever had."

Her heart thumped. Did he mean it? The best sex of his life? This shouldn't make her feel so… happy, but it did.

A crash, followed by breaking glass, caught their attention as they whirled toward their abandoned table.

Teddy had managed to catch the edge of the tablecloth and topple a dinner plate. He gulped down what was left of Madison's hamburger.

"Great," Collin said, rolling his eyes. "That useless dog did it again."

She ran ahead of him to make sure the puppy hadn't cut himself on any glass, even as a waiter appeared with a broom and a dustpan.

Madison scooped up the dog and Collin kneeled down to help the waiter get some of the bigger shards.

She glanced at him. Was he worth a chance? Could they really *be* something? Then, as soon as the thought entered her mind, she rejected it. No. Suddenly, she needed some air. She needed some space.

She moved back from the mess he and the waiter were cleaning up and carried Teddy away from them both, heading over to the trail that would take her home.

"Madison!" she heard Collin shout. "Where are you going?"

"I just… I need to be alone," she said, not turning around, not looking him in the eye.

"Come on. I'm trying here." Collin sounded earnest, but it wasn't enough. Also, if he really cared about her, why would *trying* sound like such a chore?

She paused, noticing again how perfectly his features fit together, how annoyingly handsome the man was. She knew if she stayed any longer, he'd start making more sense. She needed to clear her head.

"Come on, please," he called. "Stay."

But she didn't. With the dog in her arms, she turned and left him, and she kept on walking, trying to keep her spine straight.

CHAPTER NINE

THIS WASN'T EXACTLY how Collin had planned the evening. He watched Madison hop into her golf cart and fire it up. He let her go, observing in consternation as the dog took his place in the seat next to her.

"How am I supposed to get back?" he shouted after her retreating cart.

"Walk!" she shouted distantly, before she disappeared down the winding trail, the top of her cart slapping a low-lying palm branch.

"Great," he muttered aloud. He glanced back at the bar and the wedding guests, a few of whom had caught the little exchange. He needed a drink.

The Earthquake earned her name once more, he thought ruefully.

He ambled back to the bar, where the bartender held up a pitcher full of premade margaritas. "You look like you could use a drink. Margarita?"

"How about straight tequila? You have Patron?" he asked, and the bartender nodded.

Collin wasn't sure what was going on. Had the thing he said about the dog sent her running?

Nope, she just hates your guts, man.

How had he been so…off?

Their night together had been spectacular. He just assumed she'd be willing to give *them* a shot, like he was. But the more he pressed, the more she balked.

His phone lit up with a text from his sister, Sophia.

How'd it go?

He sighed.

Not so well.

She said NO?!

Collin was about to confirm that when he hesitated.

She said no—for now.

Maybe it's for the best.

It didn't feel like it. For him, marrying Madison wasn't just about responsibility, it was also about *possibility*. The idea of having the family he'd always wanted—even if it hadn't happened quite the way he'd planned—made his whole future light up with hope. He didn't want to let go of that.

The bartender set the shot glass in front of him, and he pinched it between two fingers, then threw it back, the strong amber liquid burning his throat. He didn't even bother to chase it with a lime. The burn reminded him he was still alive, still here, and that meant he wasn't beaten for good. Yet.

Before Madison had told him she hated him, they'd been hitting it off. That wasn't the kiss of a woman who didn't like him, was it?

He'd have to think of a plan to win her over. To convince her that marrying him was a *great* idea.

EXHAUSTED AND DESPONDENT, Madison slipped into an oversized shirt and a pair of shorts and went to bed. Her clothes were starting to get tight, the waistband of her shorts more snug than usual. She rubbed her stomach through her T-shirt, thinking that in a few months, that waistline would get a heck of a lot bigger.

She lay down on the bed and stared at the ceiling fan making slow loops above her. What to do about Collin? Sometimes she felt tempted to consider the marriage proposal, but at other times…she was sure it was the worst idea in the world.

She rolled onto her side and clicked off the lamp. She needed sleep, and then she could figure all this out. Her phone, however, dinged with an incoming message. She thought about ignoring it, but curiosity got the better of her. She rolled over and grabbed the phone, seeing a text from her uncle.

Don't know if you heard, but Jimmy Reese escaped from jail. Just wanted you to know, in case he tries to contact you.

Madison felt her blood run cold. Jimmy Reese. Built like a boxer, icy blue eyes, tattoos so thick they completely covered his neck and both arms. A swastika on his neck, hate bubbling in him like boiling water. He'd muttered a racial slur under his breath when she'd been assigned as his attorney by the court. Honestly, she'd wanted to hand off the case—to anyone—but her uncle had thought it would be a useful lesson for her to go through with it. She had to learn how to defend even the indefensible, he'd said. It was part of her job.

She kept thinking Reese would fire her. Why would a white supremacist keep her—a brown woman—as counsel? Sure, he was a public defender case, but still. He could've asked the judge for another attorney.

Everyone had the right to a good defense, but she had despised Jimmy Reese. Skinhead, seething with hate, wanting to kill people who didn't look like him—yet, ironically, he'd ended up killing a white girl.

Madison's own dark hair and eyes made him detest her as well. He rarely said much, but the cold look in his eyes had told her he'd have been more than happy to harm her. She'd been so glad when the jury found him guilty—for once, happy to see Collin Baptista on the other side of the aisle. She knew that no matter how hard she defended Reese, a jury would put him away, especially once the girl's parents, small-restaurant owners, took the stand, crying their eyes out and showing pictures of little Monica jumping rope and in her soccer uniform, complete with auburn braids.

She went through the motions of cross-examination, but truth be told, her heart hadn't been in it. Jimmy Reese had known it, too. When they were about to read the guilty verdict, he leaned over and whispered, "Better hope I get outta here scot-free or they put me away a long time, you Pakistani bitch. I'll make you pay for every night I spend in jail."

Never mind that Madison was half-Indian,

not Pakistani—she doubted he cared about the distinction. Or the fact that her father was a second-generation Indian-American—all Reese saw was a person who wasn't like him, which meant she was less than human.

And now he was out!

Madison felt her heart speed up. Then she willed herself to calm down. *Jimmy doesn't know where I am. I'm not any place he'd know to look for me. And besides, normally these guys get caught within forty-eight hours. Jimmy will be no different.*

She thought about phoning Collin. He'd prosecuted the case. He had a right to know... But something stopped her.

What? Aside from the fact that he'd probably make a snide retort about how bad guys were bad, and how Reese should've been put in jail for longer than twenty years... No, she didn't want to admit to him that she was a little scared. Wouldn't he just use that as an excuse to push marriage even harder?

She opted to call her uncle instead.

"Hey, Maddie," he said, sounding cheered to hear her voice. "You all right?"

"Fine," she said, hoping her anxiousness didn't show. "Jimmy escaped? How?"

Uncle Rashad sighed. "Looks like an ad-ministrative mix-up. You know he was already serving a term for burglary in the county prison. Then he was scheduled to be transferred over to the state institution to start his murder sentence. But somehow the county records were out of date. When his burglary sentence was up, they let him go."

"They *let* him go?" Madison felt her blood pressure rise. "But he's dangerous! And he's violent and…" She swallowed hard. "And he hates me. He blames me for a bad defense. Or he just hates me because of what I look like."

Because my skin is darker than his.

"I know." Uncle Rashad sighed again. "It's my fault. I should've never encouraged you to take this case."

"The court assigned it to me," she pointed out.

"Yes, but I could've encouraged you to decline."

"You were simply trying to make sure I saw all sides of the law," she said. She knew he'd had no idea the defendant would be so hateful…so dangerous. Besides, just because Reese loathed her didn't necessarily mean he was coming for her, did it? After all, a man like Jimmy Reese hated a lot of people. Surely, she wasn't at the top of his list.

"Does Mom know?"

"Not yet."

"Good. Don't tell her. She'll flip out." Madison imagined her mom in an all-out meltdown. "Does… Does Collin Baptista know?"

"I assume so, or he will soon. I haven't talked to the prosecutor's office, but I'll bet they were the first ones contacted," Uncle Rashad said. "Why do you ask?"

"He prosecuted Jimmy." *And he's the father of my baby.*

"I know." Uncle Rashad paused, as if reading her mind. "Is that the only reason? I heard… It's none of my business, but someone said there was a rumor you and he…"

Madison felt her face burn. Who knew about them? Unless Collin had been spreading the word that he planned to propose, Madison hadn't told anyone about their one-night stand. And, given that they'd barely had a relationship afterward, she couldn't imagine anybody at the courthouse picking up on that.

"No. I mean…not exactly."

"Is there something you want to tell me?" he asked.

Like Collin Baptista showing up on my doorstep with an engagement ring and his ego the size of Mount Everest? No, she didn't.

"No. Not…right now."

"He's there with you, isn't he?"

"Uncle Rashad! How did you—"

"Yvana might have told me," he said quickly.

"She wanted to make sure everything was okay. She was worried about you."

Madison groaned. Of course, Yvana had told Rashad. They were close friends, and Madison hadn't exactly sworn her to secrecy.

"It's...complicated," Madison said.

"It always is," Uncle Rashad agreed. "At least, it always is until it isn't."

"What does that mean?" Madison released a frustrated breath. Her uncle often talked in riddles, like some kind of infuriating Buddhist monk.

"You'll see," he said and she could almost feel him grinning through the phone. "You doing okay? Feeling...okay?" The concern in his voice was real. It made Madison's heart feel full. No matter what, she had family who cared for her. Family like Uncle Rashad.

"Yes. A little morning sickness, but nothing I can't handle."

"You can handle anything. Always have, always will," her uncle told her. "I'll let you know if I hear any more about Jimmy, but don't worry. Since it was a clerical mistake, everybody's out looking for this guy. They'll bring him in soon."

"I hope so," Madison said. "For everyone's sake."

She hung up and then tossed and turned,

unable to go to sleep as she thought of Jimmy Reese's mean, hateful face.

She thought about Collin, too. Did he know? He had a right to know, whether or not she wanted to be the one to tell him. Jimmy would hate him as much as he did her, would be out for revenge against him as much as her.

She texted Collin.

Jimmy Reese escaped.

Instantly, her phone rang in her hands. "What do you mean, he escaped?" Collin asked.

"Clerical error, or so Uncle Rashad said. I don't know the details, but…"

"Hang on, I'm coming over." The line went dead before Madison could argue. *What the…?* Not five minutes later, she heard a furious knocking on her front door. She pulled herself out of bed and padded down the stairs to answer it. Collin was standing there in just his shorts, sans shirt, carrying a small bag. Teddy barked happily when he saw Collin and came trotting over to the glass door, tail wagging.

She swung the door open and he brushed past her. Teddy followed, nipping at his heels. "Are all the doors locked?" he asked, setting down his bag without permission on the foyer tile.

"Yes. I think so...but..."

Collin went to each door and window, methodically checking them all. "I've left a message with the prosecutor's office, so I'll get more details soon, but for now, I need to stay with you."

"Why?" Madison didn't understand the urgency, but Collin being so concerned was starting to make her even more worried. Sure, Jimmy was a threat. But he had to know where to find her first.

Collin turned, glancing at her as if she was delusional. "Because a convicted felon and a crazy white supremacist who swore vengeance is on the loose and he might kill me, or you, or both of us."

"I didn't prosecute him. I defended him."

Collin gave her a shrewd look. "I know he was trying to intimidate you in that court room. I didn't hear what he said, but I could read his body language as clear as day."

"He never said he'd kill me."

"No, but I bet he just implied it." Collin stopped fiddling with the window in the living room and crossed over to her. He put his hands on her elbows. "I know you're a strong, independent woman who doesn't need my help, but *let* me help you. This one time."

He pulled her into a hug and Madison melted

into his embrace, suddenly very grateful for Collin's presence. She could wait it out alone, she could lie awake worrying about Jimmy, but with Collin here that became much more bearable.

"Thank you," she whispered, her voice so low she wasn't sure if Collin heard. He squeezed her harder against his chest, and she felt a rush of emotion that nearly overpowered her. There was something so wonderful about his arms, so safe and comforting.

Just then, Teddy started sniffing the ground. He wandered away from them, into a corner of the foyer. Madison recognized the signs too late. He lifted his little leg and peed.

"No!" Madison cried, breaking the embrace.

"Bad dog!" exclaimed Collin as he lunged forward, too. The dog finished his business and then ran to hide under a nearby table.

"Well, that's one way to be distracted from the likes of Jimmy Reese," she said shaking her head at the yellow puddle on the white marble tile.

"Bad dog!" Collin shouted at the dog once more. Teddy cowered under the foyer table, looking scared as he ducked his fuzzy head.

"Don't yell at him," Madison chided, putting a hand on his arm.

"Why not? How else is he going to learn? He needs boundaries. Rules."

Madison let out a sigh of frustration. Honestly, she didn't understand this man. What would yelling at a puppy do? "We need to take him outside. Show him where he's supposed to go."

"Well, I sure as hell am not going to pee on the grass so he learns."

Madison couldn't help grinning. "No! Of course not. I mean, we need to take him out. When he pees outside, we give him a treat. That's called positive reinforcement."

"Sounds like spoiling him to me."

"I don't get you. One second, you're coddling him and the next, you're yelling at him. What kind of dad does that?"

Collin froze. "You said *dad*."

Madison wished she could swallow the word. Take it back. "Dad to a dog."

"I think you meant more than that," he corrected, and his eyes flashed with triumph. "Much more."

"No. I didn't." Did she? Her head swam. Surely not. Collin wasn't ready to be a dad. Hell, she wasn't even convinced she was ready to be a mother. So far, taking care of a dog for twelve hours had more than tried her patience.

Collin stared at her for a long time, during

which she was keenly aware that he *wore no shirt*. Madison broke the gaze and scurried to get a paper towel and some spray cleaner to wipe up the mess.

"I've got that," he said, and took them from her as he stooped to clean. A few wipes and the puddle was gone.

"Outside," Madison said in a gentler voice to Teddy. "We do that *outside*." She studied the puppy, doubtful he understood her, although he did come out and trotted over to her bare feet where he gave her toes an apologetic lick. She picked him up and carried him to the front door.

"No, let me," Collin said, retrieving the dog from her. "Jimmy might be out there."

"He wouldn't know where I am," she said.

"You're right, he probably doesn't. But let me take him outside. There are mosquitos out there, too."

"Fine." Madison watched as Collin took the dog out, walked him down the stairs to the small patch of grass and set him down.

The dog sniffed around on the grass but was in no mood to do anything, since he'd just relieved himself all over the floor inside. After a minute, Collin reached down and picked him up. He brought him back into the house, tucked in the crook of his arm. Teddy felt warm and surprisingly small. His fur made him look like a bigger dog than he actually was.

"Why don't we try to take the dog upstairs," Collin said, setting Teddy down. "See if he'll sleep in your room."

Madison reluctantly agreed. She wasn't wild about the idea of him possibly having an accident there. She gathered up a few folded towels from the utility room, then followed Collin as she carried Teddy upstairs. Madison carefully made a bed of towels near the bed and put the dog in it. Teddy gave a little puppy yawn and a stretch before he lay down. Madison sat on the edge of the bed, watching Collin carefully tucking the towels around the dog and felt a sudden tenderness for the man. He could be caring and gentle, at least when he wanted to be.

The puppy's eyelids grew heavy and then closed. Collin grinned. "Looks like I was right—again."

Madison frowned. She'd been feeling grateful to the man. Why did he have to go and ruin it by gloating?

"Please. The stick this morning was just luck," she said, crossing her arms.

"Brilliance, you mean." Collin flashed her a smile, and she felt the annoyance in her chest loosening. It was hard to stay mad at him, that was for sure. "You say I always *think* I'm right, but what if I just *am* always right?"

Madison wrinkled her nose at him. She yawned. "Someone so brilliant can no doubt let himself out, then." Madison, suddenly feeling exhausted, leaned back on her pillows.

"No, I'm staying. I told you. Until they find Jimmy Reese."

Collin took a step closer, leaning over her on the bed. She almost thought he might kiss her.

"You should sleep on the couch, then," she said, her voice a whisper. In a way, she hoped he'd argue with her. But he didn't.

"The couch. That's fine." He turned to leave, pausing at the door. "Good night, then."

"Good night," Megan called softly, not sure whether to feel disappointed or relieved.

He glanced once at the dog, still sleeping, and then started to open the bedroom door. But he'd only gotten it halfway open when Teddy woke, lifting his small golden head and giving a sharp bark. Collin's shoulders slumped in defeat. He turned to see little Teddy emerge from his towel bed and head toward him.

"No, no," he scolded the dog lightly as he picked him up and took him back to his bed. "You're supposed to go to *sleep*."

Madison watched as the dog lay down once more, staring at Collin.

"I think he wants me here," Collin said as he sat next to Madison on the side of the bed.

Madison snorted. "That is the lamest excuse I've ever heard for a man to share my bed," she said.

"I mean it. Watch." Collin got up and walked to the door. Immediately, Teddy was on his feet, scampering toward him. But the second Collin returned to the bed, the puppy went back to his own and settled in.

Madison shook her head. "Unbelievable. Well, then, *you* take him."

"Me? I'm not going to take him."

"He wants to sleep with *you*, so why don't you take him downstairs? To the couch." Madison made a shooing motion with her hands. She didn't like the fact that Teddy seemed to suddenly prefer Collin. Was he the dog's favorite now? She knew it was childish, but still. Did Collin charm *everyone*?

Collin's shoulders slumped. "Okay," he agreed. "I'll take him downstairs with me." He stooped to pick up the dog. Madison noticed how small the puppy was in his muscular arms, how easily he lifted the squirming furball. His forearms kept the dog safely tucked against his chest. The picture would have been adorable, except that Madison still felt a sense of rejection.

Collin trudged toward the door, but as soon as he got there, the puppy whined and kicked, fighting to free himself.

"What the...?" Collin managed, as Teddy wriggled out of his grasp and jumped to the floor, scampering back to his towel bed.

Madison felt relief. So, the dog *didn't* want to leave. He just didn't want Collin to leave, either. The realization hit her—Collin had been right.

"I think he wants us both here," Madison admitted. Part of her didn't mind that idea. Not with Jimmy Reese on the loose.

"It's what I've been *saying*." Collin studied her, and she found the look in his eyes unsettling. Not to mention the swath of bare skin... Why didn't the man wear a shirt?

"Fine," she said. Then she made a pillow wall, dividing the bed in half.

Collin slid his fingers into the waist of his sleep shorts. He tugged downward. "I'll just..."

"No!" Madison exclaimed, blocking her eyes with her hands. "No, keep those on."

"I was kidding. It was a joke."

"Not a funny one." Madison parted her fingers and glared at him. Collin sighed.

"Besides, you've already seen it," he said.

"Yes, but maybe I'm *still* scarred."

"Ha, ha." Collin made a face and then shrugged. "Fine. I'll keep the shorts on. For your sake." He walked over to his side of the bed and scrutinized all the throw pillows she'd lined up down the center. "Is the great wall of pillows *really* necessary?"

"Yes, it is," Madison declared, pulling the covers over herself. Collin settled in on his side, and she felt the mattress lurch beneath his weight.

"Just to warn you, I'm a cuddler," Collin said. "These pillows probably won't even stop me."

"Cuddler? You? No way." Madison couldn't possibly imagine him spooning. Then again, he *had* been cuddly after the sex they'd had. She tried not to think about the way their naked bodies had fit together... The pillow wall might not be enough, after all.

"I am. I might spoon you by accident, so be prepared."

"That's what the pillows are for," Madison said, as she rolled over. She gazed fondly at Teddy on the floor next to the bed. The puppy could barely keep his eyes open now, as he lay on his bed of towels. Sneaky dog. "Good night, Teddy," she said, reaching up to click off the lamp on the bedside table.

Collin coughed. "I don't get a good-night?"
"No. No, you don't," Madison said, but in
the dark of the bedroom, she grinned.

CHAPTER TEN

COLLIN THOUGHT HE might never fall asleep. Hearing Madison's steady breathing and the dog's occasional shifting on the floor, he was hyperaware of every little sound and movement in the small dark bedroom. Collin was used to one-night stands. He preferred them to the sticky entanglements of relationships. His longest relationship to date was a year and that was with a fellow law student years ago. She'd been destined for corporate law, he for prosecution, and both held a definitive understanding that their relationship was temporary, a mutually beneficial agreement until graduation.

Madison was different, and not just because she was carrying his child. Okay, that did make a huge difference, but maybe it was just the difference he needed. Collin had always thought he'd *one day* start a family, but *one day* never came. Now, he had to seriously consider that this might be the best chance he'd ever get to settle down. He'd never really been forced to think about it, and he knew himself well enough to realize that without proper motivation, he'd keep putting family on the back burner.

He glanced at the wall of pillows between them and had to laugh a little. She kept surprising him. She'd be harder to win over than he'd thought. He shut his eyes, thinking that being in her bed was closer to his goal than being out of it, pillows or not.

Then, he remembered Jimmy Reese and his muscles tightened. He knew the man probably had no idea the two of them were on this island, but he also knew that he couldn't take any chances. Not with Madison. Or the baby.

COLLIN WOKE TO the feeling of warmth and softness in his arms. For a second, he forgot where he was as he snuggled up to the warm body next to him. Then, distantly, he remembered—North Captiva Island. Madison's bedroom. Madison was pregnant with *his* baby. The thought sent a shiver of satisfaction through him, even though he lay with his eyes closed against the rising sunlight. So, sometime during the night, Madison had softened toward him, moved away the barrier of pillows and snuggled into him. Maybe the standoffish defense attorney had a soft spot for him after all. Maybe she didn't dislike him as much as she said she did.

He pulled the warm body closer, and then, suddenly, got a wet lick across the face.

That wasn't Madison.

His eyes flew open and he saw Teddy sitting on top of a pillow, licking his face. He glanced around the bed but there was no sign of Madison. Just the puppy in all his furry glory.

"Well, this is great," he mumbled, as the puppy continued to cover his cheek in saliva. "Stop it," he growled, pushing the animal away. But the yellow dog wouldn't be deterred as he gave Collin's face another slobbery dog kiss, tail thumping hard against the covers. Collin propped himself up on one elbow to see that he was alone in the bedroom with the pup. Where had Madison gone?

Then he heard a telltale retching sound from behind the closed bathroom door. This was followed by a flush of the toilet.

He swung his legs out and got up, hurrying across the floor. He knocked softly.

"You okay?" he asked the closed door.

"Fine," Madison grumbled. But then, she heaved again.

"You don't sound fine," he said, trying to turn the doorknob, only to find it locked. "Madison, let me in."

"Be out…one minute," she called and flushed the toilet once more.

Collin felt an urgent need to help. Worry flicked across his mind. Did she eat something bad? Was it the flu? Could either one hurt the baby? Or was this morning sickness? He rattled the doorknob a second time.

"Madison, come on, let me in."

He could hear the faucet running, and then it stopped. The bathroom lock clicked open as she swung the door wide.

"I said I'm fine." She looked pale, her hair disheveled, her mouth wet from where she'd splashed water. She was anything but fine.

"You don't look…"

Suddenly, her eyes grew wide, she clapped a hand on her mouth and pivoted on her heel. In seconds, she'd run back to the open toilet and threw up once more. Collin jumped quickly into the room, holding back her hair into a makeshift ponytail. It brought him back to his college days, when he used to work at a local bar. He'd held back the hair of many a girl he knew in that restroom.

Madison was too weak to fend him off, so she let him help her. Teddy, concerned, sat at the door of the bathroom and whined. Madison's last dry heave stopped and she straightened, wiping her mouth with the back of her hand.

"Are you okay? Fever?" Collin let her hair go and put a palm on her forehead. She felt cool, no fever.

"No." Madison shook her head. "Morning sickness." She pointed to her lower abdomen.

"How long has this been going on?"

"Since I peed on a stick, pretty much," she said. Madison moved to the sink and turned on the faucet, running her hand beneath the tap and rinsing out her mouth.

"*Every* morning?" Collin couldn't believe it. Suddenly, he realized how Madison had been suffering these last few weeks. Suffering alone. He didn't like that. She shouldn't have had to suffer *daily*, vomiting by herself. He should've been there. Yet, how could he have been? She'd never even told him. Maybe never planned to tell him.

"Every morning, and sometimes every afternoon," Madison said, looking exhausted.

"Can you… Can you keep anything down?" Now, Collin was beginning to worry about the baby. Was he getting any food?

Madison gave a reluctant nod. "Sometimes I can. I'm usually better *after* I eat a little."

"Then let's get you some food." Collin helped her out of the bathroom, and Madison even took his elbow for support. He shoved down his feelings of resentment that she hadn't told him, hadn't shared her burden. Right now, the priority was to get some food in her stomach. Feed mother *and* baby.

"First, could you take Teddy out?" she asked, looking pale. "I don't want him to…"

She ran back into the bathroom and retched again.

"I should stay with you. Fix you some food. If you can keep it down, that is."

She shook her head and pointed away from her. Teddy sat at his feet and whined. He looked for her belt, the makeshift leash, then hooked it onto his collar and led him downstairs to the door.

"Okay, dog, we're going out. You're gonna do your business and then we're going in," he said in his strictest voice. Teddy, however, cocked his head to one side, clearly not understanding. Still, Collin walked the dog confidently out to the small yard.

He scowled down at the puppy. "Now, you go," he said in his best do-as-I-say voice.

The dog just gazed up at him, tail wagging.

"Go," he said. "*Go*. Poop. Pee. Whatever you need to do."

The dog's pink tongue lolled out, and Collin felt his frustration rise.

"Go. Now." He rattled the belt. The dog continued to sit there, staring at him. He didn't even bother to sniff the grass.

"Go, dog." He pulled Teddy to his feet and walked him in a little circle. The dog followed happily but still didn't sniff the grass or give any sign that he was going to do anything other than follow Collin's ankles.

He tried a few more walks around the small yard; the dog didn't seem at all interested. Maybe he didn't need to go.

Collin felt he ought to get back to the house. Madison was sick, and she needed food, and she'd be in no condition to prepare it herself. He walked Teddy up the stairs and into the patio door.

Then, predictably, the dog, freed from the leash, trotted over to the corner and …peed a giant puddle.

"No, no, no, no!" he cried. "No! Teddy! No!"

"What is it?" Madison called from upstairs. She glanced down from the stairwell and saw the mess. "I thought I asked you to take him out."

"I *did*. For fifteen minutes! I ordered him to go, but clearly he prefers inside."

"You *ordered* him to go," Madison repeated. Color was starting to return to her cheeks, and she sent him a lopsided smile.

"Yes. He's a dog. I'm a human. I ordered

him to go." Collin thought the chain of command was pretty straightforward. Humans sat at the top. Period.

"I guess that didn't work too well. Maybe you can't just order people around."

"Teddy's a dog, not a person."

"We probably don't work in very different ways. Dogs and people, I mean." Madison came down the stairs as Collin got the roll of paper towels and went about sopping up the mess.

"Bad dog," he growled at Teddy, who seemed not to understand. Madison came and scooped him up in her arms, rewarding his rebellious behavior in Collin's opinion. "You're just encouraging him," he said.

Madison giggled. "Who's an adorable little puppy? You are!" she sang to the dog in a high-pitched voice as they both moved to the kitchen.

Collin washed his hands at the sink. "You still hungry?"

"I should probably try to eat something," she admitted.

Collin threw open the refrigerator door and peered in. She had eggs and yogurt, a single container of blueberries and a carton of milk. He glanced in the pantry and found some pancake mix.

"Blueberry pancakes?" he offered, and she raised her eyebrows in surprise. Teddy barked his approval.

Madison laughed again. "He obviously wants some," she said, looking at the pup.

"He's not getting any," Collin teased back as he gathered up the necessary ingredients.

"So…you cook?" Madison's oversized T-shirt slipped down one side of her arm, revealing her smooth brown shoulder. He tried not to be distracted by it, although everything about Madison was distracting. She looked just as striking without makeup as she did with it, her natural beauty evident in her smooth blemish-free skin. Her dark eyes studied him. They were large, reminding him of a doe's. Big, luminous, hypnotic.

"Since I was a kid."

"Really? I never thought you'd be…" She hesitated as she searched for the right word. She took a hairband from her wrist and wrapped her hair in a messy ponytail. "Domesticated."

Teddy got tired of sitting and waiting for his share and began wandering around the kitchen, sniffing the floor for scraps. Madison watched as he made his way around.

"It's about survival. I've been cooking breakfast since I was seven." Collin grabbed a big bowl from the cabinet and began measuring out the pancake mix. He cracked two eggs and expertly poured them in, then added some plump blueberries. He stirred, feeling Madison's watchful eyes on him.

"That's young," she said.

"Like I told you, Mom worked two jobs, sometimes three." He searched for a pan and found one in a lower cabinet. He set it on the gas stovetop, and turned the gas on with a click and a whoosh. Then he flicked a pad of butter into the pan. He wished he'd thought to bring over a shirt, but he'd just have to flip pancakes without one. At least it wasn't bacon.

"She was too exhausted to cook most of the time, so that fell to me. Sunday was the only day she didn't have to get up at four to take the morning shift at the bakery where she worked, so I'd make pancakes. My sister would fry up sausage. Then we'd go to church. That was our Sunday." Collin poured a little batter into the pan.

"Aw. That's so...sweet."

He glanced up, frowning. "Don't sound so surprised." Why did she always assume he was a jerk? He wasn't a jerk. Not *most* of the time. Just to dogs who refused to pee outside. She sat on a chair at the kitchen table.

"The thing is, you're such a..."

"Hard-ass," he finished for her.

"Well, I wasn't going to say that, exactly…" She sunk her chin into her hands as she rested her elbows on the table.

"But you were thinking it." He got a spatula from a nearby drawer and flipped the pancake. It went smoothly, and the cooked side was a perfect golden brown. He hadn't lost his touch.

She chuckled. "Yes, I guess so."

"You'd better get used to the fact that I'm deep," he said. "Lots of layers to this onion." He grinned and she broke out laughing, throwing her head back and showing her bright white smile. She was beautiful. She reminded him of his mother in that moment—his mother when she wasn't worn-out and tired; his mother when she lounged around in her pajamas, looking relaxed and not so stressed. She'd loved his pancakes, heaped praise on them. He remembered how he'd enjoyed taking care of his mother, since she worked so hard to take care of him and Sophia.

Collin flipped the pancake onto a waiting plate, then started another. Soon, he had a perfect stack. He divided them between two plates and took them to the table, adding syrup and two glasses of milk. Collin felt full of satisfaction when Madison hungrily dug in.

"Oh…" She groaned in pleasure. "These

are *so* good," she mumbled, her mouth full. She took a big drink of milk. "You really can cook."

"Get used to it," he said. "I'll be doing this a lot more often. When we're married."

She froze, a bite halfway to her mouth. "You can't be serious." She stood then, taking a little of her pancake, without syrup, and putting it on a plate.

"Better not feed him—" but she was already placing the plate down on the floor "—table food." Collin shrugged and shook his head. That dog would be spoiled soon. Probably wouldn't even eat dog food if they ever got some. Teddy instantly wolfed down his breakfast, eating so quickly Collin was afraid he might choke.

"Slow down, buddy," he cautioned, not that the dog could understand him.

"He's not too interested in taking orders from you," she said.

"He ought to be if he knows what's good for him." He glanced at Madison. "And at some point, you and I need to talk. I *am* serious. I meant that proposal." He raised his fork and popped an oversized bite of syrup-drenched pancake into his mouth.

Madison shook her head, dark strands falling loose from her ponytail and curling around her temples. "But I don't *know* you."

"We'll have the rest of our lives to get to know each other," Collin said, completely unconcerned by the prospect.

"But how is that possibly going to work?" Madison shoveled more pancake into her mouth. With each bite, Collin felt a swell of pride—he was feeding the mother of his baby. He was feeding his *baby.* He liked taking care of them, and he didn't understand why she didn't want him to.

"You've heard of arranged marriages. We know each other better than that," he said. "And those often last."

"That's different."

"How?" Collin challenged, taking a big swig of milk to wash down the blueberry goodness. "You know *why* they work?"

"I have no idea."

"Because both people *decide* to stay married. Staying married isn't about sentiment or passion or love. I know all the movies and books want you to think that way. But staying married is about two people who decide that's what they both want to do. Be married. So, for this to work, all we have to do is decide to get married and stay married."

"How can you say marriage isn't about love?" She sounded both puzzled and angry.

"Because in the end, it's just a legal document, a binding contract that says the two people involved will support each other and their children."

Madison dropped her fork onto her plate with a decided plink. "That is the least romantic thing I've ever heard."

"I told you. Marriage isn't about romance. It's a legal contract."

Madison rolled her eyes. "I can't believe you'd say that. This isn't medieval times. In this country, we're free to marry the person we love. And that's what we *should* do. I want love."

"You don't want a legal commitment?"

"I don't want a romance-free marriage. I want it *all*. Love, passion, everything. I don't want…a pity marriage." She looked at him, dark eyes serious, but showing a hint of insecurity. Was she really under the impression that he pitied her?

"You think I'm asking you to marry me because *I pity you*?" Collin shook his head in disbelief. How could she be so off?

"You do. You figure this is like some old-fashioned novel or movie, and you're supposed to swoop in and save me with an engagement ring. You didn't care about me before you found out that I'm pregnant. So…it's a pity proposal."

"No. It isn't." Collin put his fork down, grabbed a napkin and wiped his mouth, the sweet taste of blueberries suddenly turning sour on his tongue. "I don't pity you. I know you *can* take care of yourself."

That admission quieted her fast.

"I want to help. That's all. I want to take care of you when you're sick, and make sure our child has two parents who love him. It's not *pity*. It's my *duty*. And I don't run from my responsibilities. Even if you never planned to tell me about them."

"Why would I tell you when I haven't decided what to do?" Madison pushed away her chair, apparently done with her meal. She picked up her plate and headed for the kitchen. But she couldn't outrun him. How could the woman be so…infuriating?

"I get a seat at that table," Collin said, following her to the sink she dumped her dirty plate in it. "You can't decide this alone. That's *my* baby inside you."

"You don't understand."

"You're right. I don't. Why would you even *think* about an abortion when we're two adults with great jobs, who are reasonably sane and would make halfway decent parents?"

She turned to look at him, brow furrowed, big brown eyes focused. "I'm not getting an abortion," she said, voice so low he almost didn't hear her.

"You're keeping the baby?" He had to be sure.

She nodded. "Yes, I'm…"

But he didn't let her finish that sentence. She was going to have his baby! The thrill of that, the absolute pure joy of that decision, surged through him. He hadn't realized how much the threat of losing the baby had been weighing on him. How out of control he'd felt, how helpless. Now, things seemed to be back on track. She was seeing reason, finally listening to him. He swept her up in his arms and kissed her.

CHAPTER ELEVEN

MADISON COULDN'T FEEL anything but Collin's mouth on hers as pure heat pulsed through her veins. She could sense it all the way to the soles of her feet. God, the man could kiss! He held her in his strong bare arms; nothing separated her from his smooth chest except her thin T-shirt. She could feel his hard muscles beneath her hands, as he pressed herself against him. She remembered that feeling from the night they'd spent together. Of their own accord, her hands slid up to the back of his neck, and she brought her breasts fully against his chest, not caring that she wasn't wearing a bra.

Suddenly, she couldn't get enough of his mouth, their tongues meeting in a sweet dance, his lips tasting like blueberry syrup. Madison staggered back a step and hit the kitchen counter. She wanted more, much more from him, as he explored her body with his hands. They roamed downward and cupped her behind. In seconds, he lifted her easily onto the kitchen counter, her head nearly bouncing against the cabinets as he broke off their kiss.

"Maddie," he moaned, for the first time calling her by her childhood name. "Maddie…" It sounded so right. He claimed her mouth again, and this time, she leaned down to kiss him as he pressed his body against hers, and she wrapped her legs around his waist. When he drew her closer, she moved her hands to his hair, her fingers running through its thick waves. She was so hungry for him—she devoured his mouth. She felt her whole body react to his. Inside, a flame had been lit that had nothing to do with the baby. At that moment, she was just a woman who badly wanted this man.

Suddenly, he was tugging at the hem of her shirt, and she raised her arms, eager to be free of the last barrier between them. His mouth found her right nipple and she gasped, arching her back into him. He took her left breast in his hand, growling in appreciation of its weight as he carefully squeezed it. Her breasts, deliciously sore from the pregnancy, were extra sensitive, and she felt each flick of his tongue as if it were electrically charged. Instantly, she felt her innermost depths grow warm with need.

She held on to his neck for dear life as he

moved his attention to her left nipple, his teeth flicking ever so gently, making her groan. It was just like the night they'd spent together; he seemed to anticipate every one of her desires as if he were inside her head, accurately predicting exactly how she wished to be touched. Now, the only thing she wanted was for him to take her again, like he had that night, in a surge of unstoppable passion—all care about practicality out the window, all thought for the future gone in that one moment of instinct. He licked the center of her chest, in the curve between her breasts, driving her wild with want. She clutched at him with her legs, tightening her grip, and felt that he, too, was ready. Oh, so ready.

She wanted him inside her. Right now, proving once and for all that the one night they'd spent together was no accident, no mistake. The passion they felt for each other was real. It *had* to be real. No man had ever made her feel like this, so consumed by want, so oblivious to reason. Each of his kisses drove her wild, trailing like hot lava down her naked skin.

Now, he was tugging at the waistband of her shorts. *Yes*, she thought. *Take me. Right here. In the kitchen.* She didn't care if the shades were open, or if they were in full view of the patio door.

And then, before he could get her shorts down, they both heard the telltale sounds of retching.

Teddy.

They looked back in time to see the puppy hack and then throw up his pancake breakfast all over the tile floor.

MADISON SNATCHED UP her shirt and pulled away from him, breaking their embrace to look after *that dog.* Collin couldn't have been more annoyed—or more uncomfortable, his erection straining against his shorts. "He's fine," Collin said, reaching out for Madison. "Dogs throw up. He probably ate too much. Told you not to feed him table food."

Then the pup retched again, a loud, hacking sound, and puked up more blueberry pancake... and something else. Madison scurried over to the pup.

"Wait! That's an... M&M." How she could tell from the mess there, Collin had no idea, but somehow she'd picked out a little round green unchewed and barely digested M&M. "Chocolate is poisonous to dogs!"

Beneath the stool near the breakfast bar, Collin saw a chewed-up wrapper on the floor. "Looks like he's had a few," Collin said, as he snatched up the destroyed wrapper. No candies were left inside.

"What? No!" Madison hurried to his side, and took the gnawed wrapper from his hand. "This was a half-*full* bag. It was in my purse! How did you…"

Then Collin peered beneath the stools at the breakfast bar. "Looks like he found your purse."

There, under the second stool, was Madison's small bucket bag, dumped on its side, contents strewn all over the floor. They hadn't been able to see it from their vantage point at the dining room table.

"I put it on the stool," Madison said, frowning as she studied the place she thought she'd left it.

"I guess he could reach it," Collin said, then glanced at the puppy. "Bad dog," he said, shaking a finger. The dog, who'd retched twice, but now seemed fine, simply trotted away.

Madison stooped to pick up the contents of her purse. "He ate my lip balm!" She held up the small tube that had been gnawed beyond repair. It was now just four or five plastic pieces and the empty half of the tube.

"Teddy!" she scolded. The puppy, for his part, barked once and wagged his furry tail.

"Is lip balm toxic to dogs, too? Seems like

that dog has a death wish," Collin observed. *One that might come true if he interrupts us again.* His groin was only beginning to settle down, but his hunger for Madison hadn't abated. He'd wanted her, and the dog had made sure to kill the moment. He grabbed a wad of paper towels to help her sop up the puppy's mess, realizing this was the second time that morning he'd done the same thing and the roll was dwindling fast. He'd better go invest in more paper towels, and soon. Even that didn't entirely distract him from Madison. He was distinctly aware of every movement she made, and he wanted to feel her petal-soft skin against his once more.

"You don't seem very concerned," Madison said, her voice accusatory; she picked up the puppy and studied his face, as if she could tell by looking whether the dog had truly been poisoned. He didn't think the chocolate could hurt all that much, at least not that small amount.

"He'll probably be fine. M&M's are milk chocolate and isn't that—"

"What about the lip balm?" Madison interrupted. Her worry was growing, and he hated to see her so worked up over the dog. Collin felt that if Teddy was dumb enough to poison himself, then wasn't that Darwinism at work on some level?

"Since we put it *on* our own lips, I think it's fine. It's nontoxic, anyway."

"What about the plastic bits?" She pulled the dog close, as if the force of her cuddling could keep him safe. She looked beautiful, dark eyes flashing. Fierce and protective. *She's going to make one hell of a mother,* he thought and grinned at the prospect. She was willing to fight him to get that dog the care he needed.

"We have to call the vet," Madison said, then grabbed her phone from the table. "I'll call Yvana and get his number." She began dialing as she cuddled the dog against her neck.

"Is he even on the island yet?" Collin asked.

"Yvana said he's coming today, so let's hope he is." Madison pressed the phone to her ear and waited.

MADISON STOOD VERY still as the vet, Dr. Ruben, carefully checked Teddy for any signs of chocolate poisoning. They all sat in his living room, about a quarter mile from Uncle Rashad's house. Ruben had arrived on the first morning ferry and hadn't even had a chance to unpack his luggage yet, which sat in his foyer against the wall. Instead of a white lab coat, he wore black Bermuda shorts and a yellow-and-black striped golf shirt.

"Good boy," Dr. Ruben said, his salt-and-pepper hair worn thick and wavy. The fifty-something vet examined the dog, peering into his ears. The puppy licked his face and the doctor laughed. "You're a cute one," he told the golden ball of fluff as he gave the affectionate dog a pat.

"Is he going to be okay?" Madison felt like a bundle of nerves. Would half a bag of chocolate candy kill this poor stray? She didn't know how she'd live with that. She wanted to help the poor thing, not kill him. Plus, what kind of mother would she be if she couldn't even keep a dog alive?

Collin reached forward and took her hand. She felt his warm strong fingers wrap around hers and, for a second, she was very glad he was there. He'd remained quiet for most of the visit, letting the vet do his work. Yet, she appreciated his quiet confidence as he stood behind her in the vet's kitchen, the dog on the dining room table so the doctor could take a better look at him.

"Well, I don't recommend M&M's for puppies," he said as he finished his exam and then gently placed Teddy on the floor. "But, I think, given his size and the fact that there's not as much concentrated cocoa in milk chocolate, the amount he actually ingested is pretty small."

Madison felt her shoulders relax, reassured by Dr. Ruben's words. Thank goodness! Collin squeezed her hand and she squeezed back. She turned to him and he was smiling, relief in his eyes, too, as well as a tiny bit of "I told you so" in the quirk of his smile. Madison didn't care. She was just glad the pup would be all right.

She knelt down and rubbed the dog's head, cradling his furry face in both hands.

"And the lip balm? The plastic?"

"Because it's such a small amount, I wouldn't worry," Dr. Ruben said. "And the lip balm is just wax. Watch him for the next few hours, and if he gets lethargic or starts vomiting and doesn't stop, call me, but I think he'll be fine."

"Oh, thank goodness." Madison flattened her hand on her chest as she slowly exhaled. She hadn't realized how tense she'd been.

"First-time mom?" Dr. Ruben asked, which made her tense up again. Was she showing already?

"What do you mean?" she asked, unable to keep the defensive tone from her voice. Could everyone see she was pregnant? She put a protective hand across her abdomen.

"Puppy mom," he said, pointing to the dog.

"Oh." She laughed a little and exchanged a knowing glance with Collin, who chuckled.

"Oh. Yes. Sort of. I had dogs growing up, but my parents took care of them."

"And he's technically not *her* dog," Collin pointed out.

"Yours, then?" The vet turned his attention to Collin.

"Mine? No." Madison watched as Collin visibly backpedaled. "Not *either* of ours. We *found* him."

The vet shrugged. "Many new pet owners get their pets that way." Dr. Ruben folded his arms across his chest. "And I didn't feel a microchip in him, either, so if he does have an owner, that person will be harder to find."

"But he's a dog on an *island*. Someone brought him here." Teddy romped over to Collin and began playing with his shoelace. Collin gently moved him along.

Dr. Ruben nodded. "Lots of tourists do come here and rent homes, and sometimes they bring pets, and maybe…they decide they're too much trouble and don't want them anymore. We've had other pets abandoned here. A couple of cats. Another dog."

"That's horrible!" Madison felt so sad for Teddy, and all the animals like him, lost or abandoned. She almost felt like crying. When had she become so sentimental? Sure, she'd always had a soft spot for her clients—most of them—and for animals, but lately, she felt like tearing up at everything. She sucked in a breath. Must be pregnancy hormones.

"Lucky for this guy you rescued him," Dr. Ruben said, stroking the dog's head. "Domesticated dogs aren't meant to be on their own."

Collin crouched and gave the puppy a scratch behind the ears. He was so gentle and loving that Madison found herself transfixed by the sight of man and dog. The size disparity was obvious; Collin was massive compared to the pup. Was this how he'd be with a baby? She suddenly had an image of him cuddling an infant to his shoulder, gently rubbing the baby's back.

"I'm glad we found you, boy," Collin said. The dog's tongue slid out, and Collin laughed, letting down his guard. Seeing the normally tough prosecutor falling prey to the charms of a puppy made affection rise up in Madison's chest. So, he wasn't the coldhearted assistant district attorney all the time. She thought about the feel of his lips on her bare skin and realized she already knew that. He had passion in him—determined and directed—and Madison felt a pull toward him. She noticed how his strong shoulders filled out his shirt. She still had a hard time getting used to Collin without his perfect-fitting suits. Here, he wore sneakers and cargo shorts and snug faded T-shirts.

Collin seemed to sense her studying him. He looked up and smiled, the light reaching his eyes. Would the baby have his easy smile? She hoped so.

Stop thinking about it, she scolded herself. *Even if the baby did, what would it matter? They couldn't actually work as a couple, regardless of what Collin thought. He was too egotistical, too self-involved.* Deep down, she suspected he'd only proposed to her because, somehow, this would be another notch in his belt. It *was* a pity proposal, but beyond that, it was a way for him to play the martyr. *Look at me, at the noble thing I did.*

That was why he was so good at getting the jurors to give Jimmy Reese the maximum sentence. She thought about Jimmy and glanced at her phone. No new messages from her uncle. Although, if she pulled up a local Fort Myers news app, she saw Jimmy's mug shot, intimidating and fierce, staring up at her. She immediately quit the app. She'd already decided this was the safest place she could be. If Jimmy came for her, he'd no doubt go to her apartment or her office. The idea that he could somehow link her uncle's house to her seemed a bit of a stretch. Let alone the fact that he couldn't possibly know where it was. Could he?

Collin cocked his head to one side, confusion flickering across his face.

"Everything okay?" he asked her.

"Fine," she lied and then focused her attention on Dr. Ruben.

"Well," Dr. Ruben said, clearing his throat. "The puppy, if you keep him, will require some shots. I can't say for sure how old he is, but my guess is about eight weeks. He may or may not have had the first round of vaccines, but in any case, you'll need to bring him to a vet in the next six weeks or so to get his shots. Otherwise, feed him twice a day and keep those M&M's out of his reach."

"Oh, I will," Madison said, vowing to rid the entire house of chocolate. The last thing she wanted was another scare. "Should we take him to the mainland now for his shots?"

"We still need to find the owners," Collin said, straightening as the dog jumped on his hind legs and put his front paws on Collin's knees. "Down, boy," he admonished.

"You heard Dr. Ruben," Madison said, pointing at the doctor, who still stood in his living room. "He was probably abandoned."

"We don't know that for sure, and it wouldn't be fair to the people who owned him if they're searching for this dog and we give up too soon on trying to find them."

The vet glanced from Madison to Collin and back again, looking as if he didn't want to step into the fray. "There are a few lost dog websites," he said, obviously trying to stay neutral. "But you still might not find the owners."

"We'll try," Collin said, sounding determined. Why was he so eager to offload this dog? They'd found Teddy, so they needed to take care of him. To Madison, it was that simple.

"In the meantime, I've got some extra food, a spare collar and leash that might work for this guy." Dr. Ruben fingered the makeshift belt around the dog's neck. "Want them?"

"Yes," Collin and Madison both said at once. While he went to fetch them, Madison and Collin stayed locked in an uneasy silence. When he returned, he secured the collar around the dog and clipped on the leash. "The tag on the collar has my number. It's a spare I keep for my German shepherd."

"Thank you. What do we owe you?"

"On the house," Dr. Ruben said. "Don't you worry about it."

"Thank you," Madison said, as she took the handle of the blue leash. Little Teddy barked in appreciation.

"Thanks again." Collin shook the man's hand. He and Madison left, walking down the bright blue porch steps. Collin slid into the driver's seat of the golf cart and flicked on the engine. Madison sat in the passenger seat, pulling the furry puppy into her lap.

"Why are you so eager to get rid of this dog?" Madison asked, unable to contain her frustration a minute longer.

"Why are you so eager to keep him? Like I said, there could be a family out there looking for him right now." Collin glanced quickly at Madison as he threw the golf cart into reverse and backed out of the narrow driveway. Once on the main trail, he turned the cart and headed back to Madison's house, which was on the other side of the island.

"Anyone looking for him would've called Yvana." Madison hugged Teddy tighter, loving the weight of him in her lap. She felt his little chest lift as he took a breath, his ears flapping a bit in the breeze that sailed in through the open windows of the cart.

Collin took the next turn a bit too fast and Madison clutched Teddy, afraid he'd go sailing out of her arms.

"Careful," she cautioned.

"I always am," he countered, his voice clipped.

"Not always, Mr. Broken Condom." Madison half-expected Collin to be angry, but instead, he threw his head back and laughed.

"Right," he said. "But as I recall, you told me not to worry."

Madison stared out at the passing scenery, a blur of tropical flowers and juvenile palm trees. The small paths and tangled plants gave the island the feel of Jurassic Park—a little bit, anyway.

"I thought you were on the pill," he added, glancing at her briefly.

"I wasn't, a fact you would've known if you'd *asked.* Or do you assume *all* women are on the pill?"

He seemed taken aback. "Why did you tell me not to worry, then?"

"Because I figured we didn't have to worry. I mean, it wasn't anywhere close to the time I normally ovulate. I thought we were in the clear." Madison sighed, feeling exasperation welling up in her. "And, I'd planned to get the morning after pill… but then… well… didn't. Work became hectic and…"

"Well, I'm sorry I assumed. It was wrong. I had a few things on my mind."

"Like Jimmy Reese."

"Yes." He met her gaze. "Like Jimmy Reese."

Her case had been in full swing that very week. It was hard to remember every detail of the trial when her own client stared at her as if he imagined colorful ways to kill her. In fact, it was Jimmy Reese, really, who'd driven her to go to the bar the night she'd met Collin. And with such a terrible defendant, she'd felt a little closer to the prosecutor who'd put him away.

If it hadn't been for Jimmy Reese, she never would've considered sleeping with Collin Baptista. She glanced at him now thinking about how small twists of fate can change the course of a life. Or, in this case, create one. "That was one time I was glad to say you won."

Collin grinned. "Yeah, me, too."

For a second, peace descended on their golf cart and they found that elusive common ground once more.

"Do you want to tell me why you're so determined to believe that we won't work out? Seems like sometimes we do agree—on the important things." Collin glanced at her, taking his eyes off the sandy path. His hands continued to steer the golf cart.

"Keyword being sometimes," she said. Madison thought they might be going more slowly than normal. Was he being careful because she held a dog in her lap, or because he was worried about her morning, noon and night sickness? "We can go faster," she added.

"I'm trying to go slow. You're pregnant and…"

"I'm not a delicate flower. You can *go faster*." Madison leaned over and stomped on his foot, sending the gas pedal downward.

"Hey. I'm driving! Stop that…" Collin squeezed the steering wheel and regained control just as Teddy let out a high-pitched bark, and that was when Madison noticed the animal in the road.

"Look out!" she screamed as Collin slammed on the brakes.

CHAPTER TWELVE

COLLIN'S HAND SHOT out to try to keep Madison and Teddy in the cart, as he hit the brakes. The golf cart skidded to a stop on the sandy path. Madison grabbed hold of the dashboard, trying to hold herself and the dog in. In front of them walked a turtle with a shell bigger than a hubcap.

"Whoa," Collin said, as the wheels of the cart stopped just shy of the turtle's front leg. "You okay?"

Madison nodded, her heart in her throat.

"Dog okay? Baby okay?"

Madison nodded again, twice. She didn't feel hurt. She hoped the baby was all right, although it was too early to feel any movement.

Collin hopped out and inspected the turtle, who seemed unfazed by the arrival of a speeding golf cart, two grown humans and a puppy. Teddy struggled against Madison's grasp, barking. She let him down, holding tightly to his leash as he trotted forward to join Collin in examining the turtle. The creature, which

was almost as big as the dog, didn't even with-
draw his head as the puppy sniffed curiously
at his leg.

"Brave old fella, aren't you?" Collin said to
the turtle. Another golf cart came speeding by
in the opposite direction, and Teddy barked
at it.

"This path has a lot of traffic," Madison
said, frowning. "The turtle might get hit if he
stays there." She glanced back and forth at the
now-empty road, but Collin knew it wouldn't
stay that way for long.

Collin tried to shoo the turtle with his foot,
but when it became clear that it wasn't going
to move any faster, he stooped, picked up the
big turtle and hustled him to the greenery on
the other side. Teddy barked and strained at his
leash, eager to follow his new friend.

"Oh, no. You're coming with us," Madison
said, leaning down and picking him up. But
then she felt a little light-headed and reached
out to grab the front of the cart, drawing Collin's attention.

Suddenly, Collin was on high alert. "Everything okay?" he asked, rushing to her side.

"Fine," Madison said. "Just lightheaded. It
happens sometimes."

Collin studied her, concern on his face.

"Let's get you home," he said. "You need to rest. And let me hold the dog."

"You've got to drive," she said. "I'll be fine." She hoped she would be. Teddy, sitting in her lap, whined and looked up at her, as if he was worried about her, too. She cuddled him, nuzzling his neck, and he rested his snout on her shoulder.

Collin sent a worried glance her way, but she was already feeling better. "You sure you're okay?" Madison felt the sincerity of his concern…and the warmth of his affection. Was she wrong about him? Maybe he really *did* care about her.

He tentatively reached out and put his hand on her knee, and she let him keep it there as he drove down the small winding road to the house.

AFTER THEY'D PUT Teddy on a bed of towels in the utility room, he fell asleep almost immediately, exhausted from his trip to the vet. Collin stepped back and gently shut the door. The sun had set now, and it was getting late.

"You think he'll be okay in there?" Madison asked.

"I think he'll be fine," Collin said, steering her to the stairs. "You should rest. Maybe lie down? You look…tired."

Madison laughed. "Oh, really? Thanks," she muttered sarcastically. Great. She already felt bloated and exhausted, and her blood kept running hot and cold. Pregnancy hormones? She didn't know. But, loath as she was to admit it, lying down sounded pretty good. But, still, she hesitated.

"I'll go, but... I'm worried about Teddy. What if the vet was wrong? About the chocolate?"

"I'll check on Teddy, all right? I'll make sure he's fine, okay? You lie down and rest."

"But..." Collin wouldn't be denied. He guided her upstairs to the bedroom, and she was hyperaware of the strength of his hand on her elbow. He was a good six inches taller, too, with muscle to spare. Not that she was in any condition to fight him.

"Fine," she said as she let him lead her to the bedroom. Distantly, she wondered what would've happened earlier if Teddy hadn't gotten sick. She remembered Collin's mouth on hers, the way he'd explored her, the passion that lit up every one of her nerve endings. Even thinking about being without her shirt made her face grow hot. She remembered his lips on her nipples, the expert way his tongue had danced on their tips. Madison shivered, her belly suddenly feeling warm. And this time, she didn't think it was due to pregnancy hormones at all. Now, all she could think about was Collin's broad shoulders, how his bare chest had felt against the palms of her hands.

Her thoughts ventured into X-rated territory as she hit the top of the stairs, and Collin led her by the hand to the bedroom. She knew he just intended to put her down for a nap, and yet...she found her mind leaping to all sorts of possibilities, most of them without clothes. Madison was so intent on her imagination that she didn't notice the corner of the hallway runner. Her flip-flop caught on the edge and she tripped. Collin reached out to steady her and then suddenly she was in his arms. God, he was tall. And broad. And...muscular. So... many muscles. His suit hid them during trials, but now, in his snug-fitting T-shirt, she could see every last one.

"Oh," she gasped. Being so close to Collin made her feel winded. He stared at her a long time, too long, without speaking.

"Maddie," he breathed.

"Only people who knew me when I was a kid call me Maddie," she told him, feeling his eyes on her, assessing her, almost reading her thoughts.

"I want to know you as well as they do," he said, gently pushing a tendril of hair from her forehead and tucking it securely behind her ear. "Besides, I like how it sounds. *Maddie*."

She liked how it sounded, too, when he said it—a deep guttural sound she could feel in her lower belly. He was so close to her now. Was he moving even closer? Was he going to kiss her? Her stomach tightened in anticipation as she remembered the last time he kissed her and she'd ended up half-naked on a kitchen counter.

All she could do was stare at his mouth, his perfect sensual lips. She remembered the taste of them and wanted to taste them again.

"Collin…" Was it a warning? Or a request? She wasn't sure.

"I'm going to kiss you now," he said, and she didn't move. Couldn't move. This was what she wanted, repercussions be damned. And, she realized, it was exactly the way she'd felt that night in the parking lot of the bar. What was it about Collin Baptista that made her throw every last bit of good sense to the wind?

Collin put his hand firmly on the small of her back and pulled her toward him. She went willingly. Then, he dipped down and pressed his lips against hers, lightly, tenderly, with the hint of more to come. She stood on her tiptoes, eager for him, as she parted her lips and his tongue found hers. Instantly, every nerve ending in her body seemed to turn on, her blood-stream a humming highway of anticipation.

Madison felt something hard behind her and realized it was the hallway wall. They'd some-how walked there, and now Collin pressed himself fully against her, his hands roaming her curves, his mouth devouring hers. She wanted him, as badly as she had that first night, her body feeling dangerous and out of control, like the first flame of an uncontain-able fire.

Collin broke free first. "Maybe we should both lie down," he suggested.

"Yes, we should," Madison said, tugging him through the bedroom door. "On the bed."

Collin went, a smug smile at the corners of his mouth. "If we go there together, you're not going to nap."

"I'll just have to risk it."

CHAPTER THIRTEEN

COLLIN LAID MADISON gently down on the made bed, finding her lips once more. The woman tasted like some kind of addictive drug. Sweet, savory, intoxicating. She was damn near the most gorgeous woman ever, he marveled as he broke free and stared at her face. Cheeks flushed, lips pink and swollen from his kisses. Her dark eyes looked darker now that her pupils were dilated, and her thick black hair was draped on the light blue bedspread like a shadowy fan. He could've smacked that dog earlier for interrupting them, just when he'd managed to convince her to let down her guard. He'd damn near taken her right there in the kitchen.

She wiggled out of her top now, and he sucked in a breath as he admired her swollen breasts, maybe a cup size bigger since their single night together. Pregnancy must be to blame for her delicious new curves, but Collin wasn't complaining. Not in the least. He kissed her ample breasts, feeling himself grow harder against her. How could he want a woman so badly? Especially one who *already* carried his baby.

Yet, as she lay there, eyelids low, watching him, he had never wanted any other woman more. He felt there was something primal about his attraction to her, and that filled him with a desperate kind of need. He pulled off her shorts and her thong with them, and she lay before him bare. He had a flash of her in the past, just like this, flat on her back, willing and waiting for him that night. He was remembering it clearly now, as he freed himself from his shorts and underwear, kicking them off. Then he pulled her to the edge of the bed. *Yes, like this*, he thought. *Just like this.*

Madison rose up on one elbow.

"Condom?" she asked him.

"Uh… We already…" He nodded down at her belly.

"What about…" She bit her lower lip and glanced to the side.

"Well, if I have something, I'm pretty sure you've got it by this point." Collin realized how bad the joke was the minute he said it. Her eyes grew big with concern. "Kidding. I'm kidding. I got checked out a couple of months ago when I gave blood. I'm fine. Anyway, I haven't been with anybody but you for the last year."

"The last…year?" Madison looked shocked.

"Nope." *Too busy for entanglements*, he thought as he laid a trail of kisses up her belly. *Where my son is.* He reached her mouth and any protest died on her lips. She groaned into his mouth, a sound of pure want, and it drove him wild as he felt himself strain against his very skin. He moved alongside her, finding the softness between her legs, feeling her slick wetness.

"Maddie," he moaned, unable to contain himself any longer as he pushed inside, finding her deep center. Immediately, he felt her heat. Was she hotter than usual? He couldn't tell, but whatever it was, she was pushing him over the edge. With need, with passion. He was almost afraid to move at first, afraid even the slightest movement would compel him to come inside her. He moved his hips slowly at first, and then, when he was confident he would last, he went harder and deeper. He lay on his elbows, careful to keep his weight off her stomach, concerned about the baby—*but not too worried*, he thought wryly, as he moved faster. Now he realized what he'd missed that night with all his forgotten memories. He'd missed this, this truly magnificent sensation. He wasn't going to be able to hold back any longer.

"You're perfect," he told her, and it was the

truth. He'd never felt a woman so hot, so wet before. She squeezed her legs more tightly around him, and he almost came right then but managed to hold on.

"I want to be on top," she murmured, and he let her move. He lay down and she climbed on him, and in his mind's eye, he saw a flash of another memory. *This was what she did the last time.* Now, she sat on top of him, hands on his chest, full breasts spilling out between them. He arched his neck and flicked a nipple with his tongue. Her nipples were darker than he remembered. The pregnancy, maybe? He loved the color, like milk chocolate.

Then she moved atop him, raising her arms above her head, crossing them, and he reached up and cupped her full breasts, marveling at the weight of them in his hands. She was a beautiful woman. A work of art. She rocked her body faster, her hips grinding into his and then, suddenly, she reached her own climax, her nipples pointed and puckered, her head thrown back as the pure pleasure took her to another place. She fell off him, satiated, but he was far from done. He flipped her on her side and took her from behind, in strong deliberate strokes. Oh, he wanted this. He'd wanted this since their first night together, since far before that, since the moment he'd first laid eyes on her.

You're going to be my wife, he thought, determined to make it true. They did belong together, and he'd prove it to her. He wanted her in the most basic of ways. In *every* way. He could hold back the tide of his climax no longer. He came with a guttural grunt of pleasure, spilling himself deep inside her.

He collapsed against her back, wrapping her in his embrace, feeling sated at last. Finally, he remembered the sex they'd had. *Completely* remembered it. Who would've known the disapproving defense attorney could be this...free? He would never forget the way she'd ridden him, the confident way she took herself to her own climax. *What a truly incredible woman*, he thought. Even hotter than he remembered. He'd lucked out in so many ways. This intelligent, compassionate, *fantastic* woman was carrying his child.

For a full minute, he didn't want to move. She didn't, either, and he held her there, spooning against her back for what felt like half a lifetime. He didn't want to let her go, didn't want to break apart, for fear it would somehow break the spell between them. For once, they weren't fighting. Correction—for once she wasn't fighting *him*. Why she was so sure they'd make a terrible couple was beyond him. The sex was incredible, and wasn't that a good start?

"You're just perfect, Maddie," he murmured in her ear. "I mean that. You are. Truly. Exceptional." He'd been with enough women to know exactly what he wanted, what he needed, and that was Maddie.

"Are you going to give me a star rating?" she teased as she traced the outline of his chest with one fingernail.

"Five out of five stars," he declared. "Without a doubt."

She chuckled, and he felt her laugh against his chest. He loved making her laugh. He suddenly realized what he wanted more than anything was the chance to make her laugh for the rest of their lives. The possibility was comforting. He didn't have to worry about finding a wife, about figuring out if she was *Miss Right*, because the baby had done that for him. Now, he'd just have to make her Mrs. Right.

She grew silent, and he could almost hear the wheels of her mind turning. What was she thinking now? He hoped that her orgasm had knocked all the doubts out of her mind. *Yet, if anyone could find fault with their amazing sex, it would be Madison Reddy.*

Her brain never shut off. It made her an imposing defense attorney, but—at times—an infuriating woman.

"What are you thinking?" she asked him, then.

"Wondering what *you* were thinking," he admitted honestly.

"I asked you first." Somehow, this felt like a trap.

"Well," he began cautiously. He stroked her hair, loving its thickness. "I was wondering how you were going to somehow try to convince me that great sex means we're destined for divorce."

She laughed again, a little giggle that shook her back.

"I haven't agreed to marry you yet," she said.

"Oh, you will." He inhaled the sweet scent of her hair, admiring its softness as he laid his cheek against the back of her head. "You'll be Mrs. Baptista."

This caused her to peel herself away from him. "Okay, say I do marry you—which is a looong shot. Since when am I going to give up my name?"

"Because…" Well, because Collin had just assumed she would. He'd never thought of her *not* changing her name. Should he push it? Or not? Was this one of those arguments where she'd insist that this was more proof that they weren't compatible?

Madison stared at him, eyebrows arched, looking as sexy as any model. Suddenly, he didn't care whether she took his name or not, as long as he could take her body every night.

He pulled her down and kissed her, and she returned his kisses as she rolled onto her back, weaving her hands through his hair. *Saved!* Thank goodness. He broke the kiss, and she glanced at him, breathless. Her eyes seemed dazed, and very, very beautiful, framed by the thickest, fullest black lashes he'd ever seen. He could gaze at them all day.

"Maybe when we argue, I should just kiss you," he suggested.

Madison gave a frantic nod. "Yes, yes, let's do that."

He bent down and kissed her once more.

Then, his phone, lying on the bedside table, rang, the screen lighting up with an incoming call. Reluctantly, he ended the kiss to see who might be trying to reach him. That was when he saw it was his old friend, Jenny, from the prosecutor's office, his former boss.

"Hello," he said, thinking, *finally*. He'd left her a dozen voice-mail messages about Jimmy Reese. "Did you catch him? Tell me you caught him."

Beside him, Madison tensed. Pulling the top

sheet over her bare chest and sitting up, she eyed him, concern on her face.

"No, we haven't. Yet."

The muscles in Collin's shoulders stiffened. "What's the latest?" He glanced at Madison, who was still studying him. *Who is it?* she mouthed. But he shook his head, holding up a finger.

"Well, we tracked down his brother, and with a little persuasion his brother admitted Reese was hell-bent on finding you. Finding you and Madison Reddy. Said he knew he didn't have much time before he was caught, but if he's going away for twenty years, might as well kill the people responsible for putting him behind bars first."

Collin felt like someone had thrown a bucket of cold water on him. This wasn't the first time he'd ever been threatened by a con, and while he already knew Jimmy Reese was determined to get revenge, the fact that he was broadcasting it to his next of kin made it all the more real. He reached out and sought Madison's hand.

"Well, you sure know how to ruin a man's vacation," Collin joked, but inside he seethed.

"All available officers are on the manhunt, but maybe we could round up a few to give you some protection?" Collin knew she didn't make the offer lightly. She wouldn't assign anyone unless she thought Jimmy Reese posed a real threat, but right now, Collin felt the best thing to do would be to use all on staff to apprehend Reese, before he found out where they were.

"No. What are the odds he'd find Rashad's house? Use them to track down Reese. Maybe station one officer at the ferry stop, since that's the only way onto this island."

"He could get around the ferry stop. If he had his own boat. I'd feel better if I sent a couple out. Just to be sure."

"I can handle myself." Collin had taken self-defense, and he carried a conceal-and-carry permit for a handgun, which he had stowed in his bag at the rental house. Hell, he was a better shot than some of the cops were, at least those he saw at the range on weekends.

"I want you to catch him *before* he figures out where we are. You'll need all the manpower there. Not babysitting us. We'll be fine." Collin felt certain that sending cops here would be a waste of time, and he needed them all working to track down Reese.

"Okay. Watch your back, Baptista." With that, Jenny hung up.

Collin stared at his phone, then turned to Madison. "I've got some bad news. Jimmy Reese…" He paused, wondering what would be the point of telling her what she already knew. "They haven't caught him yet," he finished. "They found his brother, but then the trail went cold."

"What else?" Madison blinked fast.

"He's been talking about you. And me. To his brother."

Madison nodded, as if resigned. "I figured."

Collin regretted saying anything. Tears glistened in her eyes. He sat down and pulled Madison into his arms.

"He's not going to hurt you. I won't let him."

Madison allowed him to hold her, and he squeezed her tighter.

"I want you to know that. We're not enemies anymore, okay?"

She nodded into his chest and swiped at her eyes. He pulled away and wiped a tear from her cheek. "You okay?" he asked.

"Damn pregnancy hormones. I usually don't cry this easily." She angrily rubbed her eyes.

"Good, because I hate crybabies," he teased, and then she laughed as he stroked another tear from her cheek.

DURING THE REST of the week, worry about Reese began to fade into the background, since neither of them could do anything from the island to help catch the escaped convict. They notified Yvana and her staff, as well as everybody on ferry duty, to be on the lookout for the man and gave them all pictures. If he set foot anywhere near the clubhouse, Yvana and her crew would recognize him. They both began to feel a little safer. Things returned to normal, or as normal as they could be with a pregnant woman suffering from near-constant morning sickness and a puppy with little to no training yet.

Every day, Collin chipped further away at Madison's reluctance to get married, even as they fell into a kind of routine. They'd wake up, walk the dog, feed him with pet food they'd borrowed from Dr. Ruben and then plan the day's meals. Collin made himself useful around her uncle's house—fixing a leaky pipe and mowing the lawn. Could they be domesticated together? Living in tandem once the baby came?

As they sat on the back porch, watching the sun set on Friday, the sky in front of them was a blaze of colors from bright pink and lavender to a darkened orange. Collin drank beer from a bottle and Madison had yet another can of fizzy water. Teddy lay on the wooden boards, head between his paws as he napped. They'd had no luck finding his owner in spite of Madison's efforts. But trying to do that was much better than worrying about what Jimmy Reese might or might not be doing. No one had called the front office in search of a missing dog; a call to Yvana turned up no renters who'd brought pets they'd registered. Of course, Yvana had pointed out that plenty of people snuck them onto the island, and if the family had planned to ditch the poor dog, they wouldn't have announced that they'd brought him in the first place.

Madison studied Teddy, such a cute yellow fluff ball, and wondered who could be so cold-hearted as to leave the dog to fend for himself.

Collin reached out from his nearby deck chair and clasped her free hand. His touch comforted her despite all her reservations about him.

She glanced at his profile, wondering what it would be like to see him every day, to live with him as they were doing here. They'd slept together the last few nights, their bodies fitting as if they belonged. The sex made her hit heights she'd never thought possible, and even she had to admit they had a spark unlike any she'd ever experienced before. Maybe opposites *did* attract. Maybe she liked his law-and-order stiff persona, his overconfidence that went straight into the bedroom. Maybe she could somehow soften him, help him see that the world wasn't black and white. Maybe he could change, and she was wrong to doubt him. Maybe they could make a marriage work.

But then again, they were in vacation mode, not day-to-day living, and she knew it couldn't last. What would happen when the real world crept in? When she tried to go back to work after the baby was born? When they found themselves on opposite sides of a case once again?

The ocean breeze rustled the treetops around them, their deck porch, adjacent to her bedroom, a full two stories above the ground. She loved sitting here in the evenings, watching the sun paint colors across the sky as it dipped below the horizon, hidden in the distance by palm trees.

"You can't have much vacation time left," Madison said, bringing up the subject she'd been avoiding for the last few days. She hadn't wanted to know when he planned to leave, she realized. She was growing accustomed to his presence, his help if she needed it, his touch every day.

"I've got a few months off," he said. "And as long as Jimmy's out there, I'm not going anywhere."

Madison felt reassured by that as she stretched

out her legs on the wooden chair and gazed up at the stars in the sky above them. "Months? How did you manage that?" she asked, surprised, as she took another sip of her carbonated lime-flavored water. "I didn't think the state attorney's office gave that kind of vacation. Especially to their stars."

Collin took a deep swig of beer. He studied the moon that had just begun to rise over the treetops. It loomed, big and yellow, above the dark outline of palm trees in the distance. The ocean was too far to see, just a dark blot on the horizon. "Actually, I'm leaving the state attorney's office."

Madison sat up in her Adirondack chair and stared at him. "Private practice?" She couldn't imagine the hard-charging attorney giving up the high ground. "You joining us defense attorneys on the dark side?"

Collin chuckled, and glanced her way, the baseball cap he wore partially obscuring his face.

"No. I'm going to work for the prosecutor's office in Miami. I'm taking some time off before I start the new job. The man I'm replacing isn't leaving for four months."

Madison sat there, stunned. Miami was two and a half hours away from Fort Myers, and that was when traffic was good.

"When did this happen?"

Collin looked up at the sky and then at her. He seemed a little...uncomfortable. "I took the job a month ago. Put in my notice right away, and had my last day at the state attorney's office just before I drove out to see you."

"So...you proposed to me and you didn't think you ought to mention that you planned to live in *Miami*?" Madison felt indignation tickle the back of her throat. This was textbook Collin. He assumed that whatever he planned was *right*, and everybody else should follow along.

"Look, I know. It's a shock."

"You weren't going to tell me *before* you proposed?"

Collin rubbed the back of his neck. "Well, I was sort of hoping to break the news *after* you said yes. You know, when you were supposed to be delirious with happiness." He gave a weak laugh as she glared. "Okay, fine. Bad joke. But think about it. There are plenty of jobs in Miami. Good defense firms, better salaries."

"I don't want to work at another firm. I *like* my uncle's firm." Truth be told, she yearned for a larger family, and her work provided that. The people were great, and the fact that her uncle ran the place just made it seem cozy.

Safe. A feeling lost to her these days. Or since Jimmy Reese had become her client, anyway.

"Come on, Maddie. You can't work for your uncle forever." Collin finished the last of his beer and set the empty bottle down on the deck, by the leg of his chair.

"Why can't I? He's a great boss. And he's like a father to me. I wouldn't be the attorney I am today without him."

"I'm not saying Reddy isn't great. He is well-respected and a very smart businessman, but at some point, don't you want a challenge? Get a job on your own merits?"

Madison ground her back molars together in frustration. Suddenly, the beautiful night sky above them didn't seem so peaceful anymore. "I *did* get this job on my own merits."

"Yeah, but he's your uncle…" Collin straightened in his chair and pushed his base-ball cap back. Now, she could see his eyes—mildly annoyed, a little patronizing.

"And he wouldn't have hired me if he didn't think I was qualified. If anything, he pushed me harder than his other junior attorneys." Madison didn't like the fact that Collin thought her uncle had handed her the position. It wasn't like that. Not at all. Affection aside, he wouldn't have brought her on if he hadn't thought her one hundred percent capable of doing the job.

"Well, you could always extend your leave of absence. Be a stay-at-home mom for a while."

"No. I'm not giving up my career." Madison felt certain of this. She wanted more to offer her child—a different kind of example, one that focused on believing in oneself, and making the most of one's talents.

"Huh." Collin seemed stumped. "Well, we'll need to figure it out. Because we're going to live in Miami."

"Says who? You don't get to *dictate* where we live." A sea breeze tousled Madison's hair and blew a strand in her eyes. She angrily swiped it away. "I'm not a dog you can just *tell* to go pee outside."

"Well, it's not like that worked with Teddy, anyway," Collin grumbled. "I would've loved to ask your input *before* I took the job. But it's not like you gave me any warning that I might need to stay in Fort Myers."

Madison felt all kinds of emotions at once. First, she felt a twinge of guilt. That much was true; she *hadn't* told him. If she had, when she'd found out about the pregnancy, maybe he would've made a different choice.

But she was also shocked that he'd been planning to move away all this time, never to see her again. If she hadn't become pregnant, Collin would've been out of her life for good. That realization stunned her—and hurt her.

"You're saying if I told you about the baby a month ago, you would've reconsidered taking this new job?"

"Maybe. We could've at least talked about it. You never gave me the chance." Collin stared at her a long time.

"*You* didn't want to talk to *me*, remember?" Madison wasn't going to let Collin blame her for this. "And now you tell me you are planning to leave town. If I wasn't pregnant, would you have even given our relationship—us—another thought?"

"We slept together *one* time," Collin said. "But…"

She didn't let him finish. "Now, you're saying you only care about me because of this… this unplanned pregnancy."

"Why are you acting so hurt? *You* weren't even going to tell me about it," Collin said. "You wanted me out of your life so you could decide what to do all by yourself. If I hadn't found out by accident, would you ever have told me?"

Madison swallowed. "No."

"You would never have let me know that you're carrying my child?"

"Collin, it's not that simple."

Collin's face twisted in disgust. "How would that be fair to the baby? Never knowing his father?" He stood up. "He'd spend the rest of his life thinking his father abandoned him. Never loved him. Do you have any idea how that feels?"

"How do you even know it's a boy?"

"I just... I just know. I just have a feeling. A strong one."

Madison wondered if him wanting the baby to be a boy was partly him wanting to turn back the clock, maybe relive his own childhood and make it different. Yet, she stood by her decision. Collin had never been interested in anyone but Collin. *That's the real problem*, she thought. He'd been self-absorbed, completely focused on himself and no one else. And her pride was stung by the fact that it took an accidental pregnancy for him to even look at her twice.

"You didn't like me. You weren't interested."

"That's not true," he argued.

"It sure felt like it was true," Madison said. "And why would I tell you about a baby I wasn't even sure I was going to keep?"

"You *should've* told me. I had a right to

know. That's all." Collin stood then, grabbed his empty beer bottle and left the patio. He banged the glass door shut behind him.

CHAPTER FOURTEEN

COLLIN DECIDED TO take a walk. He needed to clear his head before he said something he'd really regret. He headed out the front door, hardly caring whether it closed behind him. The screen door slapped shut, and he figured that was enough to keep the bugs out.

The fact she'd keep the baby a secret from him still irked, and it might always bother him. How could she imagine *that* would work? A baby never knowing his father, and a father never having the opportunity to know his son. He still felt strongly that the baby would be a boy.

He went down the sandy path behind the house, the one too narrow for a golf cart, and walked until he hit the beach. Seagrass stood tall in the dunes, and the sun had already dropped below the horizon. The sky had turned from a bright pink and orange to a deep lavender. The warm breeze ruffled his hair and if he'd been less frustrated, he would've taken notice of the beautiful scene. He marched down the tapered path to the beach as the nearly full moon rose above the ocean.

He'd always vowed never to be an irresponsible parent, no matter what. After his father went to jail, he'd always felt his absence acutely and blamed him for not being there. He'd had to teach himself how to bat and how to throw a ball, how to ride a bicycle and how to shave. All the things dads were supposed to teach their sons. But he'd been long gone. Collin learned to do everything for himself, and that also meant being the one in control. He didn't like feeling *out* of control, as if someone else held the power. He'd spent his childhood feeling helpless, and he damn sure wasn't going to waste any of his adulthood feeling that way.

Then, of course, he thought of Jimmy Reese out there somewhere. The escaped convict made him feel more than a little helpless. He pulled up his text messages. No new ones from Jenny. No news.

They'll catch him before he gets anywhere close to North Captiva, he told himself. *They had to.* He was probably just lying low. But when he surfaced, he'd be caught. He wouldn't be the first escaped criminal to threaten lawyers but then get arrested in the bedroom of his girlfriend's house. Besides, Collin felt confident he could take care of himself *and* Madison—if the stubborn woman would let him. He kicked a bit of sand at his feet.

Collin took pride in his independence. He knew he could handle almost anything life threw at him, because in some sense, he already had. He'd been officially orphaned when his mom died, but since his mom had had to work multiple jobs while he and his sister were growing up, part of him had felt orphaned his whole life.

He sat on the beach as the moon rose in the sky. He could see the white foam of the waves rushing in, nearly hitting his toes. Collin rarely let himself sink into self-pity. He didn't like the feeling. Yet he also hated feeling things were out of his control. But, with Madison and the baby, none of it felt like anything he could manage or predict. He'd always looked after himself and never complained about it, and his stubborn insistence on making his own way had served him well. How else could a poor kid from the Bronx, whose dad died in jail, put himself through college and law school on a full ride?

He wasn't dumb, either. He knew Madison still resented him for not calling after their one night together, but he'd been under the impression they'd both agreed on that. How was *he* supposed to know that she'd secretly wanted him to pursue her? He'd thought it would be easier for both of them if he just let things go.

Not that he ever really had, he figured, as he watched a particularly big wave nearly slide up the beach. He'd been fighting his attraction to her for weeks. Months. He'd decided it was best if they didn't continue, and yet, he'd had every intention of pursuing her after he got the job offer in Miami. Not that she'd believe him now, and he couldn't blame her.

Part of him knew that, to her, the Miami announcement was a shock, but he'd also half-hoped Madison would be thrilled about the opportunity to get a new job away from her protective uncle. Collin admitted to himself that because he'd never had the kind of family connections that mattered, other than with his mother and sister, he didn't understand how Madison felt. He didn't know what it was like to have a family that could actually help.

Collin kept coming back to the fact that they were so good together. The sex proved it, in his mind, and so did the way they sparred on every topic from housetraining a dog to figuring out a fair deal for a defendant. He'd never experienced such electricity, such a connection before. He loved nothing more than a good debate, and Maddie gave that to him, every day. This past week they could barely keep their hands off each other, and that certainly had nothing to do with the baby. He grabbed the velvet box out of his pocket. He'd been working up the courage to ask her to marry him again, that very evening on the porch, when they'd begun fighting about Miami. He opened the box and studied the ring. It looked decidedly less impressive under the silver light of the moon, but he'd paid three months' salary for it, just as he was supposed to do. Or so he'd heard… He'd crossed all his t's and dotted all his i's, and yet, she was still angry with him.

What would he need to do to win her over? When would she trust him?

And why on earth was she so determined to break them up? He wasn't a man who believed in religion a whole lot, but it sure seemed like God and the universe were pushing them together. He didn't know how else to read the fact that a single night of sex ended up with a pregnancy.

As he wondered about this, his phone lit up with an incoming call, bathing the beach near him in artificial cell-phone light. Madison was calling. His heart leapt. Maybe her temper had cooled.

"Collin," Madison said, her voice sounding strained.

Instantly, he felt all his senses go on high

alert. "What's wrong? Are you okay?" His thoughts went to Jimmy Reese.

She paused just long enough to make his stomach drop. *Was* it Reese? The baby? Had she fallen? Collin shook the paranoid thoughts from his head. "Tell me what's wrong."

"I can't find Teddy."

"Oh." *The dog?* Collin felt almost instant relief, and then a prickle of annoyance. There were more important things to consider than the dog. He'd nearly had a heart attack worrying that something awful had happened to her, that she'd hurt herself or that somehow Jimmy Reese had found her, and it was just about the dog. Collin felt his concern go from acute to somewhere south of interested. "What do you mean you can't find him?"

"I. Can't. Find. Him." She paused after every word. "He's not inside. He's not outside." Madison sounded more and more worried. Then, she paused for a long second. "Did you leave the front door open?"

Did he? He might have.

Collin felt a stab of guilt. He'd flown through the front door, annoyed. He'd heard the screen slap behind him...but had he closed the front door? No, he didn't think he had. He hadn't thought about Teddy, about the big puppy who would have *had* to nudge the screen door open to get out to freedom. The screen had a manual latch, not an automatic one.

"I closed the screen," he said, as if that was some kind of defense, even though he knew it wasn't. "I'm not sure about the door."

Madison let out a frustrated sigh. "He got out. *You* let him out." The hurt and anger in her voice was real.

"The dog will be fine. I'm sure he'll be back before you know it," Collin offered, although his words sounded weak even to his own ears.

"Fine? It's dark! What if he gets hit by a golf cart? Or bitten by a snake?"

"That's unlikely," Collin said, though he started to feel uneasy.

"Or he could get eaten by an alligator. You know they'll be at the bay side of the island. I heard someone lost their cat not too long ago."

Collin's blood ran cold. Now, he wasn't so sure Teddy would be safe on his own.

"I'm going to go look for him," Madison declared.

"No... Maddie... Wait..." But Madison ended the call. Collin was left staring at the home screen of his phone, his imagination now filled with pictures of Teddy and Madison being devoured by a hungry gator in the dark.

Collin turned and glanced backward, only able to see the roof of Madison's house through the clump of trees that shrouded it. He ran toward it. He'd need to catch her.

MADISON COULDN'T BELIEVE how irresponsible Collin had been.

"Who leaves door *wide open*?" she cried to the open night air as she stomped down the steps leading to the front door. The humid evening air hit her, and she wrapped her hair in a hasty ponytail. Then she grabbed Teddy's leash off the porch and grabbed a bag of leftovers from the fridge. If she found him, she'd need the food to lure him in. Not to mention there was a convict on the loose. Madison shivered. Who left the door open when Reese could be out there?

Then again, who went out alone when there was a convict out for revenge?

That thought raised the hair on her arms. Suddenly, the dark shadows on the path and across the nearby shrubs didn't seem so harmless.

He's not going to find you, she thought. *He's probably sleeping in the basement of a relative's house, and might be found at any moment.*

Then Madison remembered how Reese had told her he used to spend a lot of time camping outdoors. What if he'd gone off the grid?

He was one of those people who believed the world was going to come to an end soon. He believed it would, or wished it would—she couldn't quite tell. Madison pushed memories of the cold-eyed killer out of her mind. Right now, she needed to find that puppy. Teddy was her priority.

"Teddy!" she shouted. She slung the small pack over her shoulder, containing the leash as well as the Ziploc bag of leftovers. *So help me, if an alligator eats him, I'll never talk to Collin again.* "And he thinks he can be a decent dad," she told the empty trail as she headed down the path, away from the beach. She had no idea where Teddy had gone; this was just a blind guess.

"Teddy!" she yelled into the darkness, fully aware right at that moment just how dark the island was. The only lights came from the homes nearby, small orange squares of illuminated windows, and the occasional street lamp near the path. No golf carts were out, and the path was lit only by dim moonlight.

"Teddy!" she called again, her voice echoing. The shadows grew longer as the moon rose in the sky; it seemed to get smaller the higher it went. Where had that dog gone? She considered venturing off the path, but then she thought about what she'd do if she found an alligator herself. She'd only heard of one person being bit by one on North Captiva—a teen who was lucky to get away with his arm intact. Normally, most of the gators she'd heard about were on Sanibel. But this was Florida. She had to assume the ancient reptiles could be anywhere. The thought of her adorable puppy running into one made her blood run cold. *How could Collin be so irresponsible!* Ironic, considering he was the one who was supposed to be punishing people for tiny slips, people who made mistakes. Like James Miller.

"Here, boy! Come on, Teddy!" she shouted again into the darkening night, but there was no sign of the dog. Her feet crunched on the sand beneath her feet. She walked by a patio on the second floor of a nearby house and saw a group out for an evening cocktail.

"Excuse me," she said and a woman in a sundress looked up. "Have you seen a dog run by here? Yellow?"

She shook her head. "Sorry, no," she called.

"Thanks," Madison murmured, even as laughter erupted further back on the porch, carried to her on the warm breeze, and she suddenly wished for a worry-free evening. Where she could kick up her heels. Have a glass of wine, even. Not worry about a dog... or Collin...or the baby growing inside her. Everything seemed so impossible right at that moment. She blinked back tears, wishing for a less complicated life. Nothing was working out as she'd planned, and despite the fact that she prided herself on considering all the angles, being prepared for every contingency, life still managed to throw her a few curveballs she didn't expect.

She knew she was just tired…and hungry— her stomach growled—and she was worried about the dog, worried she might never find him. She called out his name into the night and hoped for the best.

She heard rustling in some nearby bushes. "Teddy?" she called, but the rustling got louder. A creature was off the path, one she imagined was big. She pictured an alligator, slinking through the underbrush. Or something even more dangerous. Like Jimmy Reese.

But he probably wouldn't make any noise at all.

I'm being silly, she thought. Now, she felt like a child again, anxious over what went bump in the night.

"Teddy?"

Then, suddenly, Collin came tearing through the brush, nearly scaring her to death. "Nope. Hate to disappoint you. Just me."

Madison felt her heart jump in surprise. It felt like it might hammer right out of her chest.

"God, you scared me." She felt another twitch in her side, was extra-annoyed at him for causing it. "I told you, I didn't need help."

Collin tapped his phone and the flashlight app came on. He shone it brightly on the sandy ground. "Last thing I need is for you to trip and fall and blame that on me, too."

"I'm only going to blame you for what you're responsible for. Like leaving the door wide open."

Collin shook his head. "Fine. I didn't close the door all the way. I didn't think he could get out." Collin fell into step beside her on the narrow path.

"You didn't even *think* about him getting out," Madison corrected.

Reluctantly, Collin nodded, with the phone's light bouncing in his hand as they walked side by side. "No, I didn't really think about it."

"But you *have* to think about it. Teddy is depending on you, and you're just being… irresponsible."

"Me?" Collin blew out a frustrated breath and whipped his hair out of his eyes. "What about *you*? You're the one who fed him table scraps until he threw up." Collin's green eyes looked much darker in the moonlight, the smartphone flashlight casting a severe shadow across his face. Still, even in the near dark, Madison couldn't help feeling a pull toward him. He had *gravitas*, a seriousness, but also a centered confidence. It was what made him such a tough opponent in court.

"He just ate too fast," Madison hedged, although she knew he was right. He'd had too much table food, and that was her fault, not that she wanted to admit it. "Okay. Well. You messed up. I did, too. Don't make *me* out to be the irresponsible one."

For a second, Madison lost all awareness of how handsome he was, how charismatic, because right now, everything she saw was streaked with red. Was he really putting them on the same level as dog caregivers? There wasn't even a contest.

"Don't tell me you think we're equally good at taking care of Teddy," she challenged.

"Oh, I *know* I'm better than you," Collin declared, confident. "I'm the one who got him to come back after he went off-leash."

"That was luck."

"That was skill."

Madison ground her teeth. *Honestly. Was the man this...egotistical?* She couldn't believe she'd spent the last week sleeping with him. Then again, looking at the firm shape of his muscled shoulders, even in the shadowy dark, she knew why. Would she always feel this pull and tug? He was the sexiest and, at the same time, the most annoying man on earth.

"Next, you'll want me to call you the dog whisperer," Madison said with a grimace.

"Maybe." Collin flashed a playful smile. Madison felt the warmth of it spread all the way to her toes. She hated that he had that effect on her. It was hardly fair in negotiating bets. "But the point is you need *help* with this dog. Just like you're going to need help with the baby."

"Not true," Madison said, feeling absolutely confident that wasn't the case. She could do anything she had to do alone. She was self-sufficient and resourceful. She could handle a puppy by herself. And a baby, too.

"Prove it, then. Take my bet. Then we'll find out who's better at watching defenseless animals *and* who needs help."

"You're saying *you* could do it by yourself?"

Collin nodded. "Why couldn't I?"

Madison cackled bitterly. "There's no way you could. You're too…" She was going to say *self-absorbed*, but stopped herself.

"Too what?"

"Never mind." She glanced at him, more sure than ever that she'd win this bet. "Fine.

If we ever find him, and he *hasn't* been eaten by an alligator, then what do you say to a little bet? You watch him half a day, and I watch him the other half. Whoever does a better job wins."

"Wins what?" Collin stepped forward, the phone light facing their feet, casting shadows in the sand. He was so close that she nearly forgot what she'd asked him to do in the first place. Her anger faded, and she was suddenly aware of the broadness of his chest in front of her, blinded by memories of it being bare against hers, the weight of him on top of her.

Focus, Madison, she scolded herself.

"What do you want?"

Collin's lips quirked upward. "I want you to marry me."

Madison laughed defiantly, throwing her head back. "No. Not for a bet."

"Why not? Worried I'll win?" Collin nudged forward a little, kicking sand on Madison's foot. It felt cool on her skin.

"Oh, not at all." She crossed her arms as though to protect herself from his charisma, which seemed to work overtime in the dark. Standing together on this path made her all too aware of the time they'd spent alone in her house this past week. She wondered if arguing with him somehow made him sexier. Did anger fuel their passion?

"So, what have you got to lose? You'll win."

"I know I'll win."

"Then, what would *you* want?"

Madison opened her mouth and nearly said, "For you to love me," but then shut it again. What was she even thinking? *Love.* That was a big word. But it was the truth. He'd asked her to marry him, and yet he'd never once mentioned the *L* word. He hadn't even hinted that was he wanted with her. Sex? Yes. Parenting? Yes. Love? That hadn't even been on the table. She realized it was what she wanted, and yet, she couldn't make herself say it. How silly did that sound? *I want love*—like she was some silly college girl, someone who wasn't in her thirties, a successful lawyer, pregnant. *Single* and pregnant.

Besides, was love something you *asked* for? Wasn't it supposed to be *given*?

"I don't know what I want," she said instead, which seemed pretty darn close to the truth, since the fact that she'd almost asked Collin Baptista to fall in love with her sent her into a tailspin of confusion. Must be pregnancy hormones making her think about love and gooey feelings and valentine cards and happily-ever-afters.

"How about…" But then Madison heard a distant whirring sound. Before she could figure out what it was, Collin had stepped forward, wrapped both hands around her and pulled her to the side of the road. "What…"

A golf cart zoomed around the corner, smack dab in the middle of the road, and tooled straight by them, its small headlight beam shining into the darkness but not very far. He would've run her over if Collin hadn't pulled her out of the way. She saw a man in a baseball cap give a jaunty wave, unaware of how close he'd come to an accident.

Breathing heavily, she leaned against Collin, her heart racing.

"Careful," Collin said. "These drivers at night…sometimes they're not paying attention."

"I can't believe I nearly died by golf cart," Madison said, still feeling shaken. "And he didn't even slow down."

"Probably had one too many," Collin said. "And I agree. Death by golf cart has to be one of the most embarrassing ways to go."

Madison chuckled, the adrenaline of the moment dissipating in a burst of giggles as Collin released her shoulders. He kept a firm grip on her hand. "Why don't we walk on the side of the road?" he suggested.

Madison nodded, not wanting a repeat of the last few minutes.

"Thanks for that," Madison said, and Collin squeezed her hand.

"For what?"

"Saving me?"

"Oh, it was nothing. Really." Collin shrugged. "Happy I was here to help you. Or your grave-stone would've read, *RIP, Golf Cart Road Kill.*"

Madison laughed again. Then, as her chuckle died down, she thought she heard a bark.

"Did you hear that?"

"Hear what? Another speeding golf cart?" Collin asked.

"No. Wait. Listen." They both stood near the side of the road, close together and very still, holding hands. She felt her chest rise and fall, her attention focused on the warmth of Collin's hand. The ocean breeze moved through the trees near them, making a lullaby of rustling leaves. No bark. "I could've sworn I heard..."

Then the bark came again. Tiny, in the distance, but definitely a bark.

"Was that...?" Collin asked, eyes growing wide.

"That's what I heard. It's Teddy!" They both started jogging down the path. Madison let go of Collin's hand to run a little faster.

"Teddy!" she shouted, hoping her voice would reach the dog, wherever he was.

"Teddy!" Collin yelled.

A closer-sounding bark answered them as they ran into a fork in the road. A small white wooden sign indicated that to the left was the landing strip for private planes called The Salty Approach, and to the right stood the fire-house, the only one on the island.

"Teddy!" Collin shouted again, and they listened once more. They heard another telltale bark coming from the left. They both scurried down that path, Collin's phone light bouncing on the sandy road, which was only wide enough for two golf carts passing in opposite directions. Soon, they came to a clearing. The little grass airstrip stretched out before them, paved with red gravel. In the distance, an abandoned lighthouse loomed, a white tower with blackened windows. A couple of small planes were parked near the side of the airstrip, and the grass was lined with houses. *Rustic and quaint*, Madison thought, remembering that it had been years since she'd last been to this part of the island. Then, they saw the puppy, happily trotting across the mowed grass, stopping to sniff at the oversized wheel of a parked plane.

"Here, boy! Come here!" Collin yelled, and Teddy lifted his head. "See? I told you…"

Then, Teddy darted away from them, running in a big circle on the field. "Teddy! Teddy, *come*," Collin cried, but the dog took that as an invitation to play chase and began darting all around the airstrip. Collin lunged forward repeatedly, the dog just out of reach each time. Madison covered her smile with her hand and suppressed a giggle. It was hilarious to see the overconfident prosecutor scurrying around the grass like a maniac, diving after a dog who didn't want to be caught. Teddy's four legs were much faster than Collin's two. Teddy was having a ball, his yellow tail waving in the air, his fur bouncing into his eyes as he ran.

At one point, Collin, out of breath, stopped, bending down to put his hands on his knees. Teddy raced right by him, almost as if to tease, and Collin reached out, just missing the dog's neck and falling face first in the grass. Madison howled with laughter, unable to stop herself as tears spilled out of her eyes. She'd never in her life seen anything as funny as Assistant District Attorney Collin Baptista tumbling on his face while chasing after a fur ball.

"What's so funny?" Collin demanded, his face a storm of embarrassment and annoyance, which only made Madison laugh harder.

"Y-you," she finally managed to get out. "How's that dog-whispering power working now?"

"Very funny," Collin grumbled. "Teddy! Come!" he shouted, but the puppy happily ignored him, flitting away, far out of reach, tail wagging faster than an oscillating fan. Collin looked dejected and sweaty, yet he wasn't giving up as he trotted after the dog. Maybe he was finally learning that he couldn't order every creature around.

Madison's stomach hurt from laughing so hard, but she felt it was her duty to ultimately put him out of his misery. If there was one way to get Teddy to listen, it was with food.

"Teddy! Here, boy. Dinner!" Madison called and held up the plastic bag of leftovers. Teddy froze, mid-trot, his brown eyes focused on her. He paused, and for a split second Madison worried that he might turn and run away from them, darting back into the darkness. But instead, he happily romped toward them. Madison dug out a piece of chicken.

"Sit," she commanded, and after Teddy sat, she handed him the bite of chicken, which he devoured in one eager gulp.

"No fair. You cheated," Collin cried, as he grabbed the dog's collar and Madison attached the leash.

"Nope. Didn't cheat. Just used my brain, that's all. You might try it sometime, counselor."

"Ha. Funny." Collin didn't look as if he found it all that funny. His normally well-coifed hair was a mess, and sweat dripped down his red face.

"What do you think about that bet now?"

Collin shook his head and glanced at Teddy. "I don't know. He's a devil dog, that's all I can tell you. He might be possessed."

"He's not possessed! He's adorable. He's a puppy and puppies misbehave."

"Right. Devil dog," Collin grumbled, still not happy about being played by a puppy.

"Don't listen to him," Madison warned Teddy as she knelt and scratched the eager puppy behind his ears. Then she took the leash and Teddy happily walked by her side, raising his adorable brown eyes up to her. She fell in love with him a little more.

"You get him tonight for the first half of the bet," Collin said. "See how well you do."

Madison's phone rang in her pocket. She answered it.

"Hello?" she said.

"Well, well, well." Jimmy Reese's deep voice growled over the phone. "Look who's still an uppity bitch."

"How did you get this number?" She clutched the phone to her cheek and stopped in her tracks.

"I have my ways," he said. "But what you should be worried about isn't just that I have your phone number. I've got your address, too."

"What is it?" Collin asked, seeing her stricken face. But she was too busy listening to the hateful man, the violent man, the man who didn't care who he killed.

"I'm coming for you and when I find you, I'm going to kill you real slow," he said. She heard a sound in the background, but couldn't quite tell what it was. Static? Wind?

"The police are going to find you," she managed to say, glad that her voice didn't break and she sounded strong. Collin seemed to figure out what was happening. He opened his palm. He wanted the phone.

"Oh, I know," Jimmy said. "But not before I find you first."

CHAPTER FIFTEEN

THE PHONE WENT dead and Madison's knees gave way. Collin caught her, holding her tightly as she dissolved into tears. "J-jimmy Reese," she stuttered, although it was clear that Collin already knew. He stiffened.

"What did he say?"

"He wants me dead." Now that she said the words aloud, they seemed more real somehow, more dangerous.

"What did he say—exactly?" Collin wanted to comb through the details obviously, to see if there were any clues. Like a prosecutor readying himself for the cross-examination.

"H-he said he's coming for me. Gonna kill me…" She left out the *real slow* part. She couldn't bring herself to repeat it.

"Any background sounds? Traffic? Anything?"

Madison hiccupped, trying to calm herself enough to remember. "Maybe he was outside. I heard something. Wind? Trees rustling?"

Just then, she heard that same sound in the

distance. The sound of waves rushing against the beach. Madison stopped cold.

"Water," she said suddenly. "He was near water."

"You sure?" Now Collin looked even more apprehensive, his brow furrowed. "You're positive?"

"Why was he near water? My apartment is in Fort Myers, nowhere near any water. Collin... What if he found out about my uncle's house somehow?"

"He doesn't know," Collin said. "He can't." But he sounded doubtful. "Let me call Jenny," he said. "Don't worry. We're going to get this son of a bitch. I'll make sure of that."

Madison hugged Collin tighter, for once so very glad the hard-as-nails prosecutor was in her corner; she felt safer just being in his arms. If there was one thing Madison knew, it was that Collin didn't let bad guys go. She was grateful for his tough attitude just then.

Teddy looked up and whined; he came over and pressed his cold little nose against her shins, as if sensing something was wrong. She reached down and patted his head, wiping away her tears.

"Jenny? It's Collin. Jimmy Reese called Madison," he said and filled her in on the details. "We think he might've been near a shoreline. Madison thought she heard the ocean in the distance."

Collin listened and then nodded. "Got it. Yes, I think that's a good idea, too." He ended the call.

"Jenny is going to send us a couple of plain-clothes detectives, just to be safe."

"Is that really necessary?" Madison asked, but in her gut, she knew it was. Reese wasn't only violent but smart. She'd feel better with more protection. She inwardly winced when she realized she'd have to tell her uncle as well. After he found out, he'd probably insist on sending his own bodyguards if the state didn't provide them. Might even insist on them.

"They'll come tomorrow." Collin frowned as he put his arm around Madison and pulled her close. "In the meantime, you're sleeping in my house tonight."

"What?" Madison began to protest. "But I don't—"

"No buts," he broke in. "If he did somehow link your uncle's house with you, then we need to be on the safe side. Mine's a rental."

Madison saw the logic. Still, she didn't like the fact that Jimmy was already, on some level, winning by scaring them, upending their plans, making them hide.

"Just until he's caught," Collin said. "Which will be soon."

Madison hoped so.

O<small>NCE</small> M<small>ADISON</small> <small>PACKED</small> a bag, she and Collin headed over to his rental. It was smaller than her uncle's, but it did have three bedrooms, two bathrooms and a rope hammock on the extended deck, which sat, like hers, one story up. Teddy came as well, but instead of a utility room, he'd have to sleep in the bathroom on the second floor, since the utility room here didn't have a door. Despite being safely ensconced in the neighbor's house, Madison felt glum. She couldn't shake the anxious feeling in her belly, and she kept hearing the sound of Jimmy's gravelly voice.

When she and Collin arrived, they entered his bedroom, and she saw that there was a handgun on the bed.

"I'm licensed," he said. "Ever shoot one?"

She slowly shook her head.

"We'll have to change that," he said. He checked the chamber of the pistol and then double-checked the safety.

"Come here." He motioned her forward with his free hand. She didn't care for guns. They were dangerous, and given the number of clients she'd represented, typically caused more problems than they solved. Collin discharged the clip, showing her the empty chamber inside.

"Just in case you need to know," he said, and he showed her how to load the pistol, how to cock it, how to flick the safety latch. Then he gave it to her and she held it in her hands. Cold heavy steel. She mimicked his motions, pulling the side back and cocking the gun. It was harder to do than she'd thought. Would she be able to do this in a panic? With Jimmy rushing toward her? Her stomach lurched. She never wanted to have to use this on anyone. Suddenly, Jimmy Reese and his threat seemed all too real. Her bottom lip began to quiver. She was used to taking care of herself, being independent, but now the task of protecting herself seemed almost impossible.

Collin gently took the safety-locked pistol from her hands. "It's okay. I'm here." The simple words comforted her. She wasn't alone.

"Thank you," she said, expressing the gratitude she'd failed to show him. "Thank you for being here. For…looking after me."

"No need to thank me," Collin said, and pulled her into his strong arms. She felt safe there, protected. "I know what'll cheer you up." Collin threw an arm over her shoulders and pulled her close. "Let's go into the kitchen and see what we can find."

"Do you think I can eat at a time like this?" Madison asked, but then her stomach growled.

"Oh, I know you can eat at a time like this." He rooted around in the pantry. A moment later, he held up a jar of tomato sauce and a box of spaghetti.

"Yum," she said. "Spaghetti sounds delicious."

Collin grinned as he set about boiling water and warming up the sauce. He'd also gotten ground beef at the club's little grocery store, and he browned that and added it to the sauce. He used the mismatched pans left by the owners, and got to work chopping vegetables for a salad.

A little while later, they had a delicious meal—Madison digging in, not realizing how hungry she was until she put the rich pasta in her mouth. "Mmm," she murmured. "Good." She shoveled another bite in. With the baby, it was feast or famine—either she couldn't keep anything down or she felt like eating everything in sight.

"Might want to chew that first," Collin teased, but Madison didn't care. She couldn't help it. Her appetite had returned with a vengeance. And she had to admit that stuffing her face felt like a better alternative than worrying about Jimmy Reese.

"When did you want to start our bet?" he asked, eyes gleaming.

"What bet?" Madison mumbled, her mouth full.

"Teddy. Who can take better care of him?" Collin raised his fork and pointed it at the puppy, who now sat, ears at attention, as he watched the two of them eat, no doubt hoping for scraps to fall on the floor.

"Should we even do that? I mean..." With the more serious Jimmy threat, did they have time to play games?

"We absolutely should," Collin said. "You need to take your mind off Jimmy Reese. Stress isn't good for you or the baby." Collin laid his hand on her knee. "And you know Reese as well as I do. Part of what gets him off is freaking you out. He likes to get into people's heads."

That was true. Jimmy Reese wanted nothing more than to play puppet master.

"He's not in my head." *Just a little bit, maybe. Or a lot.* "And I can take care of myself."

"I know you can. But it'll be easier if you let me help." Collin squeezed her knee. She glanced at his eyes, sparkling in the low lamplight of the eat-in kitchen. "But the bet isn't that you can't take care of yourself. It's that you can't take care of Teddy."

Madison laughed. "Taking care of me is a cakewalk compared to taking care of the dog. But I can do it."

"Prove it," Collin challenged her. He withdrew his hand and she felt the coolness of air against her skin once more, missing his touch.

"I will."

"Good." Collin grinned, and somehow Madison couldn't help feeling that he'd won the first round.

THEY DECIDED TO begin the bet immediately, with Madison taking the first shift. She began the evening in full confidence, with the puppy falling asleep on her lap on the sofa, but soon found out that the tide could turn at a moment's notice. Just as Madison lifted him up and prepared to carry him upstairs to his towel bed in the bathroom, he leaped out of her arms and knocked over a vase, shattering it into a dozen pieces on the tiled floor. The dog, eager to investigate, seemed hell-bent on eating a glass shard, which made it nearly impossible to clean up the mess *and* keep him out of it.

"Are you going to help?" Madison asked Collin as she scooped Teddy into her arms.

The puppy wriggled and tried to get free, apparently on some kind of suicide mission to romp through the broken glass.

Collin sat, legs up on the coffee table, reading his phone intently, not bothering to look up from the screen. "*You're* in charge. That means no help from me."

"Since when?"

"Since I made up the rule just now." He flashed her a teasing grin. "Besides, I thought we had a bet about which one of us could take better care of him—alone. Looks like I'm winning by default."

Madison made a growling sound and carried Teddy over to the laundry room, where she popped him behind the slatted white doors. He pawed at them and whined loudly.

"Stay," she ordered him, even though the door was latched shut. He wasn't tall enough to reach doorknobs—yet. Thank goodness.

Madison got to work sweeping up the shards of glass with a broom and a dustpan, all the while watching Collin relax, feet up, nose buried in his phone. His ignoring her and the problem at hand annoyed her. Even the sight of his long tanned, muscular legs stretched, feet resting on the coffee table didn't do anything to make her feel less frustrated.

"You're really just going to sit there."

"Yep," he said, his finger scrolling across the screen, his eyes focused on the information there. "You said you were better at taking care of the dog, so here we are."

"What's so interesting on your phone that you can't help?" she asked, wondering for a split second if it was another woman. He said it had been a year since he'd had sex, but what if there were other women he'd been flirting with? Maybe another defense attorney he'd left back in Fort Myers. Rumors about the prosecutor's exploits spread like wildfire through the court. He'd even once been linked to a married judge, though no one had proof of that. Madison never understood why the rumors didn't affect his reputation. He was still respected and feared as a prosecutor, although he took loving and leaving women to a new level.

Still, he wouldn't be talking to another woman *now*, would he?

He wouldn't really be out here, on this island, proposing to her and texting other women? And he'd told her he hadn't been with anyone since her—or before her—for a long while. Maybe all those rumors were just that? Rumors.

"I'm reading a book on *babies*," he said, holding up his phone to show the e-book on his screen. "And it looks like they have quite a lot in common with puppies. For instance, the advice that you should *move all breakables high above the baby's reach*. The vase was your fault. So, that means a point for me."

"You have to be kidding me." Madison dropped the dustpan's contents into the open bin of the trashcan, and they hit the bottom of the bag with an orchestra of clinks.

"It says right here in this book that once babies are mobile and crawling, everything needs to be baby-proofed. Or in this case, puppy-proofed." He motioned around the small condo. "There's the electrical outlets…and all the breakables."

"I don't think a puppy will stick a knife in a socket," Madison muttered, although she had to admit Collin did have a point about the breakables. There were low shelves behind the couch, littered with glass figures and shells, as well as a big ceramic bowl in the center of the coffee table. There was another end table holding a blue crystal vase that once matched the one now in pieces in the garbage.

Madison finished sweeping up the finer bits of glass, then went to work removing all the breakables from Teddy-level. After that, she secured the lower cabinet doors by slipping an oversized wooden spoon through both handles—just in case the dog got smart enough to figure out how to open them. Madison put one hand on her hip and surveyed the now mostly bare living room and then went to the other rooms and did a breakables sweep there as well. She managed to collect a big armful of stuff that she locked inside a hall closet. There. Danger averted.

Suddenly, she heard the sound of Teddy jumping up and a big thumping boom.

Collin looked up from his phone this time, long enough to make a disapproving sound and shake his head. Madison felt like punching the smug prosecutor in the face.

She hurried over to the laundry and found Teddy sitting in a pile of dryer sheets, busy ripping one to shreds.

"Teddy! Bad boy! Bad, bad boy!" Madison scooped him up and pulled the sheet out of his mouth. "Would you hold him so I can clean this up?" Collin glanced up from his phone.

"Oh? Are you asking for help? Does this mean you forfeit the challenge?" He raised his eyebrows, eyes gleaming with confidence.

"No, absolutely not." She wasn't about to lose this bet. She looked around the living room and saw Teddy's leash on the kitchen table. She grabbed it, attached it to the dog, then tied it to a kitchen cabinet.

"Stay," she said, even though he didn't have

a choice in the matter. Teddy whined again and put up one begging paw. "Just stay. I'll be back."

She returned to the utility room and picked up all the dryer sheets. She managed to get some of them back in the box, and then tucked the box higher up in a closed cabinet. She was puzzled about how the little dog had reached the top of the dryer where the box had been sitting, until she realized he'd stood on top of a full basket of folded towels to manage it. Little sneak.

"Uh-oh, uh… Madison?" Collin said from the living room. "You *might* want to come see this."

Madison rounded the corner in time to witness Teddy, still tied to the cabinet, sniffing the floor. He hunched his back and pooped, right there on the kitchen floor.

"Teddy! No! Bad boy!" she scolded, rushing over, but it was too late; the damage was already done. She got a whiff of the earthy pile, which almost made her retch. Guess the pregnancy made her sensitive to smells, too. Either that or Teddy's accident smelled worse than should be possible. What had the dog eaten? And then she remembered—all her table scraps. Oh, sweet irony.

"You *sure* you don't want help cleaning that up?" Collin asked.

"No," Madison muttered through clenched teeth. "I don't need *your* help." Whatever happened next, she wasn't about to lose this bet. No matter how disgusting Teddy's mess was. She reached for the paper towel roll on the kitchen counter, held her breath and knelt down.

"Oh, Teddy," she groaned. "Outside. We go *outside*." After dumping the mess into the kitchen trash, she took Teddy by the leash and led him down the steps and to the grassy patch of yard. She stood beneath the stars and glared at the dog, who sat in the evening air, wagging his tail, looking completely oblivious to the fact that he'd caused any trouble.

"I guess it's not like you really need to go or anything," she told the puppy. "Not anymore." She couldn't wait until Collin had *his* turn managing the dog.

THE NEXT MORNING, as Collin lay sleeping, Madison stood by the bedside with Teddy in her arms. Collin hadn't heard the dog whine, but Madison had awakened immediately, having always been a light sleeper. She'd taken him outside, but rain from the night before had left a layer of mud across the yard. She'd picked him up on his way in and was heading to the master bathroom to clean his paws.

Collin peacefully slept, and lay sprawled, shirtless in bed, one bare leg outside the covers. She admired his impressive chest, the well-defined pecs, the tanned skin she'd explored just two days ago. But the night before, Madison had slept on the couch, determined not to be near Collin and his expert hands. She'd gone to sleep furious at him for leaving her to her own devices with Teddy, angry that he hadn't even helped her take out the stinky garbage bag full of his accident and the shards of glass.

Collin, for his part, had just chuckled to himself and happily taken the bed. He hadn't even slept on the couch like a true gentleman would have! No. He'd shrugged and said, "Suit yourself," when she'd declared her intent to sleep in the living room. Teddy had curled up at her feet and they'd both gone to sleep.

The fact that Collin looked so very comfortable, and so *very* sexy in the bed, made her all the angrier. She glanced at Teddy, who looked up at her with his big puppy-dog eyes. His paws, sandy and a bit muddy, had already left smudges on Madison's pink tank top. She scowled at her shirt and at the sleeping Collin. Why shouldn't *he* share in this fun? And then it occurred to her that it was technically *his* day now, his turn to look after the dog and prove he could do it—alone.

She dropped Teddy on the covers, muddy paws and all, and let him jump right on Collin. The dog began licking Collin's face, and rubbing mud all over his chest. Madison felt a little bad about it, but then she remembered how he'd refused to help her the night before and all guilt vanished.

"Hey… What the…?" Collin cried, waking up to find himself being attacked by a dirty dog.

Madison snickered. "Your turn to take care of him," she sang, then whirled around and left. Now it was *her* day to sit in a chair, put her feet up and read a book.

She waited in the hallway for a second, almost expecting to hear a string of curses from Collin, but instead, a calm quiet descended. Hesitantly, she opened the door and saw him calmly stripping the sheets. Bath water ran in the adjoining bathroom and she heard a happy bark and splash from behind the closed door.

"Don't worry," Collin said with an annoying grin on his face. "I've got this."

He shut the door, leaving Madison staring at it. *Well*, she thought, *the day was long*. Give him three more hours with that dog and *then* see how he felt about it.

COLLIN BADLY WANTED a nap. He'd taken Teddy out every hour on the hour to make sure the dog didn't have any accidents inside the house, *and* he'd played with him long enough to tire him out. So, the dog, at least, had a little siesta. Honestly, Collin was close to losing it, but pretended that caring for the puppy was the simplest thing in the world, in part because it drove Madison mad. Also, he wanted to keep her mind off Jimmy Reese and the plainclothes cops who'd be arriving today to act as babysitters.

Nothing about taking care of the dog was easy. Teddy tried to eat a pencil, nearly swallowed a bottle cap he'd found in the garbage and managed to completely destroy a fishing fly lure and a kitchen tea towel. He barely had any interest in the dog food they set out for him, but dug happily in the garbage for scraps that he dragged all over the kitchen floor.

And that was just the first hour.

Collin needed a break already, but he couldn't show it. Not with Madison watching his every move, waiting for him to mess up so she could claim victory. Collin didn't think he'd ever done anything as hard as taking care of this puppy—and he'd stayed up two nights straight studying for the bar exam. He'd put murderers behind bars. But this... Well, this was a whole new problem. None of his life's three rules applied here: 1) Never lose (except that a puppy didn't seem to know how to keep score); 2) Bad guys deserve the book thrown at them (except the puppy wasn't a bad guy, just an animal who hadn't been trained); and 3) Never sleep with the enemy (except that right now, all he wanted to do was get Madison naked and in his bed).

He sighed. Life was so much simpler when the three rules worked. Here, with this puppy, he was adrift, not quite sure what he was supposed to do, and his three rules were no help whatsoever.

Teddy ran over and tripped on his big puppy paws, skidding into the middle of the living room floor. He looked goofy and adorable.

"He's so cute," called Madison, watching him from her perch on the couch and laughing. She had a bowl of vanilla ice cream in her lap and an open magazine on her knees. "See? All paws!"

"He's just getting by on his looks," Collin grumbled. "He wouldn't survive on his charm."

"Oh, Teddy's charming. Aren't you, boy?"

Teddy galloped over and gave Madison's waiting hand a lick. She dissolved into giggles.

Collin imagined her delight with a baby. She had such a big heart, and she'd give any child a loving home. He already knew that all the discipline would fall to him. If Madison had her way, the kid would be hopelessly spoiled, like this puppy. Teddy sniffed at her bowl of ice cream, but she lifted it up and out of his reach.

"Mama's not done yet," she cooed at him. The dog sat near the couch, his tail thumping against the floor.

"Don't feed him sweets," Collin said. The last thing he needed was the dog having a runny accident in the house.

"I won't." Madison sounded defensive as she took a spoonful of ice cream. God, the woman was sexy, just sitting in cutoffs and eating ice cream. He felt his groin tighten. How did she have that effect on him?

While he was distracted by her absently eating ice cream and thumbing through her magazine, Teddy got up and wandered into the dining room. Collin, transfixed by Madison, hardly noticed. Then he glanced up and saw Teddy pee on a chair leg.

"No!" he cried, jumping up. "Outside! Outside!" Yet, he knew it was partially his fault. He'd waited past the recommended hour to take him out, and this was what happened. He'd done online research. He was supposed to take the damn puppy out every hour, just in case, and when he did pee, he was supposed to receive lavish praise (or treats). Or both.

Collin was almost beginning to wish he was back in court facing evildoers like Jimmy Reese. They, at least, presented a comparatively straightforward problem.

"You might want to clean that up," Madison called from the couch, her feet elevated, still eating her ice cream. All she had to do was put a pickle in it and she'd be a living stereotype. She'd eaten nearly everything in the fridge, including a jar of olives. Now, she was taking a page out of his mockery book, and he didn't like it.

"No worries. I've got it," he said, trying to keep his voice light and unstressed as he grabbed cleaning spray and a roll of paper towels, which were all but gone. Inwardly, he cursed the dog, who seemed to have a bladder smaller than a lima bean. Mentally, he ran through every swearword he knew as he lifted up the little dog and opened the screened patio door, dumping him unceremoniously onto the mat.

"Careful!" Madison called after him. "Be gentle!"

"I am being gentle!" he called back over

his shoulder, thinking that *not gentle* would look like opening the back door and letting him run away—again, only this time not bothering to look for him. The puppy cocked his head, floppy ears looking adorable. He might be cute, but he was a menace.

Furiously, Collin cleaned up the pee puddle using the last of the paper towels and inwardly cursed again when he realized they didn't have any upholstery cleaner, which meant that the white and ivory swirling pattern on the leg of the chair would most likely be forever stained puppy-pee yellow.

"Now, are you willing to admit that being a parent is hard?" Madison asked Collin, standing over him as he uselessly wiped the chair with paper towels.

"I never said it was easy," he grumbled. Angrily, he picked up the spray cleaner and doused the chair leg with it. *Better than nothing*, he thought.

"You acted like it would be a breeze."

Collin sat back on his haunches. "*You're* the one who thought it would be so easy you'd just go it alone! Are *you* ready to admit that you need help?"

"I'm not the one who just sprayed Clorox on the chair leg."

Collin glanced down and realized he'd sprayed bleach on the upholstery. "Is that bad?"

"Terrible," she said, unable to hide a smile.

"Seriously?" He stood and backed away, studying the upholstered chair leg for damage. He read the back of the bottle; it didn't say anything about not spraying on furniture.

"Don't worry about it. It'll probably be fine. Just wet a…"

Before she could finish, Collin got a handful of tissues and wet them under the tap, then scrubbed the chair leg—only to have the whole wad disintegrate in his hands. Madison giggled again.

"I meant a *towel*. Let me help you."

"I don't need help." Collin stood and tossed the wet tissues. He went back to the kitchen sink, but Madison was already there with a damp sponge. Before he could do anything else, she knelt down by the chair and began mopping off the pieces of tissue.

"See? Not so bad."

"You don't need to help. I already told you that."

He gazed down at her, at her beautiful dark eyes and the cleavage he could see down the V-neck of her cotton top. Despite his annoyance with Teddy, he felt a surge of attraction. Why did she look so damn ravishing all the time? With her on her knees and him standing... All kinds of dirty thoughts raced through his mind. Oh, what he wanted to do to her. *With her.* For her. All he wanted to do was lie down with her, cuddle her in his arms, and...not think about the puppy anymore.

"What's wrong?" she asked, pausing mid-wipe.

"You're just so...damn beautiful." The truth felt good. She seemed surprised, as if no one had ever told her things like that before. But he couldn't believe that. He saw the way other men looked at her, the way their eyes followed her around the courtroom.

"I don't have any makeup on."

"You don't need any." Her cheeks looked rosy, her lips eminently kissable.

Madison self-consciously tucked a stray piece of hair behind one ear. "You're just saying that." She stood, swaying awkwardly on her feet. She might be brilliant in the courtroom, but she couldn't take a compliment to save her life—at least when it came to her appearance. "Besides, I thought that seeing me...that morning...with no makeup was one of the reasons you... Well, you didn't call." She squeezed the sponge in her hand and didn't meet his eyes.

He felt his gut twist a little. How could

she not know the effect she had on him? He guessed he'd bluffed too successfully when he'd acted uninterested before. That was his fault. He'd definitely been interested. She had no idea how hard he'd had to fight not to call her, to ignore her texts. He'd done it through sheer force of will.

"No. You are gorgeous. With makeup or without." Collin crossed the kitchen to stand in front of her. "Do you remember the first time we met?"

"The Addison case," she said, still not quite meeting his eyes. Did she remember it, too?

He nodded. "That's right. It was a case of identity theft. You walked in wearing those sexy heels—the black ones with the strap across the foot? And that burgundy suit. It fit you like a second skin. You looked completely businesslike, but you were…breathtaking. Honestly, you walked into that courtroom and time just stopped for me."

Madison laughed a little. "You can't be serious."

"I can. And I am. It's no joke."

Madison studied him warily, as if waiting for him to admit he was kidding. But nothing about this admission was fake.

"You remember what I wore that day?" she asked him, sounding incredulous.

"Of course. I remember everything you did and said, every time we were ever in court together." That was just fact. Madison was not only gorgeous she was whip-smart. Any man who ever met her would know she was the marrying kind. The kind to make a life with. And now, he could, free and clear, and she needed to see that he was sincere about his offer.

"No, you don't." Madison jabbed her hip with one fist.

"Quiz me."

Madison raised an eyebrow in challenge as she flung the sponge in the sink. "The Johnson case."

"Gray suit. White shirt. Might have switched to just skirt and shirt by day three."

Madison studied him, as if unsure herself about what she'd worn. "How about Abbott?"

"Black pencil skirt. Pink blouse."

Collin moved closer to Madison. She didn't flee.

"Chambers?" she asked him.

"Was that the money launderer?"

She nodded.

"Red blouse. Black pants. Black boots."

Madison's mouth dropped. "You *do* remember almost every outfit. How is that…"

"Because I liked looking at you." Collin grinned as he moved closer to Madison, so now they were both leaning against the kitchen sink.

"So you mentally cataloged my wardrobe?" Madison seemed genuinely shocked.

"I appreciate beauty in my environment."

"What did I wear yesterday, then?"

Collin squinted. "Cutoff jean shorts. White tank."

"Day before that?"

He could feel the electricity zipping between them. They had *chemistry.* He knew it existed, but he'd never experienced it on this level. Being near Madison felt like taking a drug he couldn't get enough of; somehow his senses were always overloaded by her scent, her touch, the way she flipped her dark hair off her shoulder.

"Pink flowered sundress." He moved a little closer. Now he could smell the scent of her shampoo, the hint of jasmine.

"And the day before that?"

Collin stood so close she had to crane her neck to meet his gaze. "The day before that," he said, "you were naked in my bed."

She didn't move. He wanted her naked in his bed again. He reached out and put his hand on the small of her back, and then he lowered his head and kissed her, his tongue searching for hers as she melted into him. He felt every curve of her body, his own body coming alive as she wrapped her fingers around the back of his neck. He lifted her up onto the counter, and she devoured his mouth.

Distantly, he heard a scratching on the patio door.

Madison broke free of their kiss.

"It's Teddy," she breathed. "Should we…"

"He's fine where he is," Collin growled, picking Madison up and carrying her to the couch. He couldn't wait any longer. Two days without this was already far too long. The dog could stay on the porch forever if he could keep tasting Madison. He just couldn't get enough of her.

He pushed up the hem of her dress, feeling the soft skin of her upper thighs. He tugged off her thin cotton panties and then stepped out of his shorts. He dove inside her, hungry, greedy, eager to be where he knew he belonged. She arched her back as he took her on the couch, pushing against him in a way that nearly made him lose his resolve. He'd make her come first, and then he'd finish. He wanted to see the joy on her face.

He started placing kisses down the side of her neck and she moaned in pleasure. Oh, but he loved this woman. He wanted her to be his—now and always. She breathed heavily beneath him, moaning again, and he could feel her need growing, her want, as he moved faster.

"Collin," she murmured, his name like an aphrodisiac on her tongue.

Oh, how he wanted to hear that again and again. She clutched at his back, fingernails digging into his shoulders as if she feared she'd fly away from him in that moment. He went deeper, harder.

"Yes, that's it. Come for me," he murmured in her ear. She cried out in pleasure, tightening against him, riding wave after wave of ecstasy. He felt alive, every nerve ending in his body satisfied as she tumbled into oblivion, her face reflecting pure wonder.

"Oh," she cried. "Oh, Collin. I… I love you."

The word hit him like a ton of bricks.

Did she say she *loved* him?

"What did you…" But she grabbed his neck and pulled him down, kissing him so hard he nearly lost his breath. Then she wrapped his legs around him and her motion became too much to resist. He came with a shout, unable to contain himself any longer.

"Maddie, I love you, too," he said in her hair.

"I didn't mean to say that," she murmured, still breathing heavily.

"But you did, so now I've said it, too."

He lay unmoving on top of her, their breathing and their heartbeats the only sounds until Teddy scraped one paw against the screen door.

"That dog," grumbled Collin, pushing himself up on his elbows. He glared at the puppy barking in front of the screen, pressing his snout against it.

"He wants to come in."

"I don't want to get up."

"Well, *I'll* let him in, then." Madison pushed at him but he wasn't about to budge.

"Who says I'm done with you?" Collin pulled her closer to him. Madison giggled and then tickled him between the ribs. He shouted and rolled off her. She walked to the patio door and let in the little mood-wrecker. Teddy skipped in, happy to be inside. He trotted over to the coffee table and sniffed a leg.

"I hope you're worth it," Collin told the dog.

"Lucky for you, I'm in a pretty good mood right now, thanks to your mama."

"Well, considering *you* just lost our bet, you might have to rethink that," Madison said.

"What do you mean?" Collin stood and yanked on his shorts.

"*I* helped you. *You* accepted my help. *I* win."

Collin realized she was right, but he didn't like it. "Oh, come here, you," he said as he chased her around the living room. She squealed and took off running, and Teddy thought it was the best game of his life. He joined in, happily romping after both of them.

The doorbell rang.

Collin stopped, feeling suddenly tense. But then he figured, Jimmy Reese wouldn't ring the doorbell. Madison stopped, too, and bent down to pick up Teddy.

Collin was careful to look through the side window before opening the front door. He saw Yvana there on the stoop, as well as two burly guys in polo shirts. The plainclothes cops. *That was some timing*, he thought. Five minutes earlier and it might've been awkward.

He swung the door open.

"Hey, Collin," Yvana said. "These lovely gentlemen are here to see you." She glanced back and forth between them, clearly not sure she approved.

"Thanks, Yvana," Collin said, as Yvana nodded and headed back to her golf cart. "Come on in, guys."

CHAPTER SIXTEEN

MADISON WATCHED THE plainclothes cops set their suitcases inside the foyer.

"I'm Mark Hernandez," said the bald, heavy-set one in his mid-forties. He was tall, a little soft in the middle, with a receding hairline, but his handshake had a vice-like grip.

"Hi, Mark," Madison said. She remembered him from when he'd given testimony in court. During the Jimmy Reese case, actually. He'd been the investigating detective, the one who'd interviewed the ex-girlfriend Reese had abused, the woman who'd testified about his many connections to white hate groups.

"This is my partner, Steve Hillard." Mark nodded to the taller, broader and blonder Steve, who seemed to be a man of few words; he just gave her a quick nod as he set the suitcase down in the foyer.

Madison bit her lower lip, the Jimmy-threat was suddenly far too real now that she had two off-duty police officers as bodyguards. She was happy to have them there, but wished they didn't need to be.

"We're just here as a precaution," Mark said, as if reading her mind. "Don't you worry, because he probably won't even make it this far. Cons like him, they let hate blind them. They make mistakes."

Madison hugged Teddy closer to her chest, and Collin stepped over and put a protective arm around her shoulders. She leaned into him. Teddy whined softly and then nestled his head into the crook of Madison's elbow. The dog seemed to automatically sense her moods; he was trying to comfort her by pressing his wet nose into her arm.

"I hope so," Madison said.

"I've been on the force for fifteen years, so I know what I'm talking about." Mark had warm brown eyes and a fatherly disposition that made Madison feel reassured. He looked like a man who could get things done. "So, this is your house or your uncle's?"

Collin explained the current living situation, and Mark and Steve then went about canvassing the perimeters of both Collin's rental and Uncle Rashad's house. Madison continued to hug Teddy to her chest, even as the little dog whined and kicked his legs, eager to get down and trot after the new bodyguards.

"Teddy, they've got a job to do, so you let them be," Madison whispered. "They're here to work." The puppy snuggled against her.

"Have you notified any officials on the island?" Mark asked them, while his partner checked all the doors and windows, looking for weak spots. "About Reese?"

"The club manager, Yvana, has his picture, and so do the ferry captains," Madison said. "We've also sent out notices to the full-time residents to be on the lookout."

"Yeah, a scumbag like Jimmy with a big Nazi neck tattoo would stick out around here," Collin added.

Mark nodded. "We heard he called you." He studied Madison.

"Yes. I don't know where he got my personal cell number, but he did."

Even though Mark kept a solid poker face, Madison was sure he didn't like that bit of information. Madison didn't, either. If he had her phone number, he might have other information.

"And…" Mark cleared his throat. "It's none of my business, but…" He looked uncomfortable as he glanced from Madison to Collin. "But you want to tell me why the prosecutor and the defense attorney on this case happen to be vacationing together?"

Madison felt her face go beet red.

"She's my fiancée," Collin announced, putting his arm around her again.

Madison didn't protest the word. Fiancée sure sounded better than "We had a drunken one-night stand and I knocked her up! Congratulate us. We're going to be parents!"

Mark eyed them both, clearly understanding that there was more to this story than either was telling, but decided to let it go. Madison hugged Teddy to her chest, almost like a shield.

"How long have you…"

"Since the Jimmy Reese case, actually," Collin said easily. They both realized how short a time that was. Once again, Madison felt her face flame. Two months, and they were already engaged? What else could that be but a pregnancy? Yet, Mark didn't let on that he'd put the pieces together.

He nodded slowly. "Does Jimmy know?"

Collin and Madison looked at each other. "No," she said. "I mean, I don't think so."

"I'm just saying, if that crazy man thought you two had a thing going, it would fuel his conspiracy theories." Mark folded his bulky arms across his chest. "He'd figure you two worked together to set him up. Not that he needed anybody's help. That maniac did enough damage all on his own."

Madison felt a shiver run down her spine. She hadn't thought of it that way before, but if he *did* know…he'd be even angrier with her than he already was. He'd hate her more, if that was possible. She remembered his dead-eyed stare. Collin put his arm protectively around her, giving her shoulders a squeeze.

"He can think what he wants," Collin said, "but he's got twenty years to serve, and I intend to see that he serves his sentence in full." Madison loved the look in his eyes, determined and stoic. A man not to be messed with.

"Me, too." Mark nodded at Collin, and a promise seemed to pass silently between the two men. They were equally committed to seeing Jimmy back behind bars. He glanced up at the staircase. "I think it's best if you stay in the rental for now, and Steve and I will take Mr. Reddy's house."

"Keep us informed when you come and go. Here are both our numbers," Mark said, giving Collin a business card. "We have your numbers from the prosecutor's office, so we think we're good. Do these look right?"

He showed Collin his phone with numbers programmed in. Madison recognized hers right away and nodded. "Yvana gave us keys to your place as well as ours. Otherwise, we'll try not to infringe on your vacation too much."

"Thanks," Collin said. The officer retreated with his silent partner, Steve, to the porch. Madison watched out the window as they descended the stairs and then went to her uncle's house. The lights came on inside and she sighed.

"You'll be safer with them staying next door," Collin said, as if sensing her hesitation.

"I know, but…" Madison put Teddy down and he sniffed the floor where the officers had been standing. "But I guess having them here makes it harder to forget that Jimmy's coming."

"He probably won't even make it this far," Collin said. "Remember what Mark said? They're just here as a precaution. That's all. He could've been at the beach, whatever beach, for any number of reasons. We can't assume he knows your uncle has a house here or that you'd be in it."

"True," Madison agreed, although she still felt the knot of fear tightening in her stomach. Teddy licked her hand. She reached down and patted his head with her free hand. "I just want this over. I want him to be caught."

Collin pulled her and Teddy into his arms. "I know. Me, too," he whispered in her ear, and then hugged her tightly to him, a gesture that felt warm and protective all at once. Madison leaned into him, grateful for the contact, even as Teddy whined between them, stuck in the middle of a group hug. Suddenly, she felt tears spring to her eyes. *Crying? Again?* God, she hated these pregnancy hormones.

She sniffed and pulled away from him, wiping at her eyes.

"Are you crying?" he asked.

"No," she lied.

"Are you okay?"

"Yes. It's just…the pregnancy," she said with a sigh.

Collin shook his head and laughed. "You're allowed to feel things, you know."

"Am I?"

"You keep everything so tightly wrapped up. So contained. It's okay to let loose once in a while." Collin caressed her chin with one finger.

"Says Mr. Control-Freak-Prosecutor."

"I'm not a control freak," Collin exclaimed. And Madison just threw her head back and laughed as she gave his arm a playful shove.

"You are *the most* control freaky of control freaks." Teddy wriggled, trying to get loose, so she set him down. He immediately trotted off, sniffing under the dining room table for crumbs.

"I am not."

"You are. Who proposes to a woman and *doesn't tell her* he plans to move to Miami? Except one who just *assumes* when he says 'jump' everyone else says, 'how high'?" Madison crossed the room and headed to the kitchen, where she poured herself a glass of water.

"One who knows that the common sense move is for you to come to Miami with me." Collin followed on her heels.

"Why? Because your career is more important than mine?" She whirled at him from the sink, still clutching her glass of water.

"No, because—" But Collin didn't get to finish.

Just then, Teddy jumped on the couch in the living room, surprising them both. "Off the furniture!" he shouted and the dog jumped down in fright.

"See? Control freak."

"I just don't want dog hair on the couch. And at least this time he listened to me."

"Only because you bellowed at him. He has no idea what you're saying."

"No, but he knows I'm mad."

"Anyway," Madison said, setting her empty water glass on the counter, "he's a golden doodle. Part poodle. They don't shed." She knelt by the puppy and scratched him behind the ears.

"Technicalities," Collin joked. He eyed the puppy, who was still hiding beneath a dining room chair.

Madison laughed. "How about this… *I'll* feel more if you let loose a bit."

"Like how?"

"Like allowing Teddy to sit on that couch. It's not even *your* couch."

"But that's even more reason why he shouldn't sit on it."

"He won't hurt it," Madison argued.

Collin's face looked pinched and uncomfortable. "I don't know…" Madison stared at him expectantly. "Fine, but just five minutes."

She put Teddy on the couch and watched as Collin squirmed. Having the dog on the furniture did push all his buttons…

"How long has it been?"

Madison glanced at the stopwatch on her phone. "Twenty seconds."

"Argh," Collin said, grinding his teeth.

"Thirty," Madison called out. Teddy walked in a little circle on the couch and then sat down, making Collin flinch. "Forty," Madison said, eye still on the phone.

Then, Teddy raised one paw and began cleaning himself with his tongue.

"Nope, no way, that's it." Collin, unable to make the full five minutes, stomped over to the couch and shooed the dog off. Teddy jumped down and scurried over to the corner. Still, presumably feeling bad, Collin bent down to scratch the pup behind his ears. Teddy perked up instantly.

"You've got a soft spot," Madison said. "Admit it."

"Absolutely not," he declared, but he was still scratching Teddy's ears.

THE NEXT DAY, Madison put Collin to work building a makeshift fence in the yard so they could easily let Teddy in and out without having to keep him on his leash. Since they had to take him outside every hour, the schedule was exhausting them both. Next door, the police officers were dressed in vacation mode with board shorts and T-shirts, but their clothes didn't hide the bulk beneath or the guns strapped to their belts. Guns always made Madison nervous, even on the bailiffs in the courtroom, but now it felt that much more disconcerting. Sure, she was glad Collin had one, kept inside the bedside table drawer, but she definitely never wanted to have to use it herself. Besides, the guns reminded her that she was the one who needed protecting at that moment. Madison stood on the deck looking down on the green space between the two homes. She saw Collin walking around the yard, carrying a big roll of chain link fence for their temporary dog run. Mark nodded at Collin as he passed by.

Mark saw Madison and raised his coffee mug. Madison returned the salute with her own mug filled with green tea. She went back inside, glad Mark was there but also hating the constant reminder—Jimmy Reese was out there, and he was angry. Very, very angry. The toaster oven dinged, announcing her breakfast was ready and she sauntered over to retrieve her warm English muffin. She buttered it, all the while watching Collin out the kitchen window. He'd been on a mission to get the dog run built that morning, calling Yvana, having her clear it with the owners who, as it turned out, didn't care about what temporary fencing they put up in the yard. Collin had insisted on getting it done immediately and it was hard to argue with him. Once he got an idea in his head, it stuck. He was controlling, stubborn and downright infuriating at times.

Like him deciding that his new job in Miami was more important than hers.

Madison sat at the kitchen breakfast bar and tried not to think about the time when Collin would have to start his new job in Miami. She still couldn't believe he'd left that little tidbit out. She sighed, feeling the weight of the impossible decision before her.

Would she really give up everything she'd worked so hard for, everything she'd built, just to follow Collin to Miami? What if their marriage didn't work, like so many relationships that were rushed to commitment too soon. The statistics—and she'd looked them up—were grim. Divorce rates were already high, higher still for couples who didn't know each other well when they tied the knot. *Especially those who were getting married for a baby, not for each other.*

Yes, she'd accidentally let it slip that she loved Collin. But did it count if she said it in the middle of a…delicate moment? She didn't even know if she'd meant it. She had while she was in the storm of passion, but now? Did she really love this man? Or was she simply trying to make it work for the baby's sake? Maybe she didn't want to acknowledge the fact that he was trying hard, too. Would either of them be working to create a relationship if there wasn't a baby in the picture? She didn't think so. And wasn't that the wrong reason to be together?

Madison rubbed her still-flat stomach as she watched Collin hammer in a fence post in a corner of the yard. She might not be show-ing, but she seemed to be retaining every-thing she ate. The waistband of her shorts felt a little tighter, and she was feeling bloated. She thought about all the women in the court-room who made eyes at Collin Baptista and, hell, some of the women who'd slept with him. Would she be able to keep his attention when she had a huge belly? Somehow, she just knew she wasn't going to be one of those adorable pregnant women who looked like they were carrying a basketball under their shirts. She'd be a bloated monster with three double chins.

She sighed, already feeling hungry, even though they'd just had breakfast. Teddy whined at her feet and put a paw against her bare in-step. He must be hungry, too.

"You want to eat all the time, too, don't you, boy?" He was adorable—big brown eyes, clumsy puppy paws, soft yellow fur. "You probably are getting by on your looks, aren't you? Well, in your case, it's a brilliant strat-egy."

She studied Teddy, wondering if Collin would be all right with the dog coming to Miami—if she agreed to go. A puppy and a baby, talk about a lot of new guests. Then she wondered what it would be like to go to sleep with Collin every night and wake up with him every day. She could get used to the idea of this man in her bed, and his mesmerizing green eyes watching her over breakfast, and yet… was she just being a fool? Could he be faithful to her? Would he? Did he love her or had he just been parroting what she'd said right back at her? Collin could have any woman he wanted, so why her?

And if she moved in with him, she'd be giving up more than her heart, risking more than her pride. She'd always taken care of herself and paid her own bills. If she moved to Miami, she'd be jobless, friendless. She'd need to rely on Collin, at first anyway. Was she ready to do that? Did she trust him to follow through on his promises?

She watched him work in the backyard and almost laughed. Collin was a Boy Scout, a do-gooder, a right-is-always-right prosecutor. She knew that on some level he'd keep his promises. If he vowed to marry her, he would. If he vowed to pay the bills, he would. When he promised to present evidence to a jury he always delivered. He prided himself on keeping his promises, but so far, he'd only promised her his name if she wanted to take it. His protection. His support. He hadn't promised her his love.

Would she be willing to move to Miami for

the sake of security? Didn't she want more than that, both for herself and her baby?

She could insist on not marrying him. She could stay in Fort Myers. But her apartment was tiny. She'd need a new place, for Teddy and for the baby.

Maybe a new house in Miami. Madison was still watching Collin work, shirtless and in board shorts, sweat glistening on his tanned arms. He carried the metal posts around as if they weighed nothing. Seeing him work made her own resolve start to melt away. He had a truly unparalleled physique, no doubt about that. Hardly surprising that nearly every woman in the courthouse noticed him.

He was handsome and sexy and strong. He made a wonderful lover... But would he make an equally wonderful dad? He didn't always have much patience, his snapping at Teddy was proof of that. He'd even wanted to give Teddy up when things got a bit tough. But, she reasoned, now he seemed to be on board with keeping him. He was putting up the fence after all, and the sweat dripping down his temples told her just how hard he was working. She had to admit, she wouldn't be sorry to go to bed with *that* every night. She absently fanned her face, glancing back at the dishes that she was supposed to be washing. She ought to get to work. She reluctantly trudged to the sink when the doorbell rang. At first, she tensed, remembering Jimmy on the loose, but as soon as she looked out the glass front door, she saw Yvana standing there, waving. Instantly, Madison relaxed.

She trotted to the door and opened it. Yvana breezed through, wearing her uniform of club polo shirt and khaki shorts and sandals.

"How y'all doing? Dog driven you crazy yet?"

"He's trying," Madison said as she nudged the puppy back behind the door. He gave a short sharp bark and tried to run outside between her legs. "Come on in."

Teddy jumped up to greet Yvana, skidding on the floor and nearly toppling over.

"That little guy is all paws," Yvana said, reaching down to pet him as he jumped up on her legs.

"Down, boy. Down." Madison pushed Teddy away but he wagged his tail happily as Yvana petted him. That was when Madison looked up and saw Collin out the back window, muscles bulging as he swung the mallet and hit a fence post. God, the man was sexy. Beyond sexy. Walking around without a shirt on made him practically X-rated. Collin met her gaze and she smiled. He flashed a tired grin in her direction and waved at Yvana as he swiped at the sweat on his brow. She felt her own internal temperature rise.

"Oooh, my lordie," Yvana said, fanning her face. "He's one handsome man. Is it hot in here or is it just me?" She tugged at her shirt collar and that made Madison laugh.

"Oh, it's hot in here, all right," she agreed.

Yvana looked beyond Collin and saw one of the police officers, Mark, sitting on the porch of Uncle Rashad's cottage, pretending to read a paper. "But not as hot as that other delicious man over there. Mmm, hmm." Yvana gave the officer an approving look. Mark, feeling her gaze, glanced up and sent her a guarded smile. Yvana waved at him and clucked her tongue. "Oh, yes, indeed. Yvana *likes*."

Madison couldn't help giggling a little. Yvana was never shy about her tastes. She'd been divorced for the better part of a decade now.

"I wouldn't mind that man watching me day *and* night." Mark went back to reading his newspaper, or pretending to. Yvana stared at him a moment longer, then turned her attention back to Madison. "How are you holding up, sugar?"

"I'm okay," Madison said. "I mean, they're watching us all the time."

"You really think that crazy man will come all the way here looking for you?" Yvana looked worried.

"I hope not," she said. "He's a...well, just a nasty dude."

"Oh, you don't have to tell me about those neo-Nazi freaks." Yvana shook her head as she adjusted her bracelets. "What I don't get is why they claim to be patriotic when they've got swastika tattoos and Confederate flags on their trucks. Didn't we *fight* the Nazis in World War II? How is that patriotic, exactly?"

Madison nodded. "They just fear what's different, I guess."

"Well, what this Jimmy Reese guy should fear is prison."

Madison couldn't agree more. "Here's hoping he gets back there sooner rather than later."

"Amen, sister." Teddy trotted up to Yvana then and sniffed at her brightly painted toes. She bent down and gave his head another pat.

"You officially adopted him?" she asked.

"Well, Collin said we should wait since the owner might want to claim him."

"Oh, I don't think there's any worry about that." Yvana made a face at the puppy.

"Why do you say that?"

Yvana glanced up sharply. "I mean, we would've heard by now." She grinned, and

Madison got the impression she might not be telling the whole truth.

"What do you—" But she didn't get to finish, because Yvana let out an appreciative whistle as she watched Mark drink coffee on the porch at the other house.

"I might just move in with you and bring a pair of binoculars." Yvana chuckled to herself and Madison couldn't help joining in.

"You're shameless," Madison said, the weirdness about Teddy all but forgotten.

"Oh, child, you have *no* idea." Yvana wiggled her eyebrows, making Madison giggle once more. "But I do have a reason for calling, other than to spy on Danny Glover over there."

"Yes?"

"I need your help. Yours and Collin's. You think you could spare an hour or two?"

"Sure. What do you need?"

"Got an older couple getting married, and I need you two to give me a hand getting the reception ready. Had two staffers miss the ferry this afternoon!" Yvana shook her head in disapproval, her big hoop earrings swaying from side to side. "Can't find good help these days! Not that I blame them for ditching work. Wedding season is the worst. And did I mention how much I hate wedding season?"

"You might've said that once or twice."

Madison grinned. Yvana's hatred for the summer months was well known. People from all over descended on North Captiva, thinking it would be a wonderful spot for a wedding—which it was—but it also meant a whole lot more work and headaches, which Yvana made clear she could do without.

"Sure thing, Yvana. We'll be there."

"YOU'RE TOO NICE," Collin told Madison about a half hour later as he drove them both to the clubhouse. They were followed by Mark and Steve, who, in honor of the wedding, had swapped their T-shirts for plaid button-up shirts that they wore untucked to try to hide the guns on their belts. Collin had put *on* his shirt, a plain blue polo.

"I just want to help. Yvana's in a tight spot, and…"

"Like I said, *too nice*." Collin flashed a grin at her, his eyes darting back to the sandy path ahead of them. He took the turn around the lagoon a little hard and she held on to her seat. "But it's one of the many things I love about you." He reached out and grabbed her hand and held it, keeping his other hand on the golf cart's steering wheel.

There it was. The *L word* again. She wasn't sure how comfortable she felt saying it, just anytime, anywhere. And that made her worry she might only want to make that proclamation when they were both naked.

"Yvana's been good to me, and I owe her *many* favors. You wouldn't believe the trouble I used to get into on this island."

"You? Trouble?" Collin's sarcasm came through loud and clear. "I can't believe that."

"Yeah, when I was nine, I stole a golf cart once. Just to go driving it around. Yvana caught me, but she didn't tell my uncle or my mom. Thank goodness. Or they would've grounded me for a month." Madison laughed, remembering her young, impetuous self. The summer she turned ten, she'd decided none of the rules applied to her anymore.

Collin laughed. He had an easy command about him that she found herself admiring.

"You can't be serious. You carjacked a golf cart! That's a felony, counselor." The way he said it sounded like he was a cop pulling her over for speeding. His mirrored sunglasses added to the effect. He looked commanding, handsome, in control. As much as she hated his control-freak nature, she had to admit, it also attracted her.

"Hardly. The keys were in it. The cart belonged to the club, and Yvana didn't press charges." The sun above them broke free of the clouds and Madison squinted against the glare. She dug around in her purse for her sunglasses and put them on.

"She should have! Little hooligan," Collin teased. She still wasn't used to seeing this playful side of him, the man who had a sense of humor, who let his guard down. She liked this Collin.

"You more attracted to me now that you know I have a criminal record? I'm a bad girl." The sunglasses threatened to slide down her nose and she pushed them up with a finger.

Collin sent her a flirting sidelong glance, casually steering the golf cart with one hand. "Oh, I *already know* you're a bad girl. In bed."

She giggled at that, as Collin reached over and squeezed her bare knee. Madison felt her cheeks grow warm. She liked this—him driving, her in the passenger seat, his hand on her leg.

Would it be like this even after the baby came? Madison wondered. Would they still flirt like this?

"We're going to be in trouble if you have a girl," Collin declared, as he took the right turn at the fork, to the path that skirted the tennis courts and the pool.

"Why do you say that?"

"Because if you're having a boy, which I

think you are, then he'll take after me and he'll
be perfect. If you have a girl, well…"

"You can't be serious." Madison gave Collin a playful punch in the arm. "Genes don't
work like that."

"They don't'?" Collin took the path by the
lagoon and they sped past a row of bright yellow flowers. "Well, it doesn't matter, I'll give
either one an amazing name." The path became bumpier and Madison held on to the railing. "What do you mean when you give them
a name?"

Collin pretended to be shocked. "I thought
the father got to name the baby."

"Since when is *that* a thing?" Now, Madison
was starting to get irked. The sexy cop persona
had begun to grate. One second, she liked his
domineering nature and the next, she didn't.
Was this him or the pregnancy hormones?

They reached the end of the lush lagoon
and a large white crane carefully waded in,
its beak poised above the mirrored water, ready
to spear a fish. The huge green palm trees lining the sandy path swayed in the gentle ocean
breeze. Their path joined another and a second golf cart drove ahead of them. The path
was particularly dry, and sand kicked up from
the back of the other cart. Madison ducked her
head to avoid getting sand in her face. Collin

eased up on the gas, and Madison glanced behind them, seeing Steve and Mark slow down, too.

"In my family, Dad named me. That was it. Mom just accepted the name he wanted. Period. No discussion. And, actually, my sister did the same with her baby, believe it or not." Collin kept his eyes on the sandy road ahead, eyes hidden behind his polarized sunglasses.

"And you think that's how it should be done?"

Collin shrugged. "It worked fine for me and for my niece." He turned the wheel, leaning into a curve. A few tropical flowers brushed by Madison's knee and the golf cart was suddenly filled with their fragrance.

"Why should the father get to pick out the name? The mother does all the work—carrying the baby. Delivering him or her. You know about labor, right?"

Collin let out a frustrated breath. "Fine, then. Have you thought about names?"

She hadn't. Not really. "Well, I don't know. I guess not."

"Well, I've got two names already picked out. Jamie for a boy, after my best friend in grade school, or Chelsea for a girl."

"Chelsea? Uh…no." They hit a little bump in the road and Madison's sunglasses slipped down her nose once more. She pushed them up.

"What's wrong with Chelsea?" Collin asked.

"Everything," Madison said, thinking about a Chelsea McAdams in second grade who used to tell her she was ugly. That was probably the only reason she didn't like the name. Still, she didn't like it.

"Give me a better name, then. What are *your* suggestions?"

"I haven't thought about it very much. But I like Ava better." Ava was a sweet name, and when she said it, she imagined a little girl with pigtails and a big gap-toothed grin.

"Ava? That sounds like an old person's name."

"It's not!" cried Madison, feeling defensive. Collin scowled at her, and Madison glared back. He whipped the golf cart around the corner and drove into a space by the club. The officers pulled in after them and took a walk around the perimeter to check for unwanted guests.

"We'll have to talk about this later." His tone reminded Madison of a disciplinary father. It was a "we'll talk about this later, but you have no chance of winning this argument" tone, which Madison did not care for in the least.

They hopped out of the cart and saw Yvana directing a few workers, clipboard in hand and the usual bright scarf around her head.

"You're just in time," she said, looking relieved. "Will y'all help with the folding tables? We just need a few more out by the pool."

"I don't want her to lift anything heavy," Collin said, indicating Madison. She both liked and hated that he was so protective. She always seemed to be of two minds about him.

"I can help with the chairs. I'm fine."

"I'd rather you sat this one out," he said, sliding his sunglasses on top of his head.

Yvana glanced from her to him and back again. "I'm not getting in the middle of this," she declared. "Y'all can figure it out. Ceremony is in less than an hour, and they'll be doing it right over there." She pointed toward a white arch with flowers near the north side of the pool. On the south side, some tables were already set up for the reception, maybe five or six. Five more were still folded and waiting to the side.

Madison marched over to a chair, determined to help.

"Madison, I don't want you lifting anything," Collin said again.

"I'm not a baby. I'm *having* a baby."

"Please. Sit." Collin pulled out a chair and urged her into it. "You can help with flower arranging."

Collin got to work sliding out one of the tables and pulling out the legs, setting it into position with a slightly red-faced struggle. But when Madison got to her feet, he sent her a warning glare that said, "don't move." She sighed and leaned back in her chair. Why was he making this so difficult? She was pregnant, not made of glass, for goodness' sake. She saw a crate full of white tablecloths and went to arrange those. Let him bark at her for lifting fabric, she thought. Collin cursed as he wheeled out another big table by himself.

"Need help?" she asked, as she carefully flipped out a white tablecloth and it billowed over the table.

"No," he grunted as he moved the table for eight into position. She watched him work up a sweat and thought, *Fine. He can just be stubborn, then.* Pretty soon, he whipped off his shirt, the heat and humidity getting to him. Now, she might not even finish the tablecloths, not with him shirtless, moving tables and chairs around. His muscles bulged and demanded her attention.

"Don't worry, I'll help him." This came from Mark, who arrived then with Steve in tow. The burly policemen added their muscle to the work, so Madison felt a bit better, but she still hated feeling helpless.

Yvana bustled out, carrying flower arrangements and putting beautiful pink and red roses in the center of each table. She glanced twice at Collin. He had a body made for a firefighter calendar. Madison wondered why there wasn't a law-and-order calendar out there somewhere, but when she thought of the other prosecutors on staff, she figured they'd never manage to get twelve who looked like Collin Baptista.

"Oh, my, you better put a shirt on soon before the guests start arriving and think this is a bachelorette party," Yvana cautioned him, grinning from ear to ear.

Collin smiled back as he stooped to pick up five folded chairs, which he carried all at once. "Nearly done, Yvana. I promise I'll be decent when the guests arrive."

"And you," Yvana called to Mark. "You want to help me with these?" She held up a vase full of flowers. Madison noticed that Mark smiled when he came over. Was there a little something brewing between those two? Madison suspected there was. She definitely saw sparks. Yvana giggled like a little girl when Mark came to relieve her of the flowers.

A tall man in a suit arrived then and walked to the bar, where he helped himself to a glass of whiskey on the rocks.

"How are you holding up, Dave?" Yvana asked the newcomer who held up one finger as he took a deep sip of his drink. Yvana gave him a pat on the arm. Madison wondered if he was the groom.

"Nervous about getting married?" Madison asked, feeling sympathetic. She remembered the shot of nerves she'd felt when Collin presented her with that black velvet box. It took a lot to commit yourself to a person—especially one as stubborn as Collin.

"Me? No, no." The tall man shook his head emphatically. "I'm not getting married. My mom is."

The man was in his fifties!

"Your mother?" Madison tried to do some quick calculations and decided that meant she was at least...

"She's eighty-six. I'm officiating the ceremony." Dave leaned in and held out his hand. "Dave. Nice to meet you."

Collin stopped working on his table and walked over in time for the introductions.

"Madison...and this is Collin."

Collin shook the man's hand.

"Dorothy and Herm, bride and groom, eighty-six and eighty-eight, respectively," Yvana explained, standing near Dave. "The family has owned the Snapper house over at the south end of the island for years."

Dave took another big sip of his drink. "I'm

going to need a few more of these before I can officiate the ceremony."

"Help yourself."

"Oh, I'm paying for it. I will, thank you." Dave finished off his first drink and went to pour himself another. "Thanks for helping out, by the way. My mother will be grateful. She's very anxious to get this ceremony done."

"Oh, she's in love, is she?" Madison asked.

"Yes, but it's not even a legal marriage," Dave explained, setting the bottle of whiskey down as he made himself comfortable at the bar. "My mother and Herm…they didn't want the legal part of the marriage, since it's expensive to rewrite their wills and nobody wants to start a fight between their grown children about who would get what when they go. They just want to make it a kind of spiritual ceremony, so they can fool around and not feel guilty. Do things I don't want to know about." He wiggled his eyebrows and Madison got the picture.

"She's worried about what God will think, so she wants it official, just not legal." Dave grinned and finished most of his second drink. "But like I said, there are just some things a grown son doesn't need to know about his mother—like what they do with their walkers when they…you know."

Both Collin and Madison laughed.

"I think it's sweet that they're getting married," Collin said, surprising Madison. "You can't ever give up on love."

"Can't you?" Dave joked. "I mean…eighty-six? Right now, my sister is decorating Mom's walker with flowers."

Collin and Dave shared a laugh.

"Where did they meet?" Madison asked.

"The assisted-living home," Dave said. "It was love at first sight, though they both have trouble remembering things, so they might have met once or twice before it really stuck." Dave took another drink. "Hey, why don't you two join me? I hate to drink alone." He offered up the whiskey bottle. He began to pour two glasses, but Madison raised her hand. "Oh, no, sorry, I can't. I'm…"

"Expecting," Collin finished, and then put a possessive arm around her shoulders, as if to take all the credit.

"Oh, congratulations, you two! That's wonderful. Boy? Girl?" Dave pointed to the soda water dispenser on the bar and Madison nodded. He filled her glass and added a wedge of lime.

"Boy," Collin announced with certainty. Madison nudged him.

"We don't know for sure yet," Madison said. "It's too early." She elbowed Collin in the ribs.

"Well, congratulations, whatever it is." Dave handed Collin a glass of whiskey and Madison her soda water. Then the three clinked glasses. A breeze made a ripple in the crystal blue pool behind them, and the sun beamed down on the deck chairs that had been tucked away to make room for the wedding tables.

Dave glanced at the bar. "Well, I think one more scotch on the rocks and then I ought to be able to handle this ceremony." He shook his head and grinned. "It's not every day your mother wants to have her fooling around blessed by God and about two dozen witnesses."

Madison smiled and Dave raised his glass to her. "I mean, God bless her, but sheesh."

"Say, do you do ceremonies for other people?" Collin asked.

"Sure do." Dave dug in his pocket and pulled out his wallet, then he handed Collin his card. Madison caught a glimpse of double rings and flowers bordering contact information. Collin took the card and studied it. "The State of Florida says I can marry you," Dave said. "Did one of those online certifications."

"Good, because we might need someone to marry us."

Madison choked on her club soda and nearly gagged.

Dave's eyes grew wide. "I might be old-fashioned like my mom, but you two aren't...?"

"No, we're not," Madison said evenly. "And we might not ever be if he keeps asking random strangers to marry us. No offense meant."

"None taken," Dave replied.

Besides, didn't they know *all* the judges in Fort Myers? One of them could perform the ceremony, if it came to that. Madison wondered if Collin was ashamed to ask. After all, then they'd know for sure that he was marrying a defense attorney.

"He's not a random stranger. We know all about his mom, Dorothy and Herm," Collin argued. Dave laughed at that.

"Well, I live in Fort Myers, so if you want a romantic little ceremony here, I'm not that far," he said. "And both of you are welcome to stay for the wedding. And as we know, there's an open bar, which I'll be utilizing to its fullest extent." Dave took another deep swig of his drink and grinned.

"What do you think, should we stay for the ceremony?" Collin asked Madison. She was still wondering about Collin's motives in asking Dave to officiate. And still a little annoyed that he was so certain she'd eventually say yes. How many times did she have to say no?

"I'd need to go shower and change first," Madison protested.

"No need," Dave said. "It's a casual affair. Don't let the white tablecloths fool you. We're going to be almost one hundred percent orthopedic shoes and compression socks around here in about half an hour."

"Let's stay," Collin suggested.

"The food's going to be fantastic," Dave said. "And like I said, there's an open bar." He turned to Madison. "Not that *you* can take advantage of it, but still…all the Shirley Temples you want!"

Madison glanced at Collin's green eyes and found herself agreeing to stay. "I guess I don't see the harm."

"Besides, if we're going to hire Dave to marry us, we need to see if he has what it takes," Collin joked. Madison made a sour face. Really, Collin's overconfidence knew no bounds.

"Oh, if I can do this, I can do anything," Dave said, leaving his empty glass on the table. He glanced at his watch. "Well, time for me to go check on the bride and groom. I'll see you kids in a bit."

Dave wandered off, back toward the main office, and Madison turned to Collin.

"Why don't you want any of the judges to marry us? *If* we were ever to get married."

Collin shrugged. "Why *would* I want them to marry us? We probably couldn't agree on which one we liked the most."

That was true enough. The judges who tended to side with Collin, she found unfair, and the ones who liked her objections, Collin would describe as bleeding hearts.

"Dave seemed nice and neutral," he said as he drained the last of his whiskey.

"You really are positive that eventually you'll convince me," Madison said, as she finished her club soda, the ice plinking in her glass as she set it back on the bar.

Collin grinned, but his eyes were serious. "Oh, I know you will."

"How can you be so sure?"

"Because we were *meant* to be together, that's why. It's why we're having this baby. It's fate."

"What if I don't believe in fate?" Madison asked.

"That's all right." Collin pushed his empty glass away. "I believe enough for both of us."

CHAPTER SEVENTEEN

THE CEREMONY FOR Dorothy and Herm went off without a snag, and was surprisingly moving, Collin thought. The bride, with her walker, wedding bouquet wired to the side rail, wore a light gray suit and a white flower in her hair. The two exchanged vows, the love apparent in both faces. Even Dave seemed to enjoy himself, and the crowd at the ceremony was nothing but loving and open. Collin thought it was proof that no matter how old people got, they weren't immune to the power of love.

Dorothy gently kissed her groom, Herm, who looked debonair in a light blue suit and tie. Herm had hardly any hair left, but he did have a sparkle in his eye and was spry enough to crack a few jokes after the kiss, causing the crowd to laugh. Then, a string quartet played classical music as the bride took to the dance floor, walker and all, and swayed a little with her new groom. Dave headed to the appetizer table but gave Collin a nod and a wink, followed by an exaggerated wipe of his forehead. *All done, thank goodness*, his face said.

Collin sat at the bar, nursing a bourbon on the rocks as he watched the other guests join the elderly couple on the floor. He wondered what it would be like to have elderly parents. He'd never know. How he wished his mom had lived to eighty-six and married someone like Herm, who clearly had a lot of affection for Dorothy. He had to admire the couple for sticking with it, for not giving up on love or happiness. His own mother had largely given up on men after his father. Still, he would've liked to have seen her happy, in love. He also wished she could've seen him happy and in love. Not that love was everything, he reminded himself. Love could fade. Loyalty remained.

His mother would've made a wonderful grandmother, and he was sorry she'd never get to meet her grandson. There was the Baptista ESP again. He *knew* the baby was a boy. He had no doubt in his mind. It was his gut that told him to trust his instincts. Like now. He and Madison belonged together. And she'd be having his son. He glanced over at her; somehow, on her way back from the bathroom, one of Herm's elderly friends had pulled her onto the dance floor. Steve, the officer who'd stayed to guard Madison, stood up to intervene, but she waved him off. Mark was on the other side of the wedding, keeping an eye on the crowd. Madison and the older gentleman slow danced—not too many fast dances for the eighty-and-up set. Madison obliged the man, who was old enough to be her grandfather, and who seemed to greatly enjoy their little waltz. It was so kind of her to dance with him, he thought, but then that was Madison. Soft-hearted to a fault. She almost needed someone to look after her, make sure no one took advantage of that big heart. That was why she needed him.

"Beautiful, isn't she?" Yvana asked, sneaking up on Collin as he stood at the bar. She nodded toward Madison. Yvana wore a colorful scarf on her head and a beautiful coordinating coral silk dress. Gone was her usual uniform of a Captiva Club polo and khaki shorts. She placed her white wine on the bar and slipped onto the stool next to his.

"I thought you had to work tonight," Collin said, raising his tumbler to his lips.

"Dave invited me to the wedding, so thought I'd come. Dave and I go way back. He's done a lot of ceremonies here," she said. "Now, back to Madison. You're supposed to be telling me how she's the most beautiful woman you've ever seen. Because, you know, she's glowing, what with all that work of carrying your baby."

Collin laughed. "Yes, she's the most beautiful woman here. Except for you, of course."

"Oh, go on, you charmer." She grinned, her smile lighting up her dark eyes. "So, you making any headway?" Yvana pulled no punches and Collin admired her directness.

"I think so. She told me she loved me."

Yvana let out a little squeal of delight and slapped her knees. "Well, now, that's something." She leaned forward, her dangling silver earrings jingling. "How about the puppy? How's he working out?"

"Oh, he's a pain in the ass," Collin said. "But Madison's in love with him, so we're probably going to have to adopt him and…why not? My son will need a dog to play with."

Yvana laughed. "Yes, I suppose so. The puppy's still with you? Y'all haven't lost him yet?"

"Not for very long, anyway." Collin pretended to sound disappointed, and Yvana laughed.

"Well, good. I say if you can look after a puppy, you can probably handle a baby just fine. Least a baby can't run away from you. Or chew up your furniture… Not right away." Yvana grinned again.

"Thank God for that." Collin held up his glass and she clinked her wineglass against it. "Though, I'm still hoping his real owner finds him."

Yvana winked at him. "Well, honey, you don't need to be looking any further." She took a sip of her white wine.

"What do you mean?"

"The owner is me." Yvana tapped her chest.

"I don't understand." Collin frowned.

"A friend of mine had a litter of golden doodles she was trying to find homes for. Couldn't get rid of this last one, and I told her I'd take him, but he was a handful."

"Oh, you're telling me."

"When I saw you and Maddie having trouble, I thought I'd give you something to bond over. I figured you'd fall in love over that puppy."

"You sly matchmaker," Collin said as he imagined Yvana sneaking around with a puppy and coming up with this elaborate plan.

"I'm the one who released the dog in her yard, and I just thought…well, the dog would probably bring you together—besides, if you can take care of a puppy, you'd damn sure be ready for a baby." Yvana grinned, showing a dimple in her cheek.

"You fooled me. Totally fooled me. Does Madison know?"

"Not yet." Yvana couldn't seem to stop grinning. "But, anyway, that dog is yours."

"I ought to make you take it back," Collin threatened.

"Why? You got a free parenting lesson out of that dog," Yvana said. "Now, you know you can take care of a baby, too. And did it work? You two going to get married?"

Collin let out a weak laugh. He had no idea what was in Madison's head—or heart—at the moment. She seemed happy to sleep with him, but not thrilled about the idea of marrying him...

"Falling into arguments, you mean." Collin studied the amber liquid in his glass, and wiped a bit of sweat from the brim. "I've asked Maddie to marry me so many times, but she keeps saying no."

"You just got to be patient with her. She's stubborn, that girl. I remember one time when she was little, she refused to wear her flip-flops around 'cause she said they hurt her toes. So, her mama got her sandals. Well, apparently they hurt, too. No matter how many different pairs her mama bought, she couldn't make that girl wear shoes. You know how many splinters she got?"

Collin shook his head. He didn't, but he could imagine.

"I don't know, either, but I pulled out at least four myself, so it had to be a lot more than that."

Collin laughed. He could almost see stubborn little Maddie refusing to wear her sandals. Or any shoes at all. He liked the idea of her being a bit wild, determined to walk her own path, even if she did so barefoot. He liked the arguments they had, and the blistering sex that usually followed. She was the Earthquake, no doubt about it.

Collin watched her do a little spin in the arms of the elderly gentleman.

"You're in it for the long haul, though, right? I might put in a good word for you, but ain't gonna do that if you're some fly-by-night." Yvana glanced at him over the top of her wineglass. The woman seemed to miss nothing. He glanced over at Madison once more. She was laughing at something her dance partner said and seeing her face full of mirth made him feel warm inside. He didn't want to be with any other woman. Madison was the woman for him, and not just because she was carrying his baby.

"I'm definitely in it for the long haul," he assured her. "No doubt about that. Now, it's about convincing Maddie to feel the same way. I think she's still looking for the emergency exits."

"So, what is it she doesn't like? What is it about you that's not hitting her right?" Yvana cradled her chin in her hand, settling in for a comfortable talk. She was easy to talk to, wise, and he was starting to forgive her for sneaking that dog into their lives.

"She thinks I'm a control freak."

"Are you?" Yvana quirked an eyebrow as she took a small sip of wine.

"Maybe a little," he admitted, shrugging one shoulder.

"We all gotta let someone else drive now and again," Yvana said, absently toying with one silver earring. "Otherwise, we're gonna run off the road. Plus, if you're gonna get married, be a family, you have to let everyone carry their fair share."

"You think so?" Collin wasn't so sure. For years, he'd been the only person he could depend on.

"I know so," Yvana said. "Now, you gonna let that old man steal her away from you?" She nodded toward Madison and the elderly man who was shuffling her around the dance floor. "He's got some serious dance moves."

"No, ma'am."

"Well, go on, then. I've gotta work on getting that fine police detective to dance with me." Yvana stared at Mark on the other side of the dance floor. He was scanning the crowd, keeping an eye out for anything suspicious.

"You've got a thing for Mark?" Collin had a hard time imagining the speak-her-mind Yvana with the reserved veteran cop.

"Tall glass of chocolate milk, that's all I'm saying." Yvana rested her chin on both hands.

"Wanna borrow Teddy? He'll help you fall in love in no time."

"Oh, hell no," Yvana said, making a face. "That's a devil dog. Cute as hell, but he's not housetrained, and he destroys everything he touches."

"Tell me about it." Collin sighed. He glanced at Mark, who still stood watch. "Maybe I'll put in a good word for *you*, then," Collin offered.

"Tit for tat, oh, yes." Yvana gave a quick nod. "I like the way you think."

Collin laughed, put down his drink and went to Madison, gently cutting in. Her partner looked sad to see her go, but graciously allowed Collin to take over.

"I'm glad he was nice about that, so I didn't have to clock him," Collin joked as he slid his hand around Madison's back and pulled her closer to him. She smelled like lavender and something else equally delicate. He loved the way she smelled.

"Counselor!" Madison exclaimed, mock outrage crossing her face as she looked up at him. "That is *awful*."

"Not as awful as watching you dance with another man." Collin could feel the deliciousness of her body pressed to his. She was so soft, so very feminine. All he wanted to do was dance with her forever. How could she not see how perfect they were together? Couples didn't dance like this, unless they had that intensity, that *love*, the heat like a flame between them. Sure, they argued, but that just meant their passion ran hot.

Madison laughed, and the sound made his groin tighten. God, he wanted her. He wanted her right here on this dance floor. He wanted her every minute of every day.

"So, what did you think of Dave? I think he'd be great to officiate our wedding."

"Collin," Madison said, a warning in her voice. "I haven't even said yes."

"Well, once you do, what do you think of Dave? He told me he has slots open next weekend. He could marry us then."

"Collin! No, we're not getting married next weekend." She glanced to the side, deliberately avoiding eye contact. Why was she so stubborn? Why did she keep refusing him? She was having his baby, so why not marry him?

Collin squeezed her tighter. This was where she belonged. Right here in his arms. "Why not?"

"Because we can't." The woman was so stubborn. And irrational. And irrationally stubborn.

"Give me one good reason why you and I shouldn't try to spend the rest of our lives together."

Madison's eyes found his once more. "Because we've only just started to date. Just because *you* want it right now, doesn't mean it'll happen. Remember what happened when you told Teddy to go pee outside? And then he did it inside."

"You're comparing us to housebreaking a dog?"

"Kind of."

He liked teasing her, he liked the constant back and forth between them.

"Seriously, though. Why not marry me?" he said again.

"We hardly know each other." Madison looked at the elderly bride and groom who were toasting each other at the head table.

"So? What I know about, I love." Collin was determined to hear them and knock each one down, the way he would with a defense attorney's closing arguments.

"You're just proposing to me because I'm pregnant."

Collin didn't see why that was a problem. Wasn't it a *good* thing he was proposing to her? "What's wrong with that? Would you rather I not propose? That I tell you I want nothing to do with the baby?"

"No." Madison looked a little flustered. She seemed to want to tell him something else, and yet she was holding it in. It was just like her to keep the most important information to herself, like the fact that she was pregnant.

"Then I don't understand. What *do* you want? You don't want me here on the island, but you don't want me to leave, either." The slow song came to an end, and they stopped dancing. A high-tempo song came on then, and the crowd around them started bouncing to the beat, but Madison just stood there.

"You don't understand," she said.

"So, explain it to me," Collin pleaded. If she'd speak some *sense*, if she opened up that vault, the one she kept closed to him, *then* he could understand. She looked at him, and for a split second, he thought she might actually share her true feelings with him. But then the moment was gone.

She shook her head and left the dance floor, with Collin staring after her, wondering what on earth he'd said.

"You look like you could use a drink," said Dave. He was sitting at a nearby table and had a bottle of wine open.

"I could, actually," he said and took a glass of red that Dave offered him.

"Don't worry. Pregnancy hormones are the worst," he said. "My wife didn't know if she was coming or going during both her pregnancies. You just have to weather the storm."

"I wish I was sure it's hormones and not that she hates me." Collin took a swig of wine as Dave laughed.

"What's it like? Being a parent?" Collin thoughtfully continued to sip his wine, thinking how much he didn't know.

"It's absolutely terrifying," Dave said. "The best kind of terrifying, though. I highly recommend it." He laughed. "I'll let you in on a little secret. Parents never really know what they're doing. We're all just winging it. You can't really control anything. You just do the best you can."

Dave peered out across the dance floor. "Uh-oh, looks like Mom lost one of her tennis balls off the feet of her walker. I'll be right back."

Dave handed Collin his wine glass, so that now Collin looked like he was double-fisting it. Dave hurried off as Collin glanced up to see another guest from the party in front of him—a woman, probably twenty-five, blond, wearing a short sundress that revealed perfect legs. "I'm Amber."

"Collin," he said. "I'd offer to shake but…"

"You've got your hands full." Amber flipped her blond hair off one shoulder and smiled, a flirty little smile. She leaned forward so Collin could see down the V-neck of her dress. The woman was definitely flirting with him. She was cute, no doubt about it, and sexy in her sandals and short dress.

"Are you here for the bride or groom?"

"Groom. I'm his great-granddaughter." She leaned forward a little more, toying with a strand of her hair, wrapping it around one perfectly manicured finger. "And you?"

"I'm actually a wedding crasher. I met the bride's son about an hour ago."

"Really?" Now, she seemed even more interested. This was the give-and-take that Collin knew so well with a woman who liked him. All he had to do was not muck it up and he could have her out of that little dress of hers in no time. He'd been at odds with Madison for so long that he'd forgotten how easy this could be—a woman interested in him, no complications, just fun.

But he wasn't supposed to do that anymore, was he? He was going to be a father. A husband. Flirting wasn't on his agenda anymore. *Yet*, he thought, *what would be the harm in just talking to the woman?* They didn't have to take it any further—and he wouldn't—but he liked the idea of simple small talk with a pretty girl. What harm could it do?

"Would you like a drink?" he asked, looking at her empty glass.

CHAPTER EIGHTEEN

MADISON CAME BACK to the reception prepared to talk to Collin, ready to apologize. With the pregnancy hormones rushing through her body, her emotions seesawed, unsteady chemicals about to mix and explode at any moment. She felt unstable sometimes, bouncing like a ping-pong ball from one extreme emotion to the next. She hoped it was just the baby, because otherwise, she might be losing her mind.

She stood near the pool, on the other side of the tables, searching the crowd for Collin. The bride and groom were sitting down, toasting with flutes of champagne, while other guests hit the dance floor. Then she saw him—broad-shouldered, dark hair, that radiant toothpaste-commercial smile. She almost waved at him, almost shouted his name, when she realized he was talking to a leggy blonde at the bar. In that instant, he handed her a drink. Madison froze. Collin was flirting, she could tell that all the way from over here.

Madison was suddenly off-balance—insecurely observing the sleek flat-stomached woman flicking her hair off her shoulder and laughing at something charming Collin must be saying. She felt bloated, thick in the middle with the start of baby-weight; but even on her best days, she wasn't sure she could compete with the young pretty girl, who was clearly fascinated with everything Collin had to say.

Here it is, she thought, the fear she'd had all along. He'd just proven it—Collin wasn't interested in *her* as much as in fulfilling an obligation. The realization cut her to the quick. He might be the father of her baby, but he wasn't ready to settle down, or be faithful, or make a life with her. He didn't understand that she wanted him free of any responsibility, any obligation. She didn't want him to marry her because he thought she was a burden, or because he felt he needed to "do the right thing." Love shouldn't be the "right thing," it should be the *only* thing, the thing he couldn't live without.

The air suddenly seemed thin. She tried to calm herself and take a deep breath, but she felt shaky. Collin wasn't going to change. He wasn't going to settle down for her. He'd marry her and make sure his son carried his last name. But the way he was smiling at the pretty girl in front of him told her that he didn't really love *her*.

Madison felt so vulnerable, so weak. She was pregnant, a slave to her emotions and hormones, and there was no way she'd be able to handle the jealousy. Everything in her life seemed to be hurtling out of her control. She just wanted to get away.

It was all suddenly insurmountable. Unsolvable. Yes, she could agree to marry Collin, but how could she when he didn't seem to understand what she wanted or needed? Could she marry him when she knew he'd flirt with every beautiful woman who batted her eyelashes at him?

"You okay, sugar?" Yvana was by her side, looking concerned.

Madison hugged herself. "Do you ever feel that you have everything under control, except then you find out you actually have nothing under control?"

Yvana chuckled low in her throat. "Honey, I feel like that all the time." Yvana put a hand on Madison's shoulder. She, too, looked at Collin.

"They're just talking," she said, seeming to read her mind. "You don't know…"

"I don't have to know," she said.

"I'm sure he's not asking her to marry him," Yvana pointed out.

"I think it's obvious he only wants to marry me out of obligation," Madison said, holding her sweating glass of club soda, the ice melting in the humid air. "And he only knows *his* way. His way is always right."

"Well, obligation is as good a reason as any to get married," Yvana said.

"But…" Madison never thought of herself as a romantic before, and yet—now, here—faced with the idea of marrying a man simply because it was good for the baby just irked her.

"And I never met a man who didn't think he was always right," Yvana was saying. "I figure that comes with the Y chromosome."

Madison had to laugh at that. Still, she felt glum. Her problems suddenly seemed to loom large, unfixable, and watching Collin smile at the blonde was making her blood boil. She ought to march over there and tell him to cut it out. But would it even make any difference? She'd seen everything she needed to see. Collin wasn't really in love with her. Otherwise, why would he have the slightest interest in that girl if he was?

"I want the whole package," Madison told Yvana. "I want a man to be so crazy in love with me he *has* to marry me, not because of a baby, but because of *me*." She watched Collin share a laugh with the girl and saw her put a hand on his forearm, a light, flirtatious touch. "Collin's not that man."

Madison just wanted to leave, then. The disappointment hit her stomach like an unexpected blow. She couldn't breathe, and if she hung around much longer, she'd probably start to cry. She felt the prick of unshed tears.

"I… I need to go."

"Want me to drive you home?" Yvana asked, placing a gentle hand on her shoulder.

Madison glanced at Collin, still involved in talking to the thin blonde. She wasn't sure how much more she could take.

"That would be great, actually."

"Come on, sugar," Yvana said. "Let's go."

Collin's phone rang in his pocket. He pulled out the cell and Jenny's name flashed on the screen. He hoped this meant they'd captured Jimmy Reese. "Sorry," he told Amber. "I've got to take this."

Disappointment wrinkled her brow, but he moved away from her, his attention focused on the phone.

"Hello?" he answered, mentally keeping his fingers crossed for good news.

"Collin." Jenny's voice sounded strained, serious. Collin felt his stomach tighten. There'd be no good news today. "Someone matching Jimmy Reese's description was seen at a boat dock on Pine Island. We're pretty sure he's stolen a speedboat. Collin, we think he's headed over to you."

"Do you have any surveillance video?"

"It's grainy, but I can send it to you."

"Do that." Collin scanned the area, looking for Madison. But he didn't see her. Where did she go? Still on his cell phone, Collin moved farther away. He looked left, by the DJ's table, and then right, by the food, but saw no sign of Madison. Steve, the plainclothes officer, stood munching on wedding cake. Collin motioned to him, mouthing "Madison?" Steve began searching the crowd as well.

"When did he take the boat?" Collin felt his attention sharpen as he scanned the room. No sign of Madison. Had she gone to the bathroom? He worked his way over to the women's restroom.

"We think maybe this afternoon."

Collin felt a cold pit of dread form in his stomach. He checked his watch. Night had fallen an hour ago. "That means he could be on the island already," Collin said.

"Yes," Jenny admitted. "I'm sorry, Collin. The officers had been to every dock, but somehow Jimmy got by us. The police chief said he'll be sending a few more officers to North Captiva."

"Tell them they'd better hurry," Collin said.

"I will." Jenny paused. "And, Collin...be careful."

"Always am." Collin clicked off the phone and then knocked on the women's restroom. "Hello? Anyone in there?" No one answered, so he pushed open the door to find it empty. He glanced at the dance floor and the tables again. Madison wasn't here. He felt panic clench his stomach. Collin rushed out to the line of parked golf carts in the gravel lot next to the pool, but saw their golf cart, keys still in it. He pulled out his cell phone and called Madison, but it went straight to voice mail; her phone was out of range. There were a number of different black holes for cell reception on the island.

Collin saw Mark, who was already on the prowl, looking for Madison.

"Any sign of her?" he asked Mark.

"I had eyes on her and then lost her. Thought she was helping Yvana, but now I can't find either of them." The detective frowned. "I tried calling her..."

"No answer?"

"Nope. Straight to voice mail," Mark said.

Even the veteran cop looked worried. Collin didn't like that, not one bit. Collin's phone dinged and Jenny's incoming video arrived. He hit Play and saw a grainy security cam video of a dock bathed in fluorescent light. Then Jimmy came into view. The dark inky neck tattoo was visible in the footage, since he was wearing a black tank top; his arms were filled with equally offensive tattoos—a cloaked KKK member, a rope tied in a noose, some quotes from Hitler in German, and, of course, the Nazi slogan, *blood and soil*. He wore a goatee and his blond hair was smashed down under a trucker's cap.

"Real piece of work," Mark grumbled as he watched the video over Collin's shoulder. The two men exchanged a glance, both knowing that if Jimmy had his way, they'd be dead, for no other reason than the color of their skin.

Collin watched the man creep onto the dock, board one boat and exit it. Then, Reese spied a faster speedboat, a white one with maroon stripes down the side. He looked furtively over his shoulder and climbed aboard. In a few seconds, he had it hot-wired and he backed up the twenty-four-foot speedboat into the darkness, disappearing from the camera's angle.

"We have to find that boat," Collin said. He

rewound the video and froze the frame to give Mark a better look at it.

"There are three docks on the island, not counting the private ones," Mark said. "Could be anywhere if he's here."

Collin jogged to the dock closest to the little marina shop and the clubhouse. Boats were docked up and down the wooden pathway. "It's worth taking a look," he said, and he hurried down the path, walking by several fishing boats. About five boats in, Mark pointed. "There!"

Near the end of the row, they saw a white boat with maroon stripes down the side. Collin ran to the boat, with its interior partly obscured by its canopy. Mark was beside him, gun drawn. Collin did a quick check of the numbers on the side of the boat against the grainy security footage.

"It's the same one," Collin whispered. "I'll go first. Can't be too careful," Mark said, his voice low, and popped ahead of Collin. He climbed onto the boat, his gun with the flashlight attachment illuminating the canopy, showing an empty captain's seat. Mark checked the door leading to the engine, but the vessel was abandoned.

He went to the back of the boat and touched the side of the motor.

"Still warm," he said. "Our guy hasn't been here long."

Fear shot through Collin. "I've got to find Madison."

YVANA PULLED THE golf cart into the little driveway by Collin's rental house, which was dark. Only now, in front of the darkened house, did Madison remember that she was supposed to tell Mark and Steve when she left the wedding party. She hated feeling jealous. She'd been so distracted by the broiling emotion, she'd all but forgotten the looming threat of Jimmy Reese. She took out her cell but got no signal, the phone completely out of bars.

"Can you tell Mark where I am?" Madison asked. "When you get back to the party? I should've told him."

"Sure, sugar," Yvana said, patting her leg. "Want me to stay? Just in case? I've got to head back to the reception at some point, but I could stay with you for a few minutes if you'd like."

Yvana yawned, and Madison realized the manager was as tired as she was, maybe more so, and Yvana still had to finish the wedding.

"No, you have work to do. It's okay. Just tell Mark and Steve, and I'm sure one of them will be here soon. I should be okay for a few minutes." All she could think about was Collin with that pretty blonde in the short dress, anyway. How long before he noticed Madison had left the party? Or would he even notice at all?

"If you're sure." Yvana eyed her once more, like a mother hen worried about her chick. "I'll stay right here until you get inside."

Madison nodded and slid off the seat. She tromped up the long porch steps, then slipped her key into the lock and opened the glass door. She flicked on the interior light, illuminating the den and the porch. She waved to Yvana, who waved back and then ran the golf cart across the sand driveway and back to the road.

Madison felt the sadness of the evening weighing on her. Collin didn't love her, not the way she needed and desired to be loved. She felt exhausted, wanting nothing more than a quick shower and bed. She walked to the bathroom, remembering they'd left Teddy inside during the wedding, but when she got there, the door was slightly ajar, the light on.

"Huh. That's funny." She frowned. Had they forgotten to close the door? "Teddy?" she called, but the bathroom was empty.

"Teddy?" Madison called again, as she searched for the dog through the living room and kitchen, even ducking under the kitchen table. "Teddy!" Where had the dog gone? Usually, he was happy to hear human voices and always ran to the foyer to greet guests. Where was he?

Madison started opening closet doors, worried that he'd somehow gotten himself trapped in one. More importantly, how had he let himself out of the bathroom? She was sure now that she'd closed it, heard the door click behind her. She wouldn't have left with the door ajar.

"Teddy?" Her voice echoed up the empty staircase, the one leading to the bedrooms. She took the wooden stairs one at a time, the boards creaking a little beneath her feet. Suddenly, the house seemed very big and very dark. She took her cell from her pocket, thinking about phoning Collin. But, again, no bars. She couldn't even send a text message.

"Teddy?" she called at the landing of the stairs and waited. Nothing. No answering bark, no scampering of claws against the wooden floor. Strange. She flipped on the light in the master bedroom, but there was no sign of Teddy. One of the patio doors was slightly open, however, and the sheer curtain fluttered in the night breeze. Had Collin left it open for air? But that didn't make sense, since the air-conditioning was on. She walked over to the patio door, worried that Teddy might somehow have gotten out. Madison stepped outside, and saw the wooden railing surrounding the patio, which was big enough for two chairs and a small table, high above the ground. Nearby, she could see the treetops of palm trees, and directly next door, the roof of her uncle's house. The house was dark, save for one light. A bedroom. Her bedroom, or had been. Did Mark leave that on? Or had they come home?

She watched for a few seconds, but saw no movement. They must've left it on. She glanced at the patio railing. The bars were too close together for Teddy to get through. Good thing, since the fall would kill him if he tried.

Behind her, a high-pitched whine pierced the air. She froze, the hairs on her forearms standing straight up. *Teddy*, she thought in recognition. That was Teddy.

"Teddy?" she called again, even more concerned as she stepped back inside the house. She heard another hesitant whine. The closet? She swung open the closet door, and saw Collin's clothes hanging there. No puppy, just shoes lining the carpeted floor. The whine came again, this time from behind her. She knelt down and pushed up the comforter, looking under the bed. Teddy saw her and his tail started to wag a little. He'd somehow wedged himself in the farthest corner, too far for her to reach. His eyes seemed worried, unsure.

"Teddy, come on, boy." The dog whined. "What's wrong, boy? Why are you hiding?"

Nerves bristled in her stomach. Why was he acting so strange? Cowering away from her? She slid one arm beneath the bed, beckoning the dog with her hand. He was out of reach, even if she stretched to her fullest.

"Teddy. Come." The dog inched forward, sniffing at her fingers. He was scared of something. But what?

Outside, she heard the distant rumble of thunder. A storm was coming. Eventually, the dog, wagging his tail, crept toward her. She grabbed the puppy and pulled him out. He licked her face.

"What's wrong with you? Thunder freak you out?"

Another low rumble outside sent the little dog's head into her armpit, as if he was trying to hide.

"Aw, Teddy, you've got nothing to worry about. I promise." She walked the puppy to the window and pulled back the blinds. In the distance, near the rolling waves of the ocean, she saw lightning flash in the darkening sky. More thunder followed. "See? It's just a storm. That's all. But you'd better go outside and do your business before it starts to rain."

She snuggled the puppy's neck, feeling

grateful for *his* love, at least. "I know you won't betray me with a leggy blonde," she told the pup, who just licked her face again. She took him downstairs and brought him outside, clipping on the leash and putting him down. The wind brought by the storm whipped her hair, and she hugged her bare shoulders. Teddy cowered by her ankles.

"Come on, boy. Do your business so we can get inside." She knew the puppy needed to go, and she also knew, if he didn't go now, the second she brought him in, he'd probably have an accident all over the kitchen floor.

Lightning flashed again in the distance. The wind kicked up and the bushes around them rattled as the storm blew in. Tiny wet spots darkened the porch near her feet. The rain had begun. Madison felt exposed again, almost as if someone was out there watching her from the thick brush.

Just my imagination, she thought, as thunder boomed across the sky and nearly made her jump out of her skin.

"Hurry, Teddy. Please." She hugged her arms and glanced at the dark shadows near the edge of the yard. *Nobody's there. It's just my imagination.* Still, she tugged on the dog's leash. "Pee-pee, okay, boy? *Pee-pee.*" She felt ridiculous coaxing the dog, but she wanted inside almost as badly as Teddy did. She glanced once more at the dark bushes. *Just bushes. That's it.*

Teddy anxiously sniffed around on the grass and then went, lifting his nose in the air and whining a bit.

Madison was relieved to see him go. "Good boy," she cried, happy as he finished and they walked back up the stairs to the front door on the second-floor landing. She looked back at the bushes, then ducked inside, bolting the glass door. For a second, she thought she saw a shadow moving in the yard. A shadow the size of a man.

She pressed her hands against the glass and peered out. Lightning flashed, showing an empty yard.

Then Teddy barked. He barked loudly, his attention entirely focused on the outside. Goose bumps rose on her arms. The dog sensed something.

"What is it, boy?" she asked, almost too scared to know.

Teddy glanced up at her and whined, and then, with a laser-like focus he stared out at the dark rain. Lightning struck once more and this time, she thought she saw the outline of a man standing on the lawn.

CHAPTER NINETEEN

WHERE THE HELL was Madison? Collin couldn't find her anywhere. Had she left the party? If she had left, she hadn't taken the cart. Panic surged through him. What if Jimmy Reese had grabbed her right from under their noses? What if she was being held by him, scared and alone, in a house nearby? Thunder rumbled in the distance. Tiny raindrops darkened the white concrete near the pool. Wedding guests began to move under the canopy, and some opted to leave.

Amber stood uncertainly, sipping her wine, waiting for him at the bar. Well, she'd just have to wait. He had to find Madison. If anything had happened to her or the baby...

Collin glanced over and saw the elderly man who'd taken Madison for a spin on the dance floor and asked him if he'd seen her. It took a few times repeating the question, but the man eventually shook his head. Hadn't seen her. Steve and Mark were looking, too, combing the entire area around the reception. Collin had tried calling her phone again, but it still went straight to voice mail. It must have been out of bars or out of battery, but either way, his calls weren't going through.

Amber waved at Collin, but he ignored her. Not to be rude, but because he had other things on his mind. He saw Dave at the other end of the bar, drinking yet another whiskey. "Dave! You seen Madison anywhere?"

"Saw her talking to Yvana a little while ago." Dave glanced up looking around. "Don't see either of them now, though."

Collin had noticed that Yvana was no longer at the wedding, either. He saw one of the groundskeepers tucking away the sound system beneath the awning to make sure none of the equipment got wet. He had a walkie-talkie on his belt. Collin was about to ask if he could use it, to call Yvana, when he saw the manager pulling up in the North Captiva Club golf cart. He trotted over to her.

"Yvana, we think Jimmy's on the island," he said urgently. "Police are coming, but for now, he's on the loose." The wind kicked up and ruffled Yvana's bright scarf. She looked worried as lightning streaked the sky above their heads.

"You serious?"

Collin nodded. "Where's Madison?"

"I just took her to your place."

Collin felt fear jolt his stomach. Madison would be all alone there. He had to hope that Jimmy hadn't figured out the address for her uncle's house. Though, why would he be on the island if he hadn't?

He signaled Mark and Steve, who started to make their way through the crowd.

"You know we're all supposed to be keeping an eye on her," he told Yvana. "Why did you leave her there alone?" Collin was irrationally angry, but Madison was in harm's way and Yvana shouldn't have left her. This was why Collin sometimes felt he was the only one who did things right, thought things through. Who left a pregnant woman alone with a killer on the loose?

Yvana frowned. "Me? Honey, she was upset about you and that blonde. If you hadn't been flirting so hard, she wouldn't have been in such a hurry to get away from you."

Guilt hit him. He should never have been flirting. "I wasn't," he lied.

"You weren't *not* flirting, either. I saw you with your Colgate smile. Made Madison think all this proposing you've been doing is just out of obligation, nothing else."

Collin let out a long sigh. He knew how it must look. He'd have to deal with hurt feelings later; right now, he needed to get to Madison before Jimmy did.

"You find her?" Mark approached, his face grim.

"She went home. Yvana dropped her off. Come on, let's go." Collin hopped into the driver's seat of Yvana's golf cart.

"No, let me drive," Mark said. "I'm faster than you."

Collin knew Mark had taken several evasive and aggressive driving courses as part of being a detective. Loath as he was to hand over the keys, Mark had a point. And this was about Madison's safety. "Fine," he said, giving him the golf cart key. "Get us there."

THUNDER RUMBLED, AND Madison peered out the window into the yard. The figure of the man was nothing more than a tall shrub, now that she got a better look at it. Teddy barked one last time. Madison scooped him into her arms and walked upstairs to the master bedroom. She wanted to forget this day had ever happened. After she tucked Teddy into a bed of towels on the floor of the master bedroom, she closed the door and then ran a shower in the adjacent bathroom. She missed her uncle's big new granite shower. The one in Collin's rental house was clean, at least, with a simple curtain decorated in shells. The blue tile was a bit out of date, but Madison hardly cared. She just wanted to wash the sticky film of Florida off her arms, get into a pair of comfy pajamas—though all she could think about was the thin blonde smiling at Collin and Collin smiling right back.

Madison knew she was overreacting. She knew it likely meant nothing, but seeing him enjoying himself so much in the company of another woman hurt her, jabbed at her like the prick of a needle. She was a fool to think he'd be faithful to her. Why would he? He didn't really love her. Hell, he could probably even use her story to pick *up* women. Was he, at this very moment, telling the pretty blonde what a victim he'd been? *I'm a father by accident. I'm going to marry the mother of my son, but I don't love her.* It sounded like the start of a star-crossed romance novel.

Madison sighed, turned on the shower and let the steam fill the small room. She slipped out of her dress, noticing as she glanced down that her waist had definitely become thicker. She looked at her toes, still visible beyond the tiny baby bulge starting in her lower abdomen. How long would she be able to see her feet before the growing baby eclipsed them entirely? She put a hand on her belly. Was she ready to be a mother? Was Collin ready to be a father? She thought of him again, laughing with the pretty girl at the reception. No. No, he wasn't.

Madison got into the steaming shower and felt tears sting her eyes as the water poured over her. She loved Collin, she realized. Truly loved him. She just wished he felt the same about her. Wished he loved her for *her.* That was what hurt so much. She knew now that she'd want to marry him whether she was pregnant or not; she'd been resisting it, but that was the truth. He didn't feel that way, though. She hated being so vulnerable, so weak, and yet, she couldn't deny her real feelings any longer. She'd been telling herself this all had to do with how *Collin* felt about her, but really, she'd been the one falling in love...

Madison washed her hair, the water calming her, although she still felt a lingering sadness as she rinsed and then stepped out of the shower, reaching for a towel. She wrapped her hair in a coral towel and used an identical one around her body She'd left her body lotion in her cosmetics bag and went to fetch it. She glanced at Teddy's pile of towels as she went— and saw that the puppy wasn't there.

"Teddy?" she called but got no answer. She knelt down to look beneath the bed, but this time she saw no dog. That was when she realized the bedroom door was wide open.

"I thought I closed that," she said aloud, wondering how it had come open. "Teddy?" she called, walking into the hallway. She glanced down and saw one half of a wet, muddy footprint on the landing near the bedroom door. Big. Menacing.

In an instant, she knew exactly who'd made that footprint.

Jimmy Reese.

"Well, Miss Lawyer," she heard somewhere behind her. She knew before she looked behind her that it was Jimmy. She'd have recognized his voice anywhere. "Don't you have some mighty fine legs? Why don't you give me a little show?"

She slowly turned in time to see the white supremacist grin. He held a pistol aimed at her chest. "We're gonna go for a ride, sweetheart."

His eyes flicked down at her towel.

"Jimmy. Please." She hoped beyond hope that somehow he'd see reason. That he'd understand whatever he'd planned wouldn't end well.

"Oh, there'll be plenty of time for you to beg, but right now, we got places to be."

"WE NEED TO go faster," Collin shouted into the wind as he hung onto the passenger seat.

Mark drove the golf cart like a bat out of hell. Collin hated that he wasn't the one driving— not being in control made him crazy, and yet, he had to admit that Mark's skills behind the wheel, even when it came to a golf cart, were superior to his.

"This is as fast as the damn thing goes," Mark yelled back as he wound their way down the narrow sandy path. Collin sat next to him in the front, and Steve sat behind them, fac- ing backward, as they tooled down the road on the fifteen-minute drive to his house. He didn't want to think about what might hap- pen if they didn't make it in time, if somehow Jimmy Reese got there first.

Rain began to fall through the open wind- shield and windows of the golf cart, as Collin mentally beat himself up for getting side- tracked by a pretty girl at the wedding recep- tion. He knew it'd been a stupid choice, letting himself get distracted, enjoying a simple mo- ment with a beautiful girl. He might be almost engaged and a dad—but he wasn't dead. And yet, he knew he'd messed up.

He sighed. He made mistakes as much as anyone else, no matter how hard he tried to be flawless. Yvana had been right; he only had himself to blame. If anything happened to Madison because he'd flirted with another woman, he'd never be able to forgive himself. But right now, he had to find her. There'd be time enough later to worry about feelings. Now, it was about making sure she was safe.

They pulled into the driveway of Uncle Rashad's house. "Madison's next door," Collin said over the wind and rain.

"But our perp is probably here." Mark turned to him. "Stay here," he shouted.

"Like hell I will!" Nobody was going to make him stay behind when Madison's safety was at stake.

"*Stay.* That's an order, prosecutor." Mark drew his gun and went. He and Steve trotted up the steps of Uncle Rashad's house. Collin, not caring about the consequences, bolted across the small path that connected the two homes. He took the steps to his rental house two at a time, his heart pounding, his stomach weak.

Just let her be okay, he prayed to anybody who might be listening. *I was a jerk, and I have to be able to make it up to her. Do not let tonight be the last time I see her.*

The door was ajar when he got there, and his heart dropped to the floor. "Maddie!" he called into the dimly lit foyer. "Maddie!"

She wasn't in the kitchen. Or the bedroom. He trotted into the bathroom, where the mirror was still covered in a fog of steam and the air was humid and smelled like shampoo. She'd taken a shower. She'd *just* been here. But where was she now?

"Maddie!" he called again, running out of the bedroom. He nearly slipped on a wet patch near the stairs and that was when he saw the mud. A man's footsteps, wet from the wet earth outside. Footsteps that weren't his own.

His stomach shrank with fear, with the horrible knowledge that Jimmy had been in this house.

"Maddie!" he cried, his voice more anguished as he started to realize he was too late. Madison wasn't here. She wasn't here because Jimmy had taken her. There was no sign of Teddy, either. What had happened to the dog?

He heard Mark shove open the front door and he glanced down at the foyer landing. The detective glared up at him. "I told you to *wait*."

"Madison's not here. The dog's not here, either. I think—"

His phone dinged with an incoming message. He saw that it was from Madison. *Thank God*, he thought. Maybe he was wrong. Maybe she was safe after all. But then he pulled up the message. It was a photo. Of her. She had silver duct tape across her mouth and her hands were wrapped in duct tape on her lap. She didn't have clothes on, wearing only a single bath towel, her wet hair falling into her face, terror in her dark eyes.

"No," Collin murmured, feeling fear, greasy and oily, spill into his belly.

"What is it?" Mark yelled up at him.

"Reese has her. He has Madison." Collin's world crumbled in that instant. The woman he loved, the mother of his child, was being held by one of the county's most dangerous escaped convicts, a man who wanted them both dead.

CHAPTER TWENTY

DON'T PANIC. MADISON kept repeating those two words in her head as she watched Jimmy Reese chain the backdoor of the small abandoned lighthouse near the beach. No one had been there for years, and one of the other property owners had long suggested turning the stone lighthouse into a museum. Distantly, Madison saw the moon rising over the water and knew they were close to the vet's house. If she managed to escape, she might even make it there or to the small fire station for help. The lighthouse was hot, without any air-conditioning, and sweat dripped into her eyes. But she was alive, and that was something. He hadn't killed her—yet.

But he was locking them both inside, causing her mind to bounce to all the other worst-case scenarios she could think of—would he hurt her? Rape her? The bulky man with the swastika on his neck was capable of anything. He had her phone tucked in his back pocket.

She'd been nearly blinded when he'd taken the photo of her.

"I'm sending it to your boyfriend," he'd told her, a leer on his face. She hadn't been able to answer, with the tape covering her mouth. She concentrated on breathing through her nose. *Stay calm. Breathe. You're still alive and that's something*, she repeated to herself.

She squeezed her arms together, trying to keep the towel across her chest up. Every so often it loosened, and she worried she'd be sitting on this folding chair naked in front of a man who'd no doubt enjoy her humiliation. She'd lost the towel on her head during the golf cart ride over and he hadn't allowed her time to grab any clothes. She suspected that he liked her vulnerable, exposed. It amused him.

"You feeling drafty, girl?" His eyes lingered on the edge of the towel slipping down her chest. "You can wear this." He offered her an oversized black T-shirt with the photo of a heavy metal band on it, holding it out as if it were a great prize. "Only I want to see you change."

She'd rather die in the towel, she thought. He leered and she looked away, glancing around the small room of the lighthouse, the rusted-out controls. The moonlight streamed in through the big windows, the storm having blown through relatively fast. Now, the sky was once again clear. She watched as Jimmy laid out his sleeping bag. She wondered if she'd spend the night sitting up, hands bound. He'd tied her ankles with bandanas, one attached to each chair leg, though she noticed one knot was looser than it ought to be. She started working her ankle a bit, trying to make it looser. He dug around in his pack and pulled out a stick of beef jerky. He opened it and took a big bite, sitting down to consider her.

"You want some?" he said, but then he laughed, because of course she had tape on her mouth. She couldn't eat if she wanted to. He took another bite. Her stomach grumbled, loudly enough for them both to hear. He ignored it. He was busy reading the messages on her phone, especially the ones to and from Collin.

"Were you two going at it before or *after* my case?" he asked, glaring at her.

She just shook her head. What was she going to do? She couldn't answer him. *Breathe in. Breathe out.* She was starting to feel panic in her throat, as if she might not be able to get enough oxygen. She thought about the baby growing in her belly. That baby needed air and needed her to be calm. Freaking out wasn't going to help either one of them.

He read more of their messages, as Madison tried to remember what she'd written him. Had there been anything about the baby? She didn't think so. God, she hoped not. If Jimmy knew she was pregnant with Collin's baby, he'd make her suffer even more.

Jimmy muttered expletives under his breath, nasty ones about her, about Collin, about the color of their skin. Madison could feel the hate rolling off him, and when he looked at her, blue eyes flat and cold, she knew he saw someone who was less than him. Less than human. The tips of her fingers tingled a little, almost numb. She wondered how long he planned to keep her like this. Inwardly, she kicked herself for storming off in a jealous rage, for not waiting until Steve or Mark could take her home. She hadn't been thinking straight after she'd seen Collin with that pretty blonde. Now that mistake might cost her her life.

"You bitch," Jimmy growled, throwing her phone on top of his sleeping bag. He stared at her with those dead eyes. She couldn't help it; fear welled up in her again. She was scared of him, as scared as she'd ever been in her life, and it wasn't just because of what he could do to *her*, but because of what he might do to the unborn baby inside her. "You work with that prick? You both work together to put me away?"

Vigorously, Madison shook her head, her still-wet hair clinging to her temples. Granted, she'd wanted him to go to jail, but she'd shown up in court every day and done her job. She hadn't been happy about it, but she'd still done it.

"You never liked me anyhow, did you?" Madison stayed very still, studying him. He was wearing a cutoff T-shirt, the brand of some southern beer on the front. The swastika was visible on his neck, as was the KKK's grand wizard on his left shoulder. *Who did that to themselves? Made their bodies temples to hate?*

"You like my ink?" Jimmy noticed her gaze and moved his arm so the glow of the phone could give her a better view. "You wanna see it up close?"

He moved his chair toward her and Madison worked on not flinching. Jimmy lifted his arm so it was nearly in front of her face, and she focused on steadying her heart, worried he'd take the opportunity to hit her, to hurt her somehow. She couldn't even talk to him, couldn't even try to reason with him, although she knew that reasoning with him would be a waste of time. Hate like that couldn't be reasoned away. Hate like that was ingrained, beaten in, never questioned.

"You like that?" He flexed his arm. "If I take that tape off, you gonna kiss it?"

Madison squeezed her eyes shut. She wished she was anywhere but here.

Jimmy came even closer, grabbing a corner of the tape and yanking hard. It came off in a rush of pain, but she managed not to yelp. Her leg kicked out, and she realized she'd loosened the bandana even more.

"There we go. There's that pretty mouth." He grinned lazily, the smile not reaching his eyes. "Gonna make that mouth scream before this is all said and done." His smile grew bigger, and he showed his crooked yellow teeth.

Jimmy pulled a knife from his back pocket and fear constricted Madison's lungs, pushing all the air out. Afraid to breathe in, she watched him cut a chunk off the end of his beef stick and pop it in his mouth. Then, he leaned forward. She pressed her knees together, and prayed her towel stayed up. He soaked in her nearly naked state, then took the edge of his knife and ran it along her bare inner thigh, leaving a tiny white scratch. She winced and he laughed, a belly laugh. He liked seeing her fear.

"You got nice legs," he said. "Too bad you spread 'em for that piece of shit." He meant

Collin. "Can't go have sloppy seconds after that prick."

Madison felt a small measure of relief. Maybe he'd spare her that. The idea of such an awful man, such a disgusting man, on her... It made her stomach roil, made her want to retch.

He chewed on some more dried beef, considering. "Still...maybe what you really need is to be fucked right. By a real man. Maybe I could breed some of that brown out of the world." He grinned once more and she felt the panic come back. She needed to get him off this train of thought. Something. Anything else.

"Why did you let me represent you?" It was a question she'd asked herself a dozen times. Yes, she'd been appointed counsel, but he could've fired her. Could've asked for a new counsel from the judge and hoped for a white man. Or he could've represented himself. The judge had made it clear to him in the courtroom that he had options. He'd taken none of them.

He shrugged. "One lawyer is the same as all the rest. Bottom feeders, the lot of you." He glared at her, hate in his eyes. *At least he's not talking about me anymore.* But the look he was giving her was dangerous. "And, hey, I'm no dummy. The jury sees you, a brown girl, representing me, well, maybe that helps 'em see past this." He gestured to the swastika on his neck. "Besides, I made you dance, little monkey. You had to dance for your master. Something I liked to make you do."

"But you believe a white person...would have represented you better...than me, right? You think white people are smarter."

"Yes," he said. "That's just genetics. We're the better race. You're just...well, a terrorist."

"I'm half-Indian. And I'm not a terrorist." She was tired of explaining this to him, and she also knew it would do no good. A person like him didn't care about facts, only hate.

He narrowed his eyes. "You still deserve to die. You fucked me over. You and that prick of a prosecutor. You aren't gonna get away with it. Hurting me. Hurting white folks."

"*What* white folks?"

"All the ones you put in jail." Now, Madison wasn't even following his logic, such as it was. He swallowed another bite of jerky. "I'm here to protect white people from people like you. I'm here to make you dance one more time."

She felt a shiver of fear dive down her back.

On some level, Madison knew his white supremacy stuff was just a cover. At heart, Jimmy Reese was a sociopath, a violent, remorseless thug, who used neo-Nazism as a cover to do bad things to people. She remembered his indifference in the courtroom, not caring one whit that he'd killed a little girl, a white girl at that. He'd been there to kill a black man, but missed. Still, he didn't show any remorse about the fact that he'd killed an innocent child.

"You feel bad about Monica?" Madison asked. *Keep him talking.*

"Who?"

"The twelve-year-old you shot and killed. At the grocery store. The one you're supposed to be serving time for."

Jimmy shrugged and looked away. "Just bad luck is all."

"No, she didn't die because of bad luck, she died because you killed her. She was white. Her family was white. You killed the very person you said you were trying to protect. Who was *her* champion?"

"The Lord works in mysterious ways."

"The Lord has nothing to do with what you've done, what you're trying to do."

Jimmy frowned, knife in mid-air. "You better watch your mouth."

Jimmy Reese was pure evil. She needed to remember that. She fell silent, wondering what she could possibly do next. Her hands were falling asleep. She doubted he'd help her or show her mercy.

Distantly, she heard a bark. A dog's bark. Teddy!

Jimmy froze. "What was that?" He got up and peered out the window. Somehow, Teddy had followed them, despite the golf cart ride.

"I don't hear anything," Madison lied.

Then came another bark, still distant but definitely a bark. At least it drew Jimmy's attention away from her. "I hate dogs," he said, and she noticed fear in his voice. Was he afraid of them? Maybe she could use that somehow.

"You're right, there's a dog," she said. "Sounds like a big one," she fibbed.

Jimmy frowned. Then he glared at her. "I'm gonna go take a look."

He sheathed his knife and then picked up his pistol. Madison felt panic. "No need to do that. Probably some resident's dog."

He studied her. "I told you. I'm gonna go see." He undid the chains on the door. She heard him clomp down the circular stone staircase. She squeezed her eyes shut. *Please don't let him hurt my dog.*

After he left, she reached down and undid the loose knot on her left leg, and then worked quickly to undo the second. In seconds, she was free and she stood and listened. She didn't hear him. She studied the duct tape binding her hands. She remembered a woman in an abduction case some time ago. She'd been a former FBI agent, and she'd had some trick about freeing herself from duct tape. What was it?

Then she remembered. Hold her hands over her head. Thrust them downward and away. She lifted her hands, and her towel fell off. She inwardly cursed but then focused again. *Gotta get out of this tape.* She thought about Jimmy, about what he'd do if he came back, and in a panic, raised her hands and threw them down, hard. To her amazement, the duct tape split in two.

She was free. She couldn't believe it!

She grabbed the black T-shirt on the sleeping bag and threw it over her head. Madison had no shoes, but that didn't matter. Couldn't matter. There was only one way out of the lighthouse, and chances were good that Jimmy was on those very stairs. She looked around, searching for a weapon. There was nothing but the beef jerky, a sleeping bag, a backpack and her towel. She grabbed the towel and slid the door open, listening. Jimmy's footsteps were nearly at the bottom now. She heard him shout, "Git, dog!"

Then she heard a loud yip—Teddy!

Slowly, quietly, she stepped on the staircase and said a little prayer.

CHAPTER TWENTY-ONE

TWO HELICOPTERS FULL of backup police units arrived within the hour, and Mark gathered them at Collin's house to form a plan. They were going to scour the island for signs of Madison. Time was of the essence, because the longer she was with Jimmy Reese, the worse it would get. Collin's nerves tingled from the adrenaline, and he felt jittery and anxious, couldn't stay still. He had to find Madison. He had to make this right. He hated feeling this much out of control. The image of Madison, fearful, her mouth and hands duct-taped, wearing nothing but a towel, made him want to strangle the life out of Jimmy Reese. The man didn't deserve to live if he so much as touched a hair on her head.

"I've got a map here of all the empty houses on the island," Mark said. "I've scanned it and sent it to all of you, so we all have it. Yvana marked all the homes with renters and without." Yvana stood in a corner of the room, looking sad and solemn. The news that Madison had gone missing had hit her almost as hard as it had Collin.

"We think he'd likely go for an empty house or even some thick brush near the beach, some secluded area, like here." Mark pointed to the north side. He glanced at his men, a dozen of them now. "You've got your partners and your sectors of the map to cover. I don't think I need to remind you all that Reese is armed and dangerous. Be careful out there, but let's bring Madison Reddy back home safe."

The officers dispersed, heading out of the home and jumping into waiting golf carts, speeding off to various corners of the island. Collin, eager to join them, followed Mark outside.

"What can I do?" he asked Mark, who wore his badge for everyone to see, as well as a shoulder harness.

"Listen, this is a police matter now. Leave it to us." Mark and Steve got into an off-road golf cart with oversized wheels. "If you're with us, you're a liability, counselor. I know this is hard for you, but keep your phone charged and stay in touch. She—or Jimmy—might try to contact you."

Mark handed him a walkie-talkie. "We're on channel five, okay?"

"But I can help. I know this island. I can…"
Collin couldn't just sit and wait.

"It's safer if you don't, counselor." Mark
looked at him with pity, clearly understanding his need to find Madison. Collin watched
the officers speed away, feeling frustration rising within him.

He glanced at Yvana. "Want me to make
you some coffee?" she asked. "It's gonna be
a long night."

Collin nodded, and the two of them went
back to his rental house. They were barely inside when he heard a telltale scratching coming
from outside. He went over to the patio door
and saw Teddy there, carrying something in
his mouth. The puppy! He was all right!

"Teddy!" he cried, feeling overcome with
emotion. "What do you have there?" He pulled
the small coral colored scrap of fabric from the
dog's mouth. He showed it to Yvana. "This is
from one of our towels, at this house. I'd know
that palm tree design. It's the one Maddie was
wearing in the photo! I know it."

Yvana's eyes grew wide. "Why would he
have it?"

"I don't know. Maybe he followed her, or
maybe Jimmy took the dog when he took Madison?"

Collin knelt and scratched the dog behind

the ears. The puppy leaned into him. "I wish you could talk, boy. I wish you could tell us what happened."

The dog gazed up at him, brown eyes wide. He whined plaintively.

"Maybe he can," Yvana said. She bent down to examine the puppy's large paws. "He's got mud and sand here. But look…" She grabbed one paw and pointed to the small red pebbles caught between his toes. "That's gravel from the airstrip. He's been over by the airfield."

"Anything abandoned out there?" Collin asked.

"No. I don't think so." Yvana thought a minute. Collin remembered the photo Reese had sent him. Could be some clue in it, something Yvana might recognize. He pulled his phone from his pocket.

"Have you ever seen this place?"

Yvana gasped. "Oh, Lord." She shook her head and clutched at his phone. "Poor Maddie."

"Look at the background, though. Anything there? Anything you recognize? Anything that could be near the airstrip?"

Yvana studied the photo. Granted, Collin could see there was precious little to go on. An old wooden chair that Madison sat on, and the background was pretty much dark except for the corner of something behind her. A metal table? It was hard to make out.

"Wait. That chair." She frowned at it. "I know that chair."

She snapped her fingers. "The lighthouse!" she said. "That's the chair up in the lighthouse. I know because the man who owns it made a big deal about trying to get it down. It's some antique or other, and he was worried someone might take it if they knew it was valuable."

For the first time, Collin felt hope, and he wanted to hug Yvana. "You might just have saved Madison's life."

He thought about jumping into a golf cart and heading over there himself, but then he realized he'd need help. Madison was right when she'd called him a control freak, but this time, he understood that he couldn't do this alone. He grabbed the walkie-talkie. "Mark?" he said into the static. "I think I know where he took her."

MADISON GOT TO the bottom of the concrete stairs, heart pounding. Jimmy could be anywhere, and he probably hadn't moved far from the lighthouse. She glanced out the cracked door but couldn't see much. Where was he? Could be on the other side of the metal door for all she knew, ready to pounce. *He doesn't know I'm here.* She tried to calm herself, keep herself alert and ready. *What's my plan? What do I do?* Madison had no idea. She glanced out again and could see a long stretch of rocky beach and then on the other side, overgrown brush. *Do I run for the beach? For the sea-grass? Do I sneak out or full-on sprint?* Her knees wobbled. She felt paralyzed by indecision but knew she was running out of time. She opened the door slowly with the tips of her fingers, so she could have a wider view. No sign of Jimmy. But he could be anywhere, waiting, lurking, ready to grab her.

She took a deep breath. *I've got to try. For the baby.* She listened carefully. All she heard were the waves rolling in from the ocean. Her feet felt like lead. *Got to try.* Once she was moving, though, she found herself running. She sprinted from the doorway, her breathing already ragged, heading for the seagrass and, she hoped, the fire station beyond. The seagrass hit her shins and thighs, slowing her down. Her bare feet sank into the sandy soil.

"Stop, bitch!" she heard behind her—Jimmy, coming around the side of the lighthouse.

Run, she told herself. *Run and don't stop running.*

She heard his big footsteps coming after her,

crashing through the seagrass. He was close, so close. But she was going to make it, she told herself. She could see the roof of the fire station ahead. All she had to do was get there. She could hear golf carts on the path, too. She saw the flash of their headlights.

"Help!" she shouted. "Here!"

The words were barely out of her mouth when she felt something strong reach out and grab her, and then suddenly she was on the ground. Big hands on her. "I told you to stop, *bitch*," Jimmy spat, coming to rest on top of her. Madison screamed as loudly as she could, hoping the nearby golf carts heard her.

That was when Jimmy reared back and slapped her. The force of his blow stunned her, and the metallic taste of blood flooded her mouth. He yanked her roughly to her feet. She was doomed. He'd drag her back to the lighthouse. Finish what he'd started. She could feel the hate radiating from him, knew he planned to do horrible things to her. He pulled her up by the arm so hard she let out a squeal of pain.

"Stop right there!" called a voice. She knew that voice. *Collin?*

She turned to see a bright light shining on them. Jimmy whipped out his gun and pressed the barrel against her temple, the cold metal making her flinch. She froze, her heart hammering in her chest, afraid to move or even speak.

"You're surrounded, Jimmy." This came from Mark, as another flashlight appeared on their left. "There's nowhere to go."

Jimmy slowly moved her in front of him, making sure she stood between the flashlights and him. Madison knew that behind those lights were guns. She saw other lights approach as well, although she couldn't see the faces beyond.

"I never had any place to go but jail," Jimmy said. "I'm still gonna get what I came for."

Madison felt his grip tighten on her arm. Hopelessness rose up in her. He doesn't care if the police shoot him, she realized suddenly. He just wants revenge, and he doesn't care if he dies getting it. She thought of the baby inside her. A flashlight wavered and Collin put it down. She saw his face in the moonlight.

"Jimmy. It's not her you want. It's me."

"Collin!" Madison called, fear choking her voice. She didn't want him to do what he was doing. He was putting himself in harm's way, and giving Reese the opportunity to kill them both.

Jimmy's grip on her arm lessened slightly. "No, I want her dead."

"Sure, but she's not the one who put you away. She's not the one who convinced a jury to *hate* you. I did that, Jimmy. That's all me."

Collin raised his hands to show he had nothing in them. Madison felt Jimmy's attention focus with laser-like precision on the prosecutor. "Madison's a good attorney, but I'm much, much better. But then, you're just a dumb piece of shit, and you probably don't know that."

Jimmy's grip on her arm tightened again. He didn't like being insulted. What was Collin doing?

"You didn't even see how you were played," Collin skillfully boasted.

Jimmy scoffed. "How?"

"I wanted your case, wanted to make an example of you. And you did exactly what I wanted you to do, needed to. Not testifying, letting me twist the jurors' thoughts about you."

"Maybe I'll kill her, then you." Jimmy pulled Madison closer to his chest. She tried not to whimper. Her fear took over, and she felt blinded by it, paralyzed.

"You only get one shot, Jimmy. You only get to hit one of us before they hit you." Collin gestured to the police officers nearby.

"Lay down your weapon, Jimmy," Mark called. "Lay it down now and nobody gets hurt."

What the hell was Collin doing? He was asking this maniac to shoot him. Madison didn't know what she felt more—anger at his recklessness or touched that he was trying to save her by throwing himself in front of Jimmy's loaded gun.

Mark and Collin exchanged glances and that's when it dawned on Madison that this was a plan. Have Collin distract Jimmy and Mark move in.

She needed to get away from Jimmy—she knew that much. She needed to give the officers a clean shot.

"You're pathetic, Jimmy," Collin went on. "You think you're tough, but you're just a dumb hick, nothing but a no-good piece of white trash. I could've put you away with my eyes closed. Hell, I slept through half that trial."

"You better watch your mouth!"

"Or what? You scared piece of—"

Jimmy moved then. He whisked the barrel away from her temple and pointed it outward. Now was her chance. She flung her head back with all her might and it connected with Jimmy's nose. He let her go and Madison dropped to her knees. He pulled the trigger and a gunshot rang out. Madison saw Collin fall.

"No!" she screamed as all the officers fired straight at Jimmy in a blur of gunfire lighting up the dark island night. Jimmy fell to the ground behind her with a hard thump as the officers advanced, flashlights bobbing, guns drawn. Behind her, she heard Jimmy's raspy bubbly breathing; he'd been hit several times in the chest. Madison didn't care; she crawled away, then leaped to her feet, rushing to Collin's side.

He lay on the ground, groaning and holding one shoulder.

"Help! He needs help!" Madison shouted, even as the officers handcuffed a dying Jimmy.

"I'm fine," Collin groaned as he sat up.

"You're shot!"

"Grazed," he said, looking at his bloodied shoulder. "I don't think the bullet went in."

Madison flung her arms around his neck. "Ow…" he muttered. "But…ow, it still hurts, though." She laughed a little and released him.

"You scared me to death," she said. "You were *daring* that maniac to shoot you."

"Better me than you." Collin's eyes grew serious in that moment, and she felt love well up in her. He caressed her cheek. "*Now* do you believe that I love you? I love you, Madison Reddy. I want you to be my wife." Collin took a big breath. "But I also respect that may not be what you want."

Madison looked at him, surprised. "Since

when does the control freak relinquish control? I thought it was just what *you* wanted that mattered."

"No." Collin shook his head. "I want to marry you, and I want you to live in Miami with me. But like you said, that's just what *I* want. I really do love you, Madison. I want you to be happy, so if you'd rather be unmarried in Fort Myers, that's where I'll stay, too."

Madison couldn't believe what she was hearing. "You'd give up your prosecutor's job in Miami?"

"I'd give up my life for you." Collin smiled weakly. "I think I almost did."

"Are you sure? You're not just doing this because you're supposed to."

"I was willing to *die* for you, Madison. What other proof do you need?" His lips rose up in a wry smile. "I love you. I want to be with you and only you. And—" he cleared his throat "—you owe me." He nodded at his shoulder.

"You're going to keep reminding me of that, aren't you?"

"Oh, yeah, for the rest of our days." Collin laughed and Madison did, too.

She flung her arms around him. "I love you, Collin."

"I just want to be with you, wherever that is."

At that moment, Madison knew that he

wanted to marry her for all the right reasons, not the wrong ones.

"I want to marry you," she whispered.

Hope and excitement lit his face. "You do?" He frowned a little. "You're not just saying that because I got shot, are you? Is this a pity proposal?" His eyes sparkled with playfulness.

"Hmm. Maybe it is."

Collin pretended to consider the consequences. "Oh, well. I'll take it. A pity proposal is better than no proposal."

"Shut up, counselor," she said and leaned down to kiss him. He kissed her back as she heard Mark calling for a medivac helicopter. "Wait. I'll say yes on one condition."

"Which is?"

"After you're better, after the hospital, I want to adopt Teddy."

Collin grinned. "I insist on it. That's one fine dog."

CHAPTER TWENTY-TWO

Seven months later

MADISON SAT ON their new couch in their tidy beachfront condo in Miami. Outside, the sun had just set, splashing color across the clouds on the horizon, and she felt enormous as she rested her small bowl of ice cream on the huge mound of her stomach.

Collin slid in next to her, grabbing the remote and clicking on the news.

"Oh, here it is." Collin turned up the volume on the local news as a picture of him in his dashing new suit appeared during a press conference. He'd put away a group of thugs who'd threatened to bomb a mosque. "I think I look fat."

"*You* look fat? Seriously?" She fed him a spoonful of ice cream and he happily took it.

"Yes. I've gained weight, but when is *my* baby due?" He patted his own nearly flat stomach. He might have gained three or four pounds, but she felt like a house.

Teddy, now almost fully grown, whined at her feet. He sat at sharp attention, watching every bite she took. He lifted a paw and she nearly let him lick the spoon, but decided against it. The dog—all seventy pounds of him—took up enough space in their three-bedroom condo.

"Okay, Teddy. Stop the begging." Collin rubbed the shaggy dog behind his floppy ears. "That ice cream is *mine*, anyhow." He took another spoonful of ice cream, the final one, and sighed. Madison dropped the spoon into the empty bowl and her wedding band sparkled on her left hand. They'd had a small courthouse ceremony three months ago and Dave had actually officiated, and toasted them with strong drinks afterward at the bar where their relationship began. Now, she was officially Madison Reddy-Baptista. The honeymoon, however, would have to wait until after the baby was born.

Pain shot through Madison's side. "Ow," she said, holding her waist, nonexistent as it was.

"What's wrong?" Immediately, Collin snapped to attention. "Is it another contraction?" He grabbed the spiral notebook he'd been using to log her pains. They'd started before dinner, but the doctor had said there was likely no rush in getting to the hospital, not for a first baby and not until the contractions came at closer intervals. They'd begun at a half hour apart, but now, as he glanced at his watch, he realized they were coming less than ten minutes apart.

He held up the notepad. "I'm going to call Dr. Goodwin." Collin whipped out his phone and dialed. He told her the latest news. "All right. Yes, we'll be there."

He hung up and squeezed her hand. "She said we should go now." He picked up the overnight bag they had ready to go as Madison put her now-empty ice cream bowl on the coffee table. He helped her up, a task that had become increasingly harder in the last few months.

"I love you," he said. "With all my heart." He squeezed her hand again as another contraction took hold and she sucked in a breath.

A few minutes later, they were both out of the apartment and at Collin's car, parked in his underground parking spot.

She went still and froze, hand on the door, as a contraction gripped her.

"Are you okay?" Collin asked, wrapping his arm around her. His face was wrinkled with worry as he watched her, his eyes concerned.

"No, I'm not okay," she sputtered, the pain making her grumpy. "I'm having a baby!"

"Well, I know, but..." Collin looked flustered, and Madison had to admit that seeing the normally cocky prosecutor so off-balance felt kind of...good. Things were completely out of his control with the delivery of this baby. This would be the ultimate test of whether or not he could really change, although even she had to admit he'd been much better lately. He'd let her choose their new home, where they were going to live together. He'd let her pick the ring she wanted to wear, taking back the one he'd bought. He'd even agreed to let Teddy sleep on their living room couch.

"I'm sorry," she muttered now, realizing that he was trying hard. "Pain makes me say things I don't mean."

"Either that, or it makes you very, very honest." Collin helped her into the front seat and shut the door. Then he scurried over to the driver's side, got in, started the car—and cursed. "Your overnight bag!" he cried and hopped out of the car again. He'd left it sitting on the kitchen floor. He darted back to the elevator.

Madison shook her head. Collin was a nervous wreck, and *she* was the one having the baby. She tried to remember the calming breaths she'd learned in Lamaze class, but none of them seemed to work right now. She rubbed her enormous belly as Collin ran back to the car, red-faced. He turned the engine, threw the car in reverse and screeched out of the garage.

"We have plenty of time," she cautioned.

"I just want to get you there," he said, voice strained.

"Then let's get there in one piece."

Collin smiled at her and reached over to grab her hand.

"What about Teddy?" Madison asked, suddenly worried.

"I texted the neighbors, so they can let him out and feed him first thing in the morning." They'd left Teddy sitting by the back door, nose pressed against the glass.

"They've been on call for weeks, so I hope they're ready to take on Teddy," Collin said as he hit the gas as they headed for Miami Hospital. It was only a ten-minute drive, and then they were parked and entering the main reception area. A fountain splashed in the lobby and gentle piano music hit their ears as they reached the maternity ward. The contractions were sharp and coming closer together now. Madison had to stop at various points and hold on to Collin's arm, the pain making it too hard to walk down the wide tiled hallway.

"I need a wheelchair, please," Collin asked the admitting nurse, who rustled one up. Madison sank into it gratefully, trying to calm her nerves. Granted, she'd never had a baby before. *But it can't be as bad as being kidnapped by Jimmy Reese.* The killer had died on the way to the hospital, pronounced dead shortly after he arrived. Madison hadn't been sorry. Even though the man's cold blue eyes still haunted her dreams, she was glad such hate was gone from the world.

"Boy or girl? Do we know?" The check-in nurse wheeled Madison toward her delivery room. Collin followed, carrying the overnight bag and an armful of paperwork, looking more nervous than she felt.

"Boy," Collin said with confidence.

"He claims to be psychic," Madison joked. "We told the doctors not to tell us, but he still thinks he knows."

"Is that right?" The nurse seemed skeptical as she wheeled Madison into her room. "Go ahead and get changed into that hospital gown on the bed, and let me know if you need anything, Mrs. Reddy-Baptista. Just ring that bell," she added, pointing to the red button near the hospital bed. "The doctor will be in shortly."

Collin helped Madison stand and slip out of her clothes. She felt awkward with her enormous belly, but Collin bent down to kiss it. "I love you, and I love this baby, and I want you to know how wonderful I think you are."

He tied the loose strands of the gown and embraced her. She hugged him back. She was so grateful he was here with her, so glad she didn't have to do this on her own. In the last few months, they'd grown so much as a couple. She'd moved to Miami for his job, but only after her uncle reassured her that she could still work for his firm, and that he'd been thinking about expanding to Miami, anyway. The stars were aligning for them, and Madison felt it was all meant to be. Watching Collin in the prenatal classes, especially the class where he learned how to change diapers, showed her how far he'd come. Fatherhood was humbling him, and he was learning how to let go, little by little.

Dr. Goodwin came in, her honey-colored hair up in a tidy ponytail, as she bustled around and examined Madison. "You're about five centimeters, so we're getting there," she said. Madison couldn't help feeling disappointed. She'd thought, with all the contractions, they'd have been further along. She'd been in labor for hours already. It felt as if they'd waited until the last possible minute to head to the hospital.

Collin caressed her hand. "I'm here. I'm not going anywhere." He took off his sweatshirt, and the hospital room light shone on the small scar on his upper arm near his T-shirt sleeve. The bullet wound had healed completely, with no real damage.

"I love you," Madison said, as another contraction overtook her.

"Let's see how you feel in a few hours," Collin joked, gently rubbing her wrist. "You do think *I* should name the baby, right?"

"No, I *never* agreed to that." It had been the one sticking point. Collin seemed to cling to this idea that the father got to pick the name. "You're giving the baby the last name, so technically, I ought to give him or her a first name."

"*Him.* And that's the father's job."

Madison felt the ripple of another contraction as it pulled at the muscles around her stomach and in her lower back.

"Mother's," Madison managed. "I'm the one delivering this baby."

"How about we flip a coin?"

Madison frowned, the pain overtaking her again. "How about you leave this room before I hurt you?"

Collin chuckled. "Do they have shots of tequila at the nurse's station? If they don't, they should."

SIX HOURS PASSED, and Collin was a nervous wreck. He hated seeing Madison in so much pain and hated feeling so helpless, but there was nothing he could do. He sat by her, he put a cold compress on her forehead, and he fed her an endless supply of ice chips. When it was finally time to push, the nurses and doctor came in, and Collin felt his heart sink down into his stomach. This was it. He prayed that Madison and the baby would be safe. He'd been staring at the monitors for both of them the entire time, panicking when they seemed to drop at all.

The nurses assured him repeatedly that both monitors were in the normal range. Collin sat and prayed and tried very hard not to stew in helplessness. Madison worked on pushing, and all he wanted was to do the work for her. But all he could do was be a cheerleader on the sidelines. But then she grasped his hand hard and he squeezed back.

"I'm here, Maddie. I'm right here."

She sent him a grateful smile between contractions.

"Okay, Madison. Get ready," the doctor instructed. "One last big push." Dr. Goodwin crouched at her feet, sitting on a rolling stool, ready to catch the baby. Madison, sweaty and red-faced, had already been pushing for an hour and a half. Despite the birthing classes, Collin hadn't really believed deliveries could take so long. On TV, they always happened in taxi cabs or in the blink of an eye. Madison was worn out, exhausted. This baby needed to hurry up.

"Ready? Now," the doctor coaxed.

Madison shouted as she pushed and then, miraculously, a baby arrived, wrinkled and tiny with a thatch of dark hair.

The nurses cleaned the baby as Collin craned his neck to see. A boy. They had a baby boy!

"Congratulations, Collin and Madison! It's a boy," the doctor said.

Madison, exhausted, met Collin's gaze. He had the good sense *not* to say, "I told you so."

The doctor put the baby on Madison's chest, and she began to cry tears of pure joy. Collin looked at his wife and baby and felt his whole body expand with love, flooded with gratitude and happiness. *This* was all he'd ever really wanted—a family of his own.

"Do we have a name?" a nurse asked Collin. He glanced up at the woman in pink scrubs. He could win the argument right here and jump in ahead of Madison, but after watching this powerful woman deliver his beautiful boy, he knew exactly what he needed to do.

"Madison is deciding," he said. "The mother gets to pick the name."

Madison smiled weakly at him. "No. We get to pick the name. Together."

Collin kissed her hand. They were a family. He wasn't alone anymore, wasn't the one calling all the shots. And for that, he was glad. She squeezed his hand as tears rolled down her face. His heart filled with love and with hope for their future.

"Our baby boy is beautiful," she said.

Collin couldn't have agreed more.

* * * * *

If you enjoyed
PRACTICING PARENTHOOD,
you'll love these other romances
from Cara Lockwood:

ISLAND OF SECOND CHANCES
SHELTER IN THE TROPICS
THE BIG BREAK
HER HAWAIIAN HOMECOMING

Available now from
Harlequin Superromance!

We hope you enjoyed this story from
Harlequin® Superromance.

Harlequin® Superromance is coming to an end soon,
but heartfelt tales of family, friendship, community
and love are around the corner with
Harlequin® Special Edition
and **Harlequin® Heartwarming**!

Romance is for life, and these stories show that
every chapter in a relationship has its challenges
and delights and that love can be
renewed with each turn of the page!

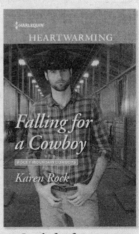

Look for six new
romances every month!

Look for four new
romances every month!

Get 2 Free Books,

Plus 2 Free Gifts -

just for trying the Reader Service!

STRS17R2

Get 2 Free Books,
Plus 2 Free Gifts—
just for trying the Reader Service!